D0042037

The Gladstone Bag

CHARLOTTE MACLEOD

The Gladstone Bag

A SARAH KELLING MYSTERY

THE MYSTERIOUS PRESS

New York • London
Tokyo • Sweden • Milan

Maine has many islands off its coast, and maybe even some pirate gold buried somewhere, because Maine is an enchanted state where anything can happen and often does. However, the place, the people, and the events in this story are all, as the old folks used to say, made up out of whole cloth. There is, as far as the author has been able to discover, no island named Pocapuk outside these pages; and if any of the characters seem to resemble actual persons the reader knows, it's either coincidence or wishful thinking.

The Mysterious Press, 129 West 56th Street, New York, N.Y. 10019

Printed in the United States of America

Quality Printing and Binding by:
Berryville Graphics
P.O. Box 272
Berryville, VA 22611 U.S.A.

For those wonderful editors
and luncheon buddies,
Sara Ann Freed
and
Susan Sandler

The Gladstone Bag

ONE

"I'm too old for this."

A fine time to think of that. She was already on the windowsill, black smoke billowing out of the room behind her, catching at her throat, filling her nostrils, making her sick. Two stories below, a ring of black-coated firemen clutched the rim of the net. She could see their red, sweat-streaked faces under their yellow helmets, all grimly upturned. She could see the crowd behind the fire lines: adults with their fists clenched in fear, semihysterical youngsters shrieking, "Jump! Jump!"

She jumped. She landed. Properly. Nothing broken, nothing sprained. She bounced once. She settled back. She sat up and waved to the crowd. Everybody cheered. She was lowered carefully to the ground, helped to stand up. She shook hands with the chief, straightened her loden-colored Tyrolean hat, dusted off her olive green tweed knickerbockers, pulled down the skirt of her Norfolk jacket, waved again, and walked away behind the engines. The firemen took off their helmets, turned them upside down, and started working the crowd. They wouldn't have gone begging for themselves, but this was for Ladderman Bechley's widow.

It was nice of Mrs. Kelling to help out. But then, Emma Kelling always helped out. It was Emma who'd organized this whole affair, as soon as she'd found out that the insurance and the Firemen's Relief Fund weren't going to stretch far enough to cover a distraught wife with bad varicose veins, three half-grown kids, a crippled mother-in-law, and too big a mortgage.

The firemen had already given their hook-and-ladder demonstration. They'd blown up a disused henhouse. They'd put out a miniature forest fire: a pile of brush contributed by the park department and two once-graceful shade trees that had most regrettably succumbed to Dutch elm disease and would have had to be destroyed anyway.

The Pirates of Pleasaunce, who normally specialized in Gilbert and Sullivan, had sung a medley of golden oldies like "Smoke Gets in Your Eyes" and "I Don't Want to Set the World on Fire." Jenicot Tippleton, their premiere chanteuse, had belted out a couple of torch songs and a torrid—torrid for Jenicot, anyway—imitation of the late Rita Hayworth singing "Fire Down Below."

As a grand finale, the Pirates had staged a semi-impromptu minimusical based on that catchy ballad, "The Fireman's Bride." They'd all been dressed in red flannel, except Emma's three grandsons. Little Bed, as the firehouse dalmatian, had worn white with black spots. Wally and Jem had been the anterior and posterior halves, respectively, of a mettlesome coal black firehorse pulling a genuine antique hose cart that had belonged to their late grandfather. Beddoes Kelling had been a notable spark; Emma still kept his fire helmet hanging in his den.

Beddoes had also established his own orchestra years ago, mainly as an excuse to keep on playing the tuba he'd carried so proudly in the Harvard Band, as had his father before him. His son and namesake, Beddoes Kelling III, still called Young Bed by his family and friends, had carried on the tradition. Young Bed was perched right now on one of the fire trucks, accompanying his fellow musicians with right good oompah. Beddoes Kelling IV was already taking tuba lessons. Little Bed had dreamed as a boy of playing quarterback on the football team, but a Kelling knew where his duty lay.

What with one thing and another, this had been a perfectly splendid afternoon. Now it was all over but the eating. Emma broke free from a clutch of youngsters clamoring for her to autograph their bubble-gum wrappers and made a beeline for the refreshment tent. She'd earned her tea, and she was jolly well going to get it.

Of course every party in the tent begged Emma to join them, but she merely kept smiling and heading for the small table in the far corner where Marcia Pence's mother, dear old Adelaide Sabine, was sitting by herself.

Mrs. Sabine had on the deep-crowned, gray straw picture hat she'd bought for Ascot in 1927. The hat was still holding up nicely, Emma thought, which was more than could be said for poor Adelaide. She had a cup of tea and a plate of miniature fruit tarts in front of her but wasn't doing much about them. Emma pulled out a chair for herself and sat down. "Adelaide, how very nice to see you out and about. May I join you?"

"Oh, please do. I'm waiting for Marcia and Parker"—Marcia was Adelaide's daughter and Parker either her son-in-law or her grandson, depending on whether she meant Parker II or Parker III—"but from the sound of things, they're still playing. Your kind Mrs. Heatherstone brought me these lovely tarts. Won't you share them?"

"Thank you, but I need something more substantial first. Jumping out of windows is hungry work, you know. We did it quite spectacularly this time. One of the men set off a smoke bomb behind me. I expect I smell like a kipper."

"Not at all," the older woman replied politely. "I'm sorry I didn't get to watch, but I couldn't face the crowd. And of course I'd seen the demonstration you gave for the women's club during Fire Prevention Week. I really don't see how you do it. Aren't you scared stiff every time?"

"I suppose I might be if darling Bed were still alive. Now that he's gone, life and limb don't seem all that important." Emma could say such things to another elderly widow. It was the young ones who'd have had fits if they'd heard her.

Even Mrs. Sabine didn't take her seriously. "Nonsense, you've a long way to go yet. If I didn't know better, I'd take you for about fifty-five."

This was perhaps stretching it a bit. Anyone would have agreed that Emma Kelling was still a fine figure of a woman, had the expression been still in vogue. Her complexion was fresh, her carriage erect, her hair as blond as it had ever been and perhaps a trifle blonder. Even her wrinkles became her. She slipped off her tweed jacket, revealing a pale green silk shirt, long-sleeved because after sixty there's really not much anybody can do about elbows, and looked hopefully around for somebody to wait on her. "But you are feeling better, Adelaide?"

"Better than I was last winter, at any rate. I'm still a bit tottery, though. Marcia's quite insistent that I mustn't go to the island this summer, and the doctor agrees with her. He says he wants me where he can get at me."

"And how do you—oh, thank you, Mrs. Heatherstone."

Naturally Emma hadn't had to wait any longer than it took for word to get to the kitchen tent that Mrs. Kelling had arrived. Naturally the tea was Earl Grey and the sandwiches all Emma's favorite kinds. Naturally she'd been served by the head woman in charge of the tea tent. Mr. and Mrs. Heatherstone had been running Emma's household for the past thirty-seven years. They were pitching in capably and cheerfully as always, ready to go along with whatever new scheme Mrs. Kelling cooked up. They'd handled bigger crowds than this, sometimes on just a few hours' notice, without turning a hair. But they were taking the summer off. How would she ever get through it without them? Emma fought off momentary despair and turned back to the frail old woman across the table. "As I started to say, how do you yourself feel about not going?"

Mrs. Sabine picked up her fork and broke a tiny corner off a strawberry tart. "Frankly, Emma, I don't much care. I keep thinking I should; Pocapuk Island has been so much a part of my life for so many years. But it's a long way to travel and a great deal of work after one gets there. I'm beautifully taken care of at Marcia's, and it's so pleasant having friends like you nearby that I find myself bearing the prospect of staying here with equanimity. Only my not going will cause a good many problems, and I'm wondering how to cope. You know about the cottages, I expect?"

"Oh yes, Bed and I spent a night in one many years ago when we were cruising the Maine coast. I'm sure you don't remember our being there; you must have had hundreds of guests over the years. Had you already invited someone for this season?"

"A full complement, unfortunately. Nobody you'd know, I shouldn't think. Most of them I've never met myself. Over the years, George and I got into the habit of letting a few what we called worthies use our cottages as summer studios. Artists, writers, people who need a quiet place to work and don't have other resources to draw on."

That was a ladylike way of putting it. Emma knew all about the Sabines' featherless chicks. "Several of your protégés have gone on to do excellent work, I understand."

"Many of them had already done good work," Mrs. Sabine replied a bit stiffly. "Besides, they've been interesting company. Some more so than others, I have to admit. On the whole, though, it's been a rewarding experience. And they don't have to be coaxed to come. In recent years, particularly since George died, that's been something of a problem. The island's not a place one can enjoy too long all by one's self unless one's a hermit, which I'm certainly not. And life is different these days, as I surely don't have to tell you. Old friends are dying off or getting to be hopeless crocks like myself, and the younger generations have more interesting things to do than dawdle away their time listening to an old woman snore in her rocking chair or maunder on about the good old days."

"How well I know!" Emma murmured.

"Nonsense, you don't know at all. Wait another ten years. Anyway, what's happened is that in recent years it's been pretty much myself and the worthies. One passes the word to another, you know, and somebody writes a letter of recommendation and it's hard to say no. This year a friend of Parker's, or a friend of a friend, recommended a Russian poet who sounded respectable if a bit dreary. Then I was approached by a Professor Wont. He and a group of colleagues were hoping they might come to the island to work on a joint project, some kind of historical thing he wasn't too clear about. Anyway, he said he'd handle all the details, so I let him go ahead and fill up the rest of the cottages, refusing to let myself admit the possibility that I mightn't be there to look after them. Now it's time to open the house, and here I am still dithering."

"They couldn't just fend for themselves?"

"Pocapuk's not that sort of place. The cottages have no cooking facilities. The arrangement's always been that people wander up for a buffet breakfast anytime between half-past seven and half-past nine, collect picnic lunches at that time if they want them, then everyone assembles in the main house at six o'clock for drinks and an early dinner. George and I thought it only fair that guests should sing for their suppers"—Mrs. Sabine laughed a little—"and they seemed to find our company agreeable enough. So I've kept on the same way."

"I should hope so," said Emma. "They're lucky you don't make them help with the housework."

"Oh, help has never been a problem. There are always college students looking for summer jobs, and I have a wonderfully capable man who acts as caretaker and general factotum. Vincent, his name is. He has a friend who cooks, and between them they round me up a staff of sorts every year. But you know how it is with temporary and usually untrained servants and a houseful of company. One's time seems to be wholly taken up with explaining what needs doing and making sure it gets done. I simply can't handle that sort of thing these days, and I don't suppose I ever shall again. It's rather restful being on the shelf, once one adjusts to the idea. But that's enough of my tale of woe. What's yours, or don't you have one?"

"Don't I ever! The Heatherstones are deserting me for the next two months. Their son and his family are in England and they've invited the parents to join them. It's a perfectly splendid chance and I wouldn't have them miss it for anything, but the housekeeping's going to be a problem, I'm afraid. My son Walter and his family have moved in with me for the summer. They had a fire in their wiring, nothing serious, but you can imagine the mess from the smoke and water. So they decided they might as well redecorate the whole place at once and get it over with."

"Then you won't be lonesome." Mrs. Sabine took another nibble of her tart. Emma ate a shrimp sandwich and sighed.

"No, I'm not wanting for company. Young Wally and Little Em have scads of friends, and of course their cousins adore having them so near. Dearly as I love them all, I'm thinking seriously of booking a cruise to the Galápagos Islands. Or possibly Antarctica. I'd hoped to bag my niece Sarah's guest house, but—Adelaide, I've just had a glorious thought! Why don't I go to your island?"

"Emma, surely you don't mean that?"

"Why not? It would be a change. Unless of course you'd rather I didn't?"

Mrs. Sabine put down her fork and reached across the table for Mrs. Kelling's hand. "Emma, my dear, how could I not want you to go? It would be the answer to everything. But are you quite sure?"

"Adelaide, consider my position. My daughter-in-law Kippy, Kristina, you know, went to school in Switzerland. I think it's charming that Kippy learned to yodel there; she yodels rather sweetly. I found it perfectly natural that she taught Walter to yodel, too. When their children came along, I could hardly wait to hear the little dears chirping their first o-le-ay-hoos. But nowadays when the lot of them get to yodeling back and forth at each other before I've even had my morning coffee, I have to say I find it a bit much."

"Good heavens! Do they really?"

"That's just the tip of the iceberg," Emma replied grimly. "Their four pet cockatoos yodel, too. Their bloodhound keeps trying to and can't. Shall I go on?"

"No, please, I can't stand it!" Mrs. Sabine was already having to dab at her eyes with a beautiful, white cambric handkerchief that smelled faintly of lavender. "I can see that your need is even greater than mine. Oh, listen, they're singing again."

The fire truck was parked directly outside the refreshment tent. The Pirates of Pleasaunce were all aboard, singing a last chorus about the fireman's bride who wouldn't stay home by her fireside. "Bed used to insist that song was written about me," Emma admitted. "I can imagine what he'd say if he'd watched me jumping out that window today. But she came to no good end, as I recall."

Mrs. Sabine was still smiling. "You're never naughty, Emma."

"At my age, when would I get the chance?" Emma stood up and put on her jacket. "Then I'd better go home and pack, hadn't I? When will it be convenient for me to stop by and pick up your keys?"

TWO

With the yodelers already in residence, getting away had been no great problem. Household arrangements could be left to Kippy and the cockatoos. Packing for so extended a stay had been easy enough; Emma was well organized and knew pretty much what sort of weather she could expect on the island, even in high summer. Warm cardigans, loose skirts of velour or corduroy, practical long-sleeved shirts went in with the summery cottons. No dinner dresses, she wouldn't need them. Her jewels could stay in the safe. Those clunky, arty pieces Emma's namesake granddaughter liked to pick out for her at craft shows would be just right for a congeries of artists.

Artists in the general sense, she meant; in fact, only two of them were involved with the visual arts, according to the list Adelaide Sabine had given her. Lisbet Quainley painted and Joris Groot illustrated. That probably meant Emma would be able to see what Groot's work was getting at and would have to guess about Miss Quainley. Then again, it might be the other way around. One never knew, these days.

It was the historian who'd organized Adelaide's guest list for her. He was supposed to be doing research, though Emma couldn't think why he'd chosen Pocapuk Island to do it on. Everard Wont, his name was; he sounded like a character out of Barbara Pym. There was also a mystery writer who'd sit and look inscrutable, she supposed, while Wont did the talking. Historians always talked; Emma had known lots of them, both professional and amateur. She'd never met a mystery writer before, though. She'd assumed they were all middle-aged women who wore odd clothes and lived in out-of-the-way places with a great many cats, but Black John Sendick sounded male as anything.

Wont was also bringing a psychologist with him, at least Adelaide thought a psychologist. She'd been even vaguer on this one than she was about the others. Either male or female or perhaps a bit of each, the name Alding Fath didn't help a whit.

And finally, Count Alexei Vassilovich Radunov, no less. He was indeed down on the list as a poet. Adelaide might have known better. The count would almost certainly be bogus, impecunious, and concerned less with poetry than with freeloading on a wealthy old widow for as long as could be managed. He might be fun, though. Rogues often were.

So that meant four men and two women, counting herself, with one iffy. Emma did hope Alding would turn out to be either female or not noticeably otherwise. If not, the dinner table would never come out right, though she couldn't think why it would matter.

When it came to passing away the idle hours, assuming she ever got any, Adelaide had told her not to worry. "You'll find the island itself an endless entertainment. There are pleasant walks, if you care for them, and wonderful bird-watching and botanizing. And of course the sea is always changing. I never tire of watching it myself. And we don't have bugs, which is a great blessing. No nasty ones, anyway."

"I'm glad to hear that," Emma had replied; "my bites always swell up and itch. What about books? Do you keep a library of any sort out there?"

"My dear, with so many writers coming and going, how could we have avoided it? You'll find plenty to read, never fear. And there's a phonograph, and radios in all the bedrooms, and television, if you care for it. There's also a piano if you care to take your music along. Vincent will make sure it's in tune."

Vincent would see to everything. He always did. Emma would

hardly have to give an order; Vincent knew how things were done. Vincent always knew.

It wouldn't be that easy, Emma was sure. Now that Adelaide had got out of having to cope, she was indulging an old person's privilege, fantasizing about the halcyon summers that ought to have been but never actually were because life wasn't like that. One of the unknowns would show up with an autocratic mother, a whiny teenage mistress, or a child who'd been dumped on him at the last minute by a vindictive ex-wife for the express purpose of stifling his creativity. One would be a drunk or a drug addict; one would come down with acute appendicitis at the first clap of a raging thunderstorm and have to be rushed to the mainland under incredible difficulties. One would be allergic to everything Vincent's friend cooked, and Vincent's friend would quit in a huff.

Emma entertained herself on the flight from Massachusetts to Maine exploring the direful possibilities and thinking up interesting ways to cope with them. It always helped to expect the worst, then one could be agreeably surprised when nothing catastrophic happened.

Most of her luggage had been shipped ahead by truck. All she carried on the plane with her—besides the tapestry tote containing her wallet, keys, cosmetics, a spare wig, a change of underwear just in case, and the photograph of her late husband with his fireman's helmet on that she always took everywhere—was a battered Gladstone bag filled with the Fairy Queen's crown and all the court jewels.

The jewels had been an afterthought. Emma had officially turned over management of The Pirates of Pleasaunce to Parker III and Jenicot Tippleton. They'd elected to do *Iolanthe* next season, with Parker as Strephon and Jenicot as Phyllis. A singer who could possibly replace Emma Kelling as the Fairy Queen had yet to be discovered.

There were always plaintive murmurs of "Couldn't you manage one more time?" but Emma was adamant. Her voice was worn out, her performing days were through. Like an old fire horse hearing the siren, though, she couldn't resist going along for the gallop. There were lots of little backstage chores she could handle better than anyone else; the jewels were one of them.

They'd been bought at Woolworth's back when glamour and

glitter were interchangeable words, when rhinestones were fashionable and cheap. Since then, they'd been through a lot of performances. Settings were tarnished and bent; stones were dirty or missing. The bracelets, necklaces, tiaras, and brooches were worthless, but at today's prices they'd be expensive to replace, even if comparable pieces could be found.

Emma had dragged the dejected bagful out of her attic, looked them over, shaken her head, and stopped in at the hobby shop for glue, silver paint, a small brush, a pair of needle-nosed pliers, and several packets of fake diamonds. These were now in the scruffy black leather satchel that had always held the fairy baubles, though Emma couldn't have said why.

That a turn-of-the-century Gladstone bag was an ugly old thing for an otherwise impeccably turned-out woman to be lugging around had not occurred to her, nor would she have given a rap if it had. She unfastened her seat belt, picked up her tote and her satchel, peeked in to make sure her wallet and the jewels were safe, carried her belongings off the plane, and found herself a taxi.

"I want the Pocapuk Ferry," she told the driver.

"Dunno's they'll let you have 'er," the driver drawled. "But I guess likely they'll let you ride 'er, long as you can pay your fare. That all the luggage you got?"

He reached to take the Gladstone bag from her; the ancient clasp gave way, and the bag popped open. "Gorry! What you got in here, the crown jewels?"

"That's right," said Emma. "I'll have it back here with me, please."

"Sure thing. What'd you do, find the treasure already?"

"What treasure is that?"

"The Pocapuk treasure. Mean to say you never heard? They run a piece in the paper about it every so often when they got nothing better to print."

"Evidently I've missed the stories. Whose treasure is it?"

"Anybody's that manages to get hold of it, I guess. It used to be Pocapuk's, which is how come they named the island after him. I dunno what Pocapuk's real name was, if he had one. Some claim he was Blackbeard's cousin or else one o' Captain Kidd's crew that struck out for himself after Kidd got hung. I think they're all full o' hogwash, but that's nuther here nor there. Anyways, Pocapuk Island's where Pocapuk used to careen his sloop."

"Careen?"

"Beach her an' scrape the seaweed off so's she'd sail faster. Some say she was a pinnace or a barkentine. I dunno. It was all a long time ago an' don't make no never mind nohow."

"And how did he get the treasure?" Emma prompted.

"Overhauled one o' them Spanish galleons somewheres down around the Bermuda Triangle, so-called, which is another pack o' foolishness if you want my opinion. Don't anything happen there that wouldn't o' happened someplace else if it was going to happen at all, which it probably didn't, is the way I look at it. Some bird named Aint or somethin' was spoutin' off about it on the TV a while back. What Pocapuk done was upped with his guns an' raked her fore an' aft, then boarded with drawn cutlasses an' chopped down the crew one after another like sheep in a slaughterhouse. Them galleons was no more maneuverable than a bathtub on roller skates, you know. Cripes, they could o' took her with a whaleboat an' a good harpooneer, like as not."

Emma was a little lost between the Bermuda Triangle and the sloop, pinnace, or barkentine. "Pocapuk did in fact capture the galleon?" This ride wasn't going to be long, and she was interested. Adelaide hadn't said anything about buried treasure.

"Well, sure. Ain't that what I was just sayin'? He made any Spaniards they had left over walk the plank, plugged up the holes in her hull, an' sailed that galleon all the way back to the island, him an' the ship's cat an' two Spanish deckhands he kept alive to work the sails."

"Are you quite sure about the ship's cat?"

"Stands to reason, don't it? Pocapuk wouldn't o' killed no cat; he wasn't a bad pirate, as pirates went in them days. Anyways, it's bad luck to kill a ship's cat. His men was s'posed to follow in the sloop, but be danged if they didn't take off on their own an' was never seen again. So Pocapuk buried the treasure an' murdered the two Spaniards so's their ghosts would guard the buryin' place forevermore, which was the standard custom in those days. He blew up the galleon with her own powder magazine and rowed to the mainland in her jolly boat with the cat an' a big sack o' doubloons."

"What happened to him and the cat?"

"Nobody knows. Some say he changed his name, dressed hisself up in some o' the Spanish captain's fancy clothes, went to Boston, an' got hisself elected mayor. Wouldn't surprise me none."

"But he never came back for the rest of his treasure?"

"Wouldn't o' needed to, would he, once he'd got his hand in the till?"

Emma had been warned about the tendency of some Mainers to regard Massachusetts as the Evil Empire to the South; she didn't try to argue the point. She was somewhat preoccupied in wondering whether that bird Aint he'd alluded to a while back could in fact have been Everard Wont. "But Pocapuk Island isn't all that big," she said. "Why hasn't somebody found the treasure by now? Haven't people gone looking?"

"Gorry, yes. That whole island got dug over so many times it's a wonder there's anything left of it. But them Spaniards was still on the job. Diggers got kilt in so-called accidents, or scared off, or didn't find nothin'. Finally, everybody got disgusted an' quit. Then some big millionaire from Boston way took it over an' built hisself a mansion out there an' posted a bunch o' No Trespassin' signs an' greased the harbor master pretty good, so you couldn't dig there now if you was o' mind to. That where you're goin'?"

"Yes, it is. I'm the new housekeeper," Emma added on a whim.

"That so? Make you dress up pretty fancy, will they?"

"Why no, I don't expect so." Then Emma realized what he must be driving at. "My goodness, you don't think this is real jewelry I have with me? It's just stage costume stuff I'm planning to repair."

The driver didn't say anything in reply. They were close to the dock now and the traffic situation was getting tricky. He pulled up at last as close to the ramp as he could manage but didn't get out this time to help her with the Gladstone bag. "Got your ticket?"

"Yes, I have."

Juggling the two bags and fishing out her money at the same time was awkward. Emma gave him a larger tip than she ought to have, rather than go to the extra bother of coping with change. The driver's eyes narrowed; he took the money without comment and pulled away.

Passengers were hurrying onto the ferryboat, so Emma hurried, too. That clasp giving way was a nuisance because now the bag wouldn't stay shut. She noticed a few interested glances being cast at the glints and sparkles that showed through the gap between the handles. Surely nobody could be fooled by such blatant fakes. Nevertheless, she took off the blue Liberty-silk print scarf she was wearing with her raw-linen Pallas knit suit and tucked it into the gap so that the bag's contents wouldn't show. "Better safe than sorry" was an axiom Emma didn't pay much attention to as a rule, but there was no sense in letting a possible annoying incident mar the beginning of her new adventure.

The ferryboat reminded her of the old *Uncateena* which she, Bed, and the children had taken out of Woods Hole years ago. It had a cabin deck with space outside to walk or sit on, an upper deck where she certainly didn't intend to go and be blown to bits, and a big door in the hull where cars and cargo could be driven straight inside. Cars were still being taken aboard, so she needn't have been in such a rush.

The cars wouldn't be for Pocapuk; the island wasn't big enough to accommodate them. The Sabines had used a pony cart when Emma and Bed visited them. Nowadays they relied on an electric golf cart, Adelaide had told her, to haul luggage, supplies, and passengers up from the dock.

Pocapuk would be the last stop on the ferry's run, and that only by special previous arrangement. Emma would probably have the deck to herself by then, unless some of the other guests happened to be making this run, too. She'd know when the time came. She chose a deck chair on what she hoped would be the shady side once they got out on the water, parked her two bags underneath, made sure the creamy broad-brimmed panama hat that had served her faithfully for many summers was securely anchored with hatpins fore and aft, and settled herself to enjoy the trip.

Sitting here, Emma had a clear though unexciting view of the dock and the parking lot. The taxi she'd come in was drawn up beside the ticket office; she supposed another boat must be due in soon and the driver hoped to pick up a fare back to the airport. Right now he was standing outside his cab, chinning with a man in a peaked cap, who broke off now and then to wave his arms at the milling cars, with no satisfactory result that Emma could see.

Perhaps they were rehashing the story of the Pocapuk treasure. It was certainly an interesting one, though a bit disconcerting to a newly appointed temporary chatelaine. What if the artists and the writers got wind of the tale and began digging up Adelaide's flower beds?

Why should they do any such thing? Surely none of their predecessors ever had, or the Sabines would have stopped letting them come. The story must be apocryphal anyway. Emma knew her Edward Rowe Snow; there were lurid yarns of pirate gold and guardian ghosts linked to islands all along the jagged North Atlantic coast. Adelaide hadn't told her because she didn't consider an imaginary treasure worth talking about. Or because she assumed Emma had already heard the legend; or because she'd simply forgotten. Adelaide's memory was none too reliable these days.

Anyway, there'd been too many other things to talk about and not much time to cover them in, considering how many other irons Emma had had to fish out of the fire before she could get away. The benefit had done well enough to ease Ladderman Bechley's family over the initial hump and show them the town was behind them. The bank had been gracious about refinancing their mortgage at an easier rate once Emma, Cousin Frederick, and Cousin Mabel, its largest depositors, had leaned on the manager just a little. Mabel was not the most forthcoming of the Kellings as a rule, but she never minded being asked to make herself obnoxious in a good cause. Some of the local merchants had come forward with generous gift certificates. Emma herself had quietly added a thousand dollars to the receipts from the benefit, Frederick another thousand. Cousin Mabel had contributed a few caustic comments, which were the most anybody had expected.

The ferryboat had steam up now; the whistle was screaming, the gangplank being taken inside. The big doors in the hull were closed and locked, the deckhands were casting off the enormous hawsers from the bollards, the propellers were beginning to churn the water. Back by the ticket office, Emma's erstwhile taxi driver was still doing his Ancient Mariner routine with the man in the peaked cap. Maybe he felt he'd already earned his day's wages, Emma thought. She'd been stupid to give him such an outrageous tip.

Oh dear, he'd spotted her. He was shouting in the other man's ear, pointing up to her. Or was he pointing to the Gladstone bag she was using as a footstool? It was foolish, of course, but Emma did find herself wishing that clasp hadn't given way while he was holding the bag.

The ferry pulled away from the pier, chugged out into the harbor. This was the sort of day to which James Russell Lowell had given such favorable mention in *The Vision of Sir Launfal*, Emma thought.

This was also the first chance she'd had in quite some time to sit still and do absolutely nothing. She'd driven all the way to Boston last night with her son, seeing the Heatherstones off on their overseas flight. She'd got up early this morning to do her last-minute fussing around, eat the enormous farewell breakfast her grandchildren had prepared for her, and be driven to Springfield Airport by her daughter-in-law and the dog. Neither of them had yodeled once; even so, Emma realized now, she was worn to a frazzle.

The monotonous chug of the ferry's engine, the slap-slap-slap of the waves against its hull were loud but somehow lulling. She'd chosen her seat well: not too much sun, not too much breeze, nobody sitting too close. The deck chair was more comfortable than she'd expected it to be. She had a longish ride ahead of her and some trepidation as to what she might find at the end of it. The sensible thing right now might be to shut her eyes and try for a short nap.

But Emma didn't want to fall asleep; people always looked so silly sprawled in deck chairs with their heads bobbing around. Maybe some coffee would help. She got up and went into the cabin, where there was a refreshment stand of sorts.

As she might have expected, the place was crammed. Passengers mobbed the counter or tried to fight their way out with precariously balanced trays of soft drinks and hot dogs. Emma managed to escape with only minor joggling and one jab in the ribs so painful that she turned her head to stare the jabber down, but failed to determine which of the crowd it could have been.

Emma carried her coffee back to her chair and took a trial sip. Thinking it couldn't possibly taste so awful as she thought, she took another. She'd been right the first time. Nevertheless, she managed to gulp down about half the cupful, then set the rest under her chair and tried to focus her attention on the paperback novel she'd brought along.

The coffee wasn't doing a bit of good. The paperback slipped from her hand. Emma didn't bother to pick it up.

THREE

She was sprawled all over the chair. Her skirt was up to her knees; her head was splitting. She had a perfectly hideous taste in her mouth. Furious with herself, Emma sat up, straightened her skirt, and took inventory. Her tote bag was there, thank goodness, tucked down beside her in the chair where she'd had sense enough to put it. Her money, her checkbook, her credit cards, her gold pen, and the blue notebook in which she'd listed all the things she needed to remember about the Sabine place were safe inside. Her wig, her spare undies, her photograph of Beddoes Kelling sitting in his hose cart were present and accounted for. She took out her compact and prepared for the worst.

She looked like the wrath of God. Her face was flushed, her hat askew. There was something awfully peculiar about her eyes; the pupils were shrunk to almost nothing. That couldn't be from the sun; she'd had them shut for heaven knew how long and now her side of the deck was completely in the shade.

How could she have let herself drop off like that? What on earth had been in that coffee? She glanced down for the plastic cup she'd parked under her chair. The cup was gone, and so was the Gladstone bag.

Was it possible she'd been doped? Emma was not given to

melodrama offstage, but her niece Sarah Bittersohn was married to a detective and often got involved in more bizarre situations than this. In fact, Sarah and Emma together had been drugged and robbed once before. Yes, it was possible; why else would the cup have been removed along with the bag? Drugs must be available on the ferry, people carried things like Dramamine and Valium when they traveled. Even aspirin might have worked. Tired as she'd been, it wouldn't have taken much to put her under.

They must have made at least one stop while she was unconscious; Emma saw distinctly fewer passengers now than when they'd set out. The Gladstone bag had gone ashore with one of the debarkers. Or had it? One glance inside would have destroyed the thief's illusions; he might have ditched his disappointing loot somewhere on the ferry. She got up, slung her tote bag over her shoulder, and began to prowl.

The fairy jewels were no great loss, the battered old Gladstone bag was certainly nothing to grieve for, but robbery was an affront. Emma Kelling did not accept affronts meekly.

Such personnel as she could find were no help at all; they merely pointed to the posted reminders that passengers were responsible for their own luggage. One young fellow did go so far as to say he'd keep an eye out, but he didn't sound as if he meant it. Emma went on combing the decks.

Naturally she saw nothing of an old black satchel. The ferry, she learned, had made not one but two stops while she lay in her unbecoming stupor. When she made her way down into the hull, which looked like a grotto for trolls and stank abominably of exhaust fumes, she saw only three cars left. There was also a skidful of grocery staples ticketed for Pocapuk, she was relieved to notice. Vincent must be on the job.

The single deckhand down here was either more lonely or more bored than those above; he listened sympathetically to Emma's plaint. No, he hadn't noticed anybody going off with an old, black leather satchel. No, none of the passengers had come below to stow an extra piece of luggage into one of the cars, but he'd help her search if she liked. Everybody's keys had to be left with the cars in case some had to be moved before the owners could get to them.

Emma felt rude and foolish peering into people's trunks and piled-up back seats, and of course it was a total waste of time. She tipped her helper a modest three dollars, not wanting to make the same mistake as she had with the cabdriver, and went back to the cabin deck hoping she hadn't erred on the side of being stingy.

It was almost half-past two by now. She still didn't feel particularly hungry after that gargantuan breakfast but supposed she ought to eat something. By now they were in sight of their next-to-final stop and the snack bar had nothing left to offer except one discouraged-looking doughnut that had been fried in rancid fat and dipped in some sticky substance alleged to have been honey. Emma took the doughnut on the premise that something was better than nothing. One bite convinced her she'd been wrong again. She dumped the revolting pastry into the trash bin and went back outside.

They were coming into a dock. Since she'd missed both previous landings, Emma felt duty-bound to stand at the rail and oversee this one like a proper tourist. There was the off-chance she'd actually spot one of the passengers walking off the ferry with her Gladstone bag in hand. And what would she do if she did? Leap over the rail shrieking, "Stop, thief"? Despite her propensity for hurling herself into firemen's nets and her many triumphs with the Pirates of Pleasaunce, Emma was no exhibitionist. Now that she faced the issue, she couldn't visualize herself doing anything at all.

As it happened, there was nothing for her to do. The dozen or so people getting off were juggling luggage of every sort but the one she was looking for. It did occur to her that a small satchel could easily have been concealed in one of those big duffel bags or some hiker's mammoth bedroll, but what if it had? There was no way she could stand at the end of the gangplank like a customs inspector, demanding that every piece be opened and searched. She'd just have to bite the bullet and go shopping in the fall for another set of court jewels.

Perhaps it was all for the best. Those old bits and pieces were really dreadfully tacky. There was no guarantee her attempts to restore them would have worked. Whoever had got hold of that junk was due for a sad disappointment and serve him or her right. Unless perhaps he, too, had a production of *Iolanthe* to mount; Emma could even have sympathized with such a motive for piracy. She knew only too well how the job of assembling props could drive a little theater group to desperation.

She must not let herself be sidetracked by any such unlikely conjecture. It wasn't a frantic prop man, it was some sleazy opportunist who'd overheard the wild tale that stupid cabdriver had been spinning on the dock and seen his chance to score off a batty old woman who didn't know any better than to carry a bagful of diamonds around with her. She ought to have shown the cabbie what useless junk it really was, instead of taking it for granted he'd have sense enough to believe her. She herself was the stupid one.

Facing up to her blunder did nothing whatsoever to lighten Emma's spirits. Now was the time when she'd planned to check the ferry for possible fellow passengers to Pocapuk. It wasn't like her not to follow through on a plan; nevertheless, she plunked herself down in a sheltered corner behind a big wooden chest with LIFE PRESERVERS stenciled on the front and settled grimly to wait out the last lap of the run. It wasn't two minutes before she was accosted by a tallish, elderly man who didn't look particularly distinguished but somehow was.

"I beg your pardon, madame, but could this possibly belong to you?"

The Gladstone bag! Emma felt ten years younger. "Oh, thank you! Wherever did you find it? I've looked absolutely everywhere."

"I think not, madame. It was in the one place where you would not have looked."

He had a slight foreign accent and a lovely voice, deep and mellow. Just now it held an undertone of amusement. Emma couldn't have helped smiling up at him even if she'd wanted to.

"The men's room, I suppose. Excuse me, I'd just like to see whether my things are still here."

She was relieved to find her blue silk scarf, rudely handled though it had evidently been. The coronets, necklaces, and bangles had been jumbled about, but she thought nothing had been taken.

"I'm afraid some would-be diamond thief has suffered a sad disappointment. This is stage jewelry, as you've doubtless guessed. I brought it along to do some badly needed repairs. It's for the fairies actually, our local Savoyards will be doing *Iolanthe* next season."

"How delightful." He really did have the most devastating voice. "And you yourself are one of the singers?"

Emma shook her head. "I used to be, but I'm past it now. And you must be one of the guests for Pocapuk. My name is Kelling; I'm your substitute hostess. Mrs. Sabine's doctor has forbidden her to make the trip."

He made her a nice little bow, neatly combining regret and pleasure. "I am sorry to learn that Mrs. Sabine is ill, but I rejoice in the good fortune that has sent you in her place."

This had to be Count Radunov. Emma had rather hoped for a fancy waistcoat and a monocle, but he was quite delicious enough in gray flannels and a taupish brown tweed hacking jacket. Savile Row, beyond a doubt, made for him twenty or thirty years ago, when he was a few pounds heavier and had not yet begun to shrink. The tan Brooks Brothers sport shirt was just right. The only touch of anything approaching the bogus was the almost invisible pattern of double-headed eagles on the dark brown silk ascot tucked in under his open collar. The ascot itself was dashing, appropriate, and merciful to an aging throat. Which reminded her. Emma took out the Liberty silk, smoothed out the wrinkles as best she could, and tied it around her own neck.

He nodded approval. "That scarf must have been chosen to match your eyes by someone who loves you very much. Excuse, I am Alexei Radunov."

"I thought you must be." Emma had in fact snatched the scarf out of a heap on a sale table during one of her rare forays into Filene's Basement, but she was too seasoned a trouper to step on so glorious a line. "Are you Count Alexei or Count Radunov? I've never been able to manage Russian titles."

"What is there to manage? Imperial Russian titles are, alas, a joke that has long ago lost its point. I am, since you ask, Count Radunov. With you, I should prefer to be simply Alexei."

He would, would he? Once she started calling him Alexei, he'd feel free to call her Emma and others would pick it up. She preferred to remain Mrs. Kelling until she found out what she had to deal with.

"I expect we'll all get to using first names once we've had a chance to become well acquainted." This should put him neatly in his place among the pack. "Are there others of our party on board?"

"There are five people on the upper deck, most of whom appear to know one another. One fellow, with the sort of bushy black beard that back in the twenties and thirties would have been the trademark of the stage Bolshevik, is sitting apart from the rest. He has a jug of red wine between his knees, of which he drinks, I have noticed, almost none. I myself do not know any of them."

"Then we may as well go up and introduce ourselves," said Emma. "I shouldn't be surprised if the man with the jug turns out to be Black John Sendick. He writes mystery stories, I've been told."

"Ah, that would explain everything."

"You yourself are a poet, Mrs. Sabine tells me."

"I am a scribbling mongrel. One does not, you understand, make a living from poetry. I write critiques of the ballet and the opera for a number of publications under several different noms de plume, offering a variety of opinions to suit every taste. I write articles with many profound hypotheses and very few certifiable facts about the paintings in the Hermitage and the expensive whimsies of the late Monsieur Fabergé."

"Really?" said Emma. "Then perhaps you've met my nephew-in-law, Max Bittersohn. He's doing a book on antique jewelry."

"Bittersohn is writing a book?" For an instant, the count almost lost his aplomb. "Mr. Bittersohn is a man of many parts."

"A few too many just now," Emma replied. "He was so unfortunate as to get his leg broken in three places during one of his business trips. The doctors put steel pins in it, and my niece had to go over to Gdansk and fly back with him. They had a terrible time getting his cast through Customs. Those steel pins kept beeping when he went through the scanner thing, and the inspectors thought he was carrying a concealed weapon."

"That could only happen to Bittersohn. Then that exquisite young woman he married is in fact your niece? I see the resemblance."

He saw no such thing, of course. There was no blood tie whatsoever between Sarah and her late uncle's wife, although there easily might have been, since Kellings had a habit of marrying their more distance connections rather than scatter the family fortune among outsiders who might want to take it out and spend it. However, Emma was willing to give Radunov good marks for effort.

"You've met my niece, then?"

"Only once, to my regret, at the French Embassy in Washington. She was the best-dressed woman there, and it wasn't even a designer model. I also cover the haute couture, you comprehend. This summer, through the generosity of Mrs. Sabine, I expect to make my fortune and release myself from the toils of hack journalism. I plan to write a best-seller under yet a different assumed name. This will be a searing romance about passion and intrigue in the court of Imperial Russia of which, in confidence, I know nothing except what I have read in other red-hot romances. It is a splendid thing Mrs. Sabine does here, to take in the beggars from the gates."

"I'm sure that's not how the Sabines have always regarded it," Emma demurred. "Sharing their cottages has been partly a way of ensuring stimulating companionship for themselves."

"But for you, madame? I find it impossible to believe you could lack for stimulation at any time."

"No, I can't honestly say that I do. In my case it's been more a matter of overstimulation."

Emma gave Radunov a thumbnail sketch of everyday life in Pleasaunce, to his sympathetic amusement. "So you see what I'm looking for on the island is simply a chance to get some rest while you clever people are exercising your brains and talents. Shall we?"

She moved toward the companionway. The count reached for the Gladstone bag.

"May I? I promise not to let it be snatched away again. Heaven forbid that your queen of the fairies should lose her crown as did our lamented czarina, with whose home life I am planning to take some shocking liberties. You see? Those must be our fellow guests."

And a scruffy lot they were was Emma's first reaction. Why did people of all ages, sexes, shapes, and conditions delude themselves that blue jeans were the ideal traveling garb?

Her mind flitted back to the girls' camp she'd attended more years ago than she was counting nowadays. Her parents would have driven her to the train, where she'd have been met by a counselor and introduced to those of the other girls whom she didn't already know. Nobody would have overdressed for the train: a plaid cotton dress with a blazer jacket or a summer-weight suit with a Peter Pan blouse would have been the thing, along with lisle knee socks and sensible shoes. Hair would have been bobbed or shingled; occasional braids or long curls were the sign of an oversentimental father. And naturally everyone would have worn a hat: a perky little cloth beret, a broad-brimmed straw, or a cloche run up by one's mother's milliner from the same material as one's suit.

Once they got to camp, they'd have changed into short-sleeved white middies with green ties and baggy green gym bloomers. Green was the camp color, of course. The chic thing had been to wear one's uniform with bare legs and not-too-new white canvas sneakers. A knot in a lace or a hole at the toe stamped one as an all-around sport and veteran camper. One had to take out the laces and dab them and the canvas with whiting once a week under the counselor's watchful eye, then set one's sneakers on the long wooden porch outside one's cabin to dry while one went bathing in rubber bathing shoes and bathing cap and a green wool one-piece bathing suit with CAMP SEETONKA embroidered across the area where one's bosom would one day be. Nobody said swimsuit in those days, although everyone was expected to master the back float, the dead man's float, the frog kick, and the dog paddle. Top girls went on to the side stoke, the back stroke, and what was modestly called the front stroke.

Life had been simpler then. Young girls didn't agonize about dates; they went to parties chaperoned by their parents and danced with the boys they'd always known. Nobody wore makeup except by stealth. Nobody read risqué books, mainly because nobody ever had the chance to get her hands on one. Nobody had any firm idea of what was supposed to happen on her wedding night, though everybody knew for a positive fact that she must on no account allow it to happen sooner.

She must really be getting old. Emma pulled herself together, put on her good-hostess smile, and walked over to the cluster of chairs. "Good afternoon. Am I correct in assuming you people are all to be guests of Mrs. Sabine?"

Various murmurs and a couple of grunts assured her that she was, and they were.

"Then may I introduce myself? I'm Mrs. Beddoes Kelling." None of that Emma stuff. "Mrs. Sabine has asked me to give you her regrets. Her doctor decided at the last minute that she's not fit to travel just now. Rather than upset everyone's plans, I've offered to fill in for her as hostess. She's given me complete instructions, and everything will go on pretty much as she'd planned."

"Well, that's a real surprise for us all," said a gray-haired woman, probably the eldest of the group, who'd had sense enough to wear a matching wraparound skirt with her blue denim jacket but erred, Emma thought, in her choice of a pink-and-yellow sun hat shaped like a parasol and tied on with a string.

The man with the jug, who'd by now evidently decided to integrate with the group, emitted a hoarse guffaw. "Mean to say you didn't know already?"

"All I knew was that Mrs. Sabine's a lady well along in years who's been ailing for quite some time," the woman replied with perfect good humor. "She had a real bad time with her chest along about February, and they thought they were going to lose her, but she pulled through. She was well enough last week to go to some kind of a big outdoor picnic. That's where she fixed it up with this lady about the island. They were having tea inside a big red-and-white-striped tent with a lot of other people around. She's not a bit sorry she's not coming; she's tickled pink to get out of it, and don't let her kid you, Mrs. Kelling. She'd been willing you to take her place even before the doctor told her she couldn't come. She has a lot of power, though you wouldn't think it to look at her. Not that you've let her pull you around by the nose. Anybody who's fool enough to try that will get his comeuppance pretty darn quick, and don't say I didn't warn you all."

FOUR

The woman glanced around the circle. One or two were smirking, but that didn't appear to bother her. "Why were you wearing that funny outfit, Mrs. Kelling? Was it because you had to jump out that high window with the black smoke coming out?"

Count Radunov was among the smilers. "And what do you say to that, Mrs. Kelling?"

"I say I'd be interested to know where this lady was last Thursday afternoon about four o'clock."

"I was in Cape May, New Jersey, giving a talk to a club there, which you can check out any time you like. I'll give you the name and address of the program chairman. Don't think I read about you in the newspaper. I can't make out the fine print, and I wouldn't have known which one to read because I don't know where you're from. The fire wasn't enough to make the news, anyway. In fact, I can't see any fire at all, just that one big puff of smoke. There'd been another fire a while before that, though. The firemen were still around. A lot of firemen. What was it, some kind of firemen's picnic?"

"Yes, as a matter of fact." Emma was still skeptical but willing to go along until she got this odd person sorted out. "It was a benefit for a local fireman who'd been killed at a fire."

"Kicked by a horse," the woman finished for her.

"Oh, come on." Perhaps it was the red wine that was making the man with the Bolshevik beard so contentious. "They don't have fire horses these days."

"They had one at the picnic," she told him calmly. "A two-headed one. From your side of the family, Mrs. Kelling?"

The remark got a good deal of rather startled laughter but not from Emma. "Yes," she said.

"Favor your husband, don't they? That's his picture you've got in your handbag, I expect. He was a fireman, too. Or was he?"

"Not really. My husband was a spark, one of those enthusiasts who go chasing after the fire engines just for the fun of it. He was active in starting our local Firemen's Relief Fund, so they made him an honorary member of Ladder One as a thank-you."

"But what about the two-headed horse?" demanded an intense younger woman who actually looked good in her jeans.

"There wasn't one. It's just that two of my grandsons dressed up as the front and back halves of a comedy horse for a skit some of the young people put on. My third grandson played a dalmatian."

"Oh. How dreary. I was hoping for a marvel. Then what about that other horse the fireman got killed on? What did he do, try to ride it up a ladder?"

Nasty little beast! "On the contrary," Emma replied coldly. "He was trying to rescue the horse from a burning building. Fire sends them crazy; the fireman was pulling its bridle and it was rearing and lashing about with its feet. I don't know whether or not the horse actually kicked him, but it well may have."

"In the stomach," said the older woman. This was really one of the oddest conversations Emma had ever encountered. "Knocked the wind out of him, then ran right over him, just in time to be out from under when the roof fell in. He'd have died anyway, I expect. There wasn't much left of him by the time that horse got through. Didn't know any better, poor thing. It's all right now, except for a big scar on its back."

"Yes," Emma had to admit. "I gather, then, that you're Mrs. Fath?" Not a psychologist, a psychic. Whatever would Adelaide Sabine say to this one?

"That's right, Alding Fath." The plump, elderly woman sounded both pleased and, for a wonder, surprised. "You've heard of me?"

"You're on the list Mrs. Sabine gave me. I must get the rest of you sorted out." Emma turned to the only other woman present, the slim one who'd hoped for a marvel. "You must be Lisbet Quainley."

"Yes, I am." It must have occurred to the young woman that she'd shown herself so far as less than amiable; she stood up and held out her hand. "It's good of you to take over, Mrs. Kelling. Did you really jump out a window?"

"I was demonstrating how to land safely in a firemen's net," Emma half-apologized.

"But weren't you scared?"

"Oh no. It's quite safe once you know how. It was only a second story window."

"In a church," Mrs. Fath amplified.

"Well, yes, but not a very big one. The church stands right up at the top of the village green, which made it the handiest place to hold the demonstration. We set off a smoke bomb for a little extra effect. It was just an easy way of winding up the entertainment and getting more people into the refreshment tent. And you're"—she decided she might as well try her luck on the man with the jug—"Mr. Sendick?"

Her will must be less forceful than Adelaide Sabine's, Emma thought. She couldn't get him to stand up, which would have been the courteous thing to do. At least he put down the jug.

"I am Everard Wont." He made it sound as if he were announcing the Last Trump. "*Doctor* Everard Wont, if you prefer to employ academic titles in your island pensorium. I am an historian, as you doubtless do not know."

"Oh, but I do," Emma told him sweetly. "Your comic history of the old Boston families was priceless! I laughed myself sick all the way through. You have the most delightful gift for the absurd."

Wont hadn't written it to be absurd, Emma knew. He'd simply made the mistake of letting some of Cousin Jeremy Kelling's buddies help with his research. Had the silly man exerted himself to check out his sources, he'd have discovered that any Comrade of the Convivial Codfish could be relied on to come up with a string of artistic and consummate lies, except for one member who was so compulsively and relentlessly truthful that nobody ever believed a word he said.

Wont no doubt had a few lawsuits filed against him by now. Emma couldn't see what was going on behind the beard, but she surmised it was something not quite nice. He grunted and went back to his jug.

The man next to him, a green-eyed redhead who'd smiled quietly at Emma's use of the word "absurd," stood to attention and waited to see whether she would offer to shake hands with him. "I'm Black John Sendick. That's my real name. My grandfather used to be crazy about some stories that ran in the *Boston Sunday Globe* about a prospector called Black John. The guy who wrote them was named Hendrix, which is sort of like Sendick in a way, so Gramp wanted to name me Black John, too. He was pretty well-off and my mother's maiden name happened to have been Black anyway, so my parents let him go ahead with it. I've thought about dyeing my hair, but I don't suppose it would do any good."

"Not unless you dyed your eyes and your freckles, too." Emma gave him her hand and a smile. "You have an excellent name for a mystery writer, at any rate. That's what you do, I'm told."

"That's what I'm trying to do, only it's sort of more horror than mystery. My first book wasn't scary enough, I guess. It sank without a shudder, but I'm still trying. I've got this really gruesome idea for a plot, only I guess I'd better not talk about it or it might go away."

"Then we must all look forward to reading your book when it's finished."

Emma had no intention of doing anything of the sort if she could help it, but she didn't want to discourage the young fellow. He couldn't be over thirty. He was clean, he was articulate, and he made no claim to omniscience. She was grateful for Black John.

"Then by the process of elimination you must be Joris Groot," she said to the last on the list.

Groot didn't appear to mind being last. He was a big man, tall and not exactly fat but generously padded. His hair was light, thin, and probably kept plastered down to his scalp when the wind hadn't been blowing it around. His nose would be peeling in a day or so; people with skin as fair as his should know enough to wear hats or stay below in the shade. Groot was forty-five or so, Emma judged, and looked like the sort of man who ought to be married by now. She wondered what he'd done with his wife.

"You're an illustrator, I understand," she said as they shook hands. "Mrs. Sabine wanted me to tell you that she had a drafting table, a stool, and a little table to hold brushes and things put in your cabin. Is that what you need?"

"Sounds fine to me, long as there's a decent light to work by." His voice was a bit on the high and squeaky side for such a big man. "I've brought my own art supplies."

She should hope so! How far did these people suppose the Sabine hospitality stretched? "You're working on a project now, are you?"

"I just finished illustrating the new catalog for Footsy-Wootsy," he told her, with no doubt justifiable pride. "Kids' styles, mostly. I did sixty-seven different pairs of Itsy-Bitsy Footsy-Wootsies."

Emma didn't know whether to be impressed or dismayed. Groot was not at all what she'd envisioned an illustrator to be. Were they all a trifle strange, or had she the ill luck to have drawn herself the one exception?

"But surely you're not planning to draw shoes on Pocapuk?" she ventured.

"Oh no," he replied. "Feet, maybe, but not just shoes. I'm kind of sick of kids' sneakers, if you want the truth. I've decided to diversify. I'll be starting the new project as soon as we get something lined up to work with."

"We?"

"Us," he amplified. "All of us, I guess. Except him." Groot nodded toward Count Radunov. "I don't know where he comes into the picture."

"Nor do I," said the count. "What is this picture?"

"Ev's book. About finding the treasure. Alding's going to psyche out where to dig, Ev's going to write a day-by-day account while the digging's in progress, and I'm going to do the illustrations. Liz is supposed to paint some kind of mood piece for the jacket, and Black John's got this great idea for a thriller, like he says. It's a really neat package."

"So it would seem. Does Mrs. Sabine know what you have in mind?"

"I'm not sure. I think Ev was intending to surprise her."

"You've certainly surprised me."

Emma hadn't expected the first bomb to drop quite this soon. Ought she to let Adelaide know right away about this cheeky proposition or wait and see whether anything came of it, which seemed unlikely to the ultimate degree. The worst that could happen, she supposed, was that Wont or one of his associates would leak word of a treasure hunt to the media for the sake of advance publicity, and they'd get a horde of sightseers trying to invade the island.

Even that mightn't be a total disaster. Vincent and his helpers could keep them from actually landing, she supposed. Adelaide's family didn't care much what happened to Pocapuk; it was too remote, too quiet, it cost too much to keep going. The Pence family compound in Connecticut suited them all much better. As soon as the old lady was in her grave, they'd be putting the island on the market; perhaps it would be wiser to sell before she went and save the inheritance tax. Some extra publicity and the hope that springs eternal whenever the subject of pirate treasure arises might enable the Pences to make a real killing on the property. She'd better not panic just yet.

"That sounds most interesting," she said. "I shan't interfere unless it becomes necessary. Naturally it will be in your best interests as well as Mrs. Sabine's to keep the project a secret, and of course you won't go rooting about digging holes in the property until you've received permission and we've made sure it won't be detrimental in any way to the buildings, the gardens, or the septic tank. There's a caretaker, I'm told, who'll be able to set you straight on what's allowable and what isn't."

Wont set down his jug with a thump and glared at her through his beard. "Is that what you call noninterference, Mrs. Kelling? May I remind you that this is *my* project?"

Emma could be very much the grande dame when she chose. "And must I remind you, Mr. Wont, that Pocapuk is not your island? Doesn't it occur to you that you've been remarkably high-handed in organizing your treasure hunt without so much as dropping Mrs. Sabine a hint as to what you were planning to do? Were you others aware that Mr. Wont hadn't bothered to get any sort of authorization from the owner before involving you in his project?"

"Ev said it would be all right," Groot mumbled.

"Mrs. Sabine did invite us to come," Lisbet Quainley put in. "I got a nice note from her."

While this discussion was going on, Mrs. Fath had been carefully unwrapping a stick of sugarless gum she'd taken from her capacious blue canvas handbag. She doubled it over, popped it into her mouth, chewed twice, and made her pronouncement. "The old lady won't care. She's made up her mind to sell the place anyway."

That was probably so, but Emma wasn't going to let this spooky, middle-aged frump make up her mind for her. "In that case, it would be doubly important for us to leave everything in salable condition," she said.

"Please understand that I see no objection to your painting or writing; I gather the Pocapuk legend has already been well publicized. I don't expect Mrs. Sabine will mind, either, though I have a feeling she thinks it's a pack of nonsense, as such tales usually are. I've been told this island has been dug over without result a number of times in the past, so I frankly don't see why you think you'll be any luckier than your predecessors. However, I'm quite aware that imaginative authors don't always need much in the way of factual material to come up with their results."

Emma smiled ever so sweetly at Everard Wont. "And now I think we'd better get our luggage together. This must be Pocapuk we're coming to."

The ferry was slowing, changing course. A line of rock and pine trees not much bigger than a few of the uninhabited islets they'd passed on their way was coming closer. Now Emma could see a pier and somebody on it, not waving, just standing there. The island wasn't all that low; she could see a knoll rising in a gentle sweep from the pier. The last time she'd come, the house had been out in plain sight. Now the pines had grown so that she caught only an occasional glimpse of brown-stained wood through their branches.

Emma couldn't see any of the cottages. They were all on the back side of the house, where there'd been and probably still was a stony little cove to bathe in if anybody cared to brave the icy water. One really did feel something of a thrill docking at an island of which one was to be suzeraine, if only for a little while. Emma did hope Everard Wont wasn't going to make a nuisance of himself. It was too bad she'd been forced to put him in his place in front of the others, but there was no earthly use trying to be tactful with an arrogant boor. Emma wondered whether Adelaide had ever run into a similar circumstance.

She also wondered whether it was one of this crowd who'd taken her Gladstone bag and ditched it in the men's room. She wouldn't be surprised to learn that Count Radunov had been both taker and finder. He mustn't have known then that she was coming to Pocapuk, too; he'd simply have spotted an elderly woman who might be a widow with tangible assets and decided on general principles to give her the old school try.

Radunov would be an agreeable antidote to Everard Wont, anyway. She wondered if the no doubt self-styled count was really planning to write a book. Why shouldn't he be? Most people were, and far too many of them did.

The ferry was reversing its engines now, gliding into the dock. The man—it was indeed a man, and a big one—was raising his arms to catch the line a deck hand was about to throw. Emma glanced around at her windblown, sunburned group of fellow travelers, said in her customary dinner-party manner, "Shall we?" and started down. She had no intention of letting Everard Wont usurp the lead.

Adelaide had promised to telephone Vincent and let him know about the change in plans. She must have done so, for the husky middle-aged man in the clean plaid shirt and khaki work pants didn't act a bit surprised to see Emma in place of his employer.

"How do you do," she said. "You must be Vincent."

"That's right, and you're Mrs. Kelling. Got the whole gang with you, eh?"

"Yes, though I didn't know it until we'd made the last stop before this one. Mrs. Sabine told me you'd have the cottages ready. I'm sure everyone would like to get settled right away."

"Ayup, we'll take care of 'em. You go straight on up to the house, Mrs. Kelling. One of the girls will help you unpack; your bags are all stowed in your room. The rest of you folks, dump your stuff on the cart and follow me. I've got the list of who goes where. Here, ma'am, I'll take that for you."

Since the men and Miss Quainley were all loaded with portable typewriters, cameras, portfolios, paint boxes, folding easels, and other tools of their respective trades, Mrs. Fath had been left to struggle along with a gargantuan blue vinyl suitcase, two paper shopping bags crammed to the ripping point, and a small, squarish hand piece. That must be what she carried her crystal ball in, Emma thought.

"Then I'll see you all in the main house at six o'clock. I believe that's the customary gathering time, Vincent?"

"That's how we've always done it. Drinks at six, dinner at seven. You manage that satchel all right, Mrs. Kelling?"

"Oh yes. It doesn't weigh anything to speak of. Thank you, Vincent."

Emma climbed the path feeling much happier now that she'd met her major domo. This was a lovely path, edged with old railroad ties, springy with inches of fallen pine needles. Flat stepping stones had been set in wherever they'd be helpful; everything was casual and natural and nicely maintained.

If there was any real treasure on this island, she decided, it must surely be Vincent. Was that his first or his last name? No matter, it was evidently what he was used to being called by the Sabines. Far be it from her to attempt any innovation in what might well be the last season this long-established ménage would ever see. Emma felt a twinge of melancholy at the prospect of its dissolution.

Once she got inside the house, though, she began to change her mind. Everything in the vast living room was in exquisite order, everything was commodious and comfortable, everything was right for its setting and function. Big jars of garden flowers and new light green pine tassels had been placed here and there by somebody with an eye for effect, or somebody who knew where similar arrangements had always gone. But it was old, not antique old or shabby old, just old and tired and ready to go, like its owner. No wonder Adelaide had not been sorry to miss coming again; there'd been too many years of sameness here. If the place were Emma's, she'd be tempted to tear it down and start again from the beginning.

But here came a youngster, she couldn't be more than fourteen or so, with a peeling nose and a hairdo inspired by Medusa. She wore a screaming yellow sweatshirt with a Smurf on the front, the inevitable blue jeans, and a smile that was pure glory.

"Hi, Mrs. Kelling, I'm Sandy. Come on up and I'll show you your room. You'll love it! This your first time on the island? Can I get you a cup of tea or anything? Want me to help you unpack?"

Emma said no, she'd been here once many years ago; yes, she'd like some tea; and it would be kind of Sandy to help her unpack, not that she couldn't have managed by herself but because Sandy so obviously burned to be helpful. She let Sandy take the Gladstone bag and followed her upstairs.

FIVE

Emma had no difficulty in sharing Sandy's enthusiasm for the room she'd been allotted. It was exactly the right size, neither barny nor coopy, all white walls, green wicker, and faded chintz. No painted board floors and rag rugs at the Sabines', of course; a couple of mellow Kirman rugs would do well enough to take the chill off the parquet. Sandy opened the big windows, letting in the smell of the ocean. The old-fashioned, painted wire screens blurred the view a trifle; nonetheless, it was magnificent.

Her window looked out over the path she'd come up, the dock, and the great wide sweep of the Atlantic. Nothing between her and Spain, or was it France? Very nice either way. However, Emma went over and shut the windows all but a crack. The air had a clammy feel, as it always does on small islands. She was relieved to notice an efficient-looking electric radiator strategically placed to the left of a deep-cushioned spring rocker that had a sensible-size lamp table drawn up beside it.

This would be a comfortable refuge from that weary perfection downstairs, she thought. She must sort out some books to bring up here. She was wondering whether a more efficient arrangement of the furniture might be worked out when Sandy bounded back with a charmingly arranged and amply supplied tea tray.

"Ah, good," she said. "That was quick, my dear." No earthly use in treating this radiant creature like a servant, she'd simply pretend Sandy was a temporary grandchild.

"Bubbles—he's the cook—had everything ready for you, Mrs. Kelling. He put the kettle on to boil as soon as he heard the ferry whistle. The sandwiches are from a salmon Bubbles caught yesterday, with cucumber and a little fresh dill he grows in his own greenhouse back home, but he can fix you something else if you'd rather. How about if I set the tray right here and turn the chair so you can look out at the water while you eat? Want me to pour?"

"Thank you, I'll manage," Emma said when it became possible to get a word in. "This is lovely, I'm starved. Would you like to open that biggest case for me and start hanging up the dresses?"

She might as well take advantage of this female whirlwind. Emma felt she'd seen almost enough water for one day. Nevertheless she took the seat Sandy had arranged for her, investigated the tea, found it exactly right, as it naturally would be, and started on the sandwiches. Absolute perfection, even Mrs. Heatherstone couldn't have done better. Hot scones in a napkin, too, with currant jam and real clotted cream to go on them. Wherever did Bubbles get clotted cream out here?

Kept a sea cow in the cove and milked her himself, perhaps. That was the sort of thing Emma's granddaughter would think of. What a pity Little Em couldn't have come, she and Sandy would get on like a house afire. And disrupt Vincent's domestic arrangements, no doubt, and get the poor child fired. Sandy was having a good-enough time now, at any rate, gurgling over the embroidered silk blouses Emma had brought along for evening wear, being ever so careful to set them just right on their padded hangers. Emma rather wished she'd put in one or two really elegant dinner frocks, if only for the fun of watching Sandy unpack them. But how could she have known she'd be assigned a personal maid? Really, this was an incredibly well-run household, even without its mistress.

By the time Emma had done with her tea, Sandy had all the suitcases emptied. Nightgowns, underthings, and stockings were folded in the drawers; shoes in the closet; Emma's toiletries on the dressing table in a commodious bathroom she wouldn't, thank goodness, have to share with anybody.

"Anything else I can do for you, Mrs. Kelling?" Sandy was by no means ready to quit.

Emma was. "Just take the tray with you, please. I'm going to lie down for a while before it's time to dress."

"Sure thing! Want your negligee?"

If Sandy got pleasure from thinking of sensible tailored robes as negligees, Emma was not about to contradict her. "Yes, the fleecy blue one. I'm beginning to feel a wee bit chilly."

"I can switch on the radiator."

"No, don't bother. A hot bath will warm me up."

"Want me to start it for you?"

"Not just now."

Even Sandy knew when she'd been dismissed. "Okay, then. Holler if you want me."

With obvious regret, the youngster took the tray and left Emma to herself. Emma slipped out of her traveling clothes, put on the blue robe, and stretched out on a chaise longue under the window. She oughtn't to be sleepy after that unfortunate nap in her deck chair, but her head still ached from whatever it was that had knocked her out and she was weary from the alternate bustle and tedium of getting here. She'd feel better after a good soak. It was unthinkable that Vincent wouldn't have plenty of hot water for her, but if by any chance he hadn't, Bubbles would no doubt boil some on the kitchen stove and Sandy would be only too pleased to lug it up in jugs, like the overworked housemaids of yesteryear.

Emma supposed she ought to have a chat with Bubbles about tomorrow's menus. Then again, perhaps she oughtn't. The odds were that he had a regular schedule to work from, laid down over years of experience. There'd be lobster in some form tonight; arriving guests always expected lobster at their first meal in a place like this. Not plain boiled, surely, that would show up at a picnic down on the beach some warmer evening than this one promised to be.

Lobster thermidor, perhaps, or a creamy lobster bisque followed by something simple but good, like chicken cordon bleu and fresh asparagus. The latter would be Emma's choice, not that she felt particularly hungry after Bubbles's elegant tea. Still, the salt air did tend to give one an appetite. She meditated a moment on her waistline, decided she was old enough not to care, pulled a lilac plaid mohair throw up over her ankles, and lay there wondering what sort of summer she was going to have.

It was too early to begin forming opinions about Adelaide's guests. Emma's guests, as she might as well learn to think of them. Whatever had possessed Adelaide to let that meretricious scribbler Wont have his own way with the invitations? Obviously she couldn't have read his latest book.

One ought at least to phone and let Adelaide know everybody arrived safely, Emma thought. She'd do that when she went down to dinner. She saw no telephone in her room; she hadn't expected one. Perhaps it was some kind of ship-to-shore radio thing such as she and Bed had had on their boat. Vincent would show her. Maybe he'd already talked with his employer; Emma wouldn't be a whit surprised.

She hoped the cottagers weren't giving him too much trouble. Wont had the makings of a first-class pest, but no doubt Vincent had run into his ilk before. Mrs. Fath was the real conundrum.

Emma knew, of course, how so-called psychics worked. They had accomplices who scouted out tidbits of personal information that could be dropped with supposedly electrifying effect at the psychological moment. Mrs. Fath must have sent someone to nose around after Adelaide Sabine in preparation for this visit. The spy would have followed Adelaide to the firemen's benefit and eavesdropped on her conversation with Emma in the tent. It wouldn't have been hard to do in such a crowd as they'd had. Once Emma had volunteered to fill in for Adelaide, she'd have become the target instead.

Maybe it had been Mrs. Fath who'd snitched Emma's satchel on the ferry, hoping to find more grist for her little mill inside. As to knowing about Bed's picture, she might even have dared to take a peek inside Emma's tote bag. That would have taken some deft burglarizing, but weren't mediums required to be experts at legerdemain? Blowing trumpets with their noses and writing on slates by means of hooks made from wire coat hangers hidden under their sleeves, that sort of thing?

Mrs. Fath didn't look like the sort of person who'd go around with a coat hanger lashed to her elbow, but wasn't protective coloration part of the deception? It was going to take more than a denim two-piece, a silly cotton hat, and a few oracular remarks to convince Emma Kelling that Alding Fath was all she cracked herself up to be.

Which was a pity, actually. Much as one enjoyed the conversation of interesting men, one did find women more serviceable companions. So far, Emma hadn't seen anything potentially congenial about Lisbet Quainley. Mrs. Fath, on the other hand, had struck her as the sort with whom one might not actually have a great deal in common, but in whose company one might pleasurably share an occasional pot of tea and an agreeable rambling chat about nothing in particular. One could hardly relax with a person who was storing up one's every inconsequentiality for possible future reference.

If one should happen to be an unprincipled rogue like Jem Kelling and his pals, one might feed that self-styled sibyl a few nuggets of outrageous misinformation, just for the fun of seeing where they turned up next. Emma tried to think up some picturesque untruths, but she'd never been any good at that sort of thing. One might as well just lie here and let one's mind drift as it would. If it happened to drift off to the Land of Nod for a few minutes, who cared?

Emma became vaguely aware that she was having a fascinating dream. She was in a strange house on a little island, lying on an old-fashioned wicker chaise longue painted green and covered in faded lilac chintz. Through the windows beside her she could see a pier that stretched out into the ocean. At the far end of the pier stood a pirate. She knew he was a pirate because he had on skintight black boots and breeches, a heavy belt of some kind around his waist—to hold his pistols and cutlass, no doubt—and a red bandanna around his head.

Emma would have preferred a bicorne to the bandanna, optimally with a skull and crossbones on its upturned brim, but one couldn't always arrange one's dreams precisely as one chose. He did at least have a bushy black beard, like that odious man she'd met on the boat. There were no burning candles stuck in it, so he couldn't be Blackbeard. Or was it Bluebeard? No, Bluebeard had been the one who kept murdering his wives. Definitely Blackbeard. Rather, not Blackbeard. This was an awfully confusing dream. She could smell salt water, she could sense the smoothness of the chintz under her, she could feel herself sitting up.

She was sitting up, she wasn't sleeping. The pirate was gone; he'd merely lowered himself off the pier into the water, and she hoped he froze his—Emma was too much of a gentlewoman to express such a hope, even to herself. It was that ridiculous Everard Wont, of course, practicing up to be a pirate ghost and scare the old woman silly because she'd laughed at his asinine book.

Emma brought herself up short. Wont might only have been posing for sketches so that Mr. Groot could get to work right away on illustrations. That would be entirely reasonable and even laudable. One must not make snap judgments based on personal antipathies. The fact that Wont had let himself be hoodwinked by the Codfish crowd didn't necessarily prove him a fool and a knave.

Not necessarily, just probably. Emma went into the bathroom and began drawing herself a tub, locking the door behind her lest young Sandy come bounding in and offer to scrub her back. She entirely approved of the late Ralph Bergengren's axiom: "Dine and the world dines with you. Bathe and you bathe alone."

She had her bath, fixed her face, and dressed herself in one of the long velour skirts she'd brought, a strange, dull old-rose shade that reminded her of the dried flower petals one might find in a bowl of potpourri. This would, she thought, nicely echo the general feeling of mild decay that the Sabine place evoked.

With the skirt, she wore one of her embroidered silk blouses, also in old rose but not too rosy. Emma liked soft, muted tints. Camouflage, Cousin Fred Kelling called them, like the stripes of a Bengal tiger. Fred was an odd old stick, she thought fondly, playing the crusty bachelor for upward of seventy years, then suddenly carrying off Jenicot Tippleton's beautiful mother because he'd decided Jack Tippleton didn't deserve her, which Jack certainly didn't. Jack was still being snippy about the divorce, so Fred and Martha were living happily the old-fashioned way, and more power to them. Emma gave herself an approving nod in the wicker-framed mirror and fastened pearl studs in her ears. She didn't feel quite up to her granddaughter's arty baubles tonight.

A shawl of wool challis splashed with improbably large peonies in those same off-reds and pinks would be her Bohemian touch for tonight. Those downstairs rooms were bound to be drafty once the sun had set. She really must quit puttering and betake herself downstairs if she was to catch a word with Vincent before the cottagers arrived.

The caretaker must have had the same idea; he was at her side as soon as she set foot in the living room. "Get you a drink, Mrs. Kelling?"

"Not yet, thank you," she told him. "I'll wait for the others. I did want a moment's chat, if you can spare the time."

"Sure thing. I'm just the bartender tonight."

"Good. First, I'm wondering whether you've phoned Mrs. Sabine yet, to let her know we've all arrived. If not, I'd like to call her myself. You'll have to show me how one goes about it."

"No problem. See here?"

Vincent fished a bunch of keys out of his pocket, selected a small brass one, and inserted it in the lock of a lacquered Chinese box that Emma had assumed must be a cellaret. Inside was a perfectly ordinary telephone, if one considered polished brass and mother-of-pearl ordinary. It worked off a signal bounced from the mainland, Vincent explained.

"But how do you hear it ring?" Emma asked him. "I should think the box would deaden the sound."

"Ayuh, that's why we got an extension in the kitchen. If there's a call for you, we come an' tell you. Somebody's always around in the kitchen. Far's the cottagers are concerned, we generally don't let on we've got one unless we have to. If they find out, we tell 'em it has to be kept shut up so's the air won't corrode the innards," he explained. "Actually the only reason for the box is so's they won't talk 'er into the poorhouse. Just don't give a hang, some of 'em. I did call, a little while ago. Mrs. Sabine was asleep, but Mrs. Pence said she'd pass the word when her mother woke up. She told me she'd phone your folks, too, so you needn't bother unless you want to."

"Then I shan't," Emma replied. "There's no sense in running up the phone bill. That was rather late for Mrs. Sabine to be napping; I hope she hasn't had another of her attacks. Did Mrs. Pence say?"

"She didn't sound too happy." Neither did Vincent.

"Oh dear." Emma wished she could think of an optimistic remark to make, but there really wasn't one. "Well, we shall just have to not bother her about whatever happens here. I'm sure you won't mind my bothering you instead."

"What I'm here for."

"I assume you got the cottagers all settled in without any trouble? Had any of them been here before?"

"Nope, all new."

"You know, that does puzzle me a bit. Mrs. Sabine told me she'd let Dr. Wont draw up her guest list for her, but I got the impression she didn't actually know him very well."

"Could be a friend of her son-in-law's."

Emma knew Parker Pence well. He was a member of her orchestra. His enthusiasms were his family, his investment business, his golf, his bridge, and his kettledrums. His friends were fellow members of the orchestra, the bridge club, and the country club. Wont might possibly be one of Parker's clients, she supposed, but that would hardly put him in a position to dictate Parker's mother-in-law's philanthropic ventures.

However, she mustn't stand here gossiping about Adelaide's guests with Adelaide's servant, not that there was anything servile about this salt-flavored colossus. "In any event," she said, "it's hardly my place to comment on her decision. What bothers me is that Mrs. Sabine appears not to have been told what Dr. Wont had in mind when he organized his team. Were you aware that he's planning a treasure hunt?"

"No!" Vincent wasn't liking this any more than she. "What do you mean, treasure hunt?"

"According to what they told me on the boat, Mrs. Fath is supposed to determine the site of Pocapuk's pirate treasure by clairvoyance. She's some kind of psychic, in case you haven't yet had your fortune told."

"Not yet."

"Dr. Wont is going to write a book about it. Miss Quainley and Mr. Groot will do the illustrations. Mr. Sendick intends to write a book, too, but his will be fiction."

"An' Wont's won't. Huh! What's Count Radunov s'posed to do?"

"He's apparently not one of Wont's group, just a friend of a friend of Mrs. Sabine's son-in-law. He told me he's planning to write a steamy best-seller and get rich. Not about Pocapuk's treasure, though."

Vincent emitted a snort that might possibly have been a laugh. "Be the first one to make anything out of it if he did. Wont fixin' to dig the place up, is he?"

"Not if I can help it. I've already told him he mustn't disturb anything until Mrs. Sabine has given her permission, assuming she does, and you've decided whether it's safe for him to dig where Mrs. Fath tells him to. I find the whole business quite absurd, myself, but I doubt if there'll be any real damage done. Knowing a bit about how Dr. Wont does his research, I'd guess that he'll simply write up a long history of previous digs, drag out the preliminaries as long as he can, make a token attempt in some picturesque location, perhaps turn up a few pieces of eight or some nice little piratical trinket."

"How can he do that?"

"Easily enough, I should think. Mrs. Fath's spirit guides will no doubt have brought one or two along as insurance." Emma was gratified to sense that Vincent was finding her more interesting than he'd expected her to be.

"Huh. Then what?"

"Oh, then the pirate ghosts will drive the diggers off. Dr. Wont's already been out on the pier in his pirate costume, rehearsing some special effects. Or perhaps he was posing for Mr. Groot; I only caught a glimpse of him."

"When was this, Mrs. Kelling?"

"About five o'clock, perhaps a little earlier."

Vincent shook his head. "Couldn't o' been him, then. Must o' been one o' the ghosts."

SIX

Emma straightened her back, thrust out her chin, and looked the caretaker square in the eyes. "Vincent, I am not a fanciful old woman. Please don't make the mistake of thinking so."

He might have flushed a little, it was hard to tell. "All I'm sayin', Mrs. Kelling, is that if it was five o'clock you couldn't o' seen Dr. Wont on the pier. I was in his cabin then, an' had been for the past half hour, tryin' to fix a light switch that didn't work. He was standin' right behind me the whole time, tellin' me what I was doin' wrong. If he'd o' gone someplace an' let me alone, I'd o' been finished a darn sight faster, but he didn't. It couldn't o' been any of the others, neither. They was all in the deck chairs down by the cove drinkin' Cokes an' such out o' their own ice chests; I could see 'em from where I was workin'. Except the fortune-teller; she was settin' in the rockin' chair on her porch doin' some kind of fancy work. You wouldn't o' mistook her for him anyways, I shouldn't think."

"I obviously mistook someone. Whoever it was had a bushy black beard like Dr. Wont's, was tall and spare like him, and dressed in—oh!"

"What's the matter, Mrs. Kelling?"

"It's occurred to me that what I took for a pirate costume may well have been one of those heavy rubber wet suits scuba divers wear. It was black and close-fitting, with a red business over the head. I suppose I saw the outfit as black boots, knee-breeches, and a red bandanna because I had pirates on the brain. The taxi driver who took me to the ferry had talked about Pocapuk and the Spanish sailors he killed to guard the treasure. Then of course I was concerned about Dr. Wont's projected treasure hunt."

"Hasn't been a summer yet that somebody didn't see a pirate or two." Vincent might have been joking, but he wasn't scoffing. "Where'd the feller go? Did he come up the pier?"

"No," said Emma, "I believe he must have stepped backward into the water. He was there and then he wasn't."

"Didn't surprise you?"

"Not really. As I mentioned, I'd decided it was Dr. Wont getting in a spot of practice. Frankly, I was more annoyed than surprised at his barging ahead without asking your permission, which shows the folly of making snap judgments. It wouldn't have been someone who works here, taking a break to do some diving?"

"Nope. They don't take breaks without my say-so and they don't none of 'em dive, not out here. You see a boat anywheres near?"

"Not a sign of one, but you know my windows only overlook the front side of the island. Do you think someone ought to check around for a trespasser? I can manage the drinks if you want to go yourself."

"No need. I'll send one of the boys."

"Where are they all? So far, I've only met Sandy, who's a perfect joy, by the way. How old is she?"

Vincent was struggling not to look too pleased. "Thirteen this past February. She's my youngest."

"Then you're a fortunate father. Is Sandy living here on the island?"

"For the time bein', her an' her friend Bernice. My wife's gone off on a dig, an' the two oldest boys are busy most o' the day haulin' traps with their uncle. Neil, he's fifteen an' a half, he's workin' here, too. I didn't want 'em stravagin' around by theirselves all summer. Figured they'd be better off with something to do where I could keep an eye on 'em."

"Very sensible of you. What is your wife digging?" Emma almost added "Pirate treasure?" but forbore.

"Indian ruins. She teaches archaeology up at the college. Pay ain't much, but she enjoys it. We got a few minutes if you want to meet the rest of the staff. They're havin' supper in the kitchen."

"By all means, if it won't bother the cook."

Vincent didn't seem to care whether the cook got bothered or not. He steered Emma through the dining room, where the table was already set with fiddleback silver and Wedgwood china in the clipper-ship pattern, through a swinging door to a serving pantry and on into a good-size kitchen.

At the business end, a stout, red-haired man wearing not only the conventional white cotton trousers and jacket but also the traditional chef's cap with its muffin top slanted rakishly over the left ear was stirring something in a pot. Lobster bisque, said Emma's nose. She'd guessed right on the menu.

At the other end, Sandy and her friend Bernice, a teenage redhead who must be Neil, a good-looking young man of twenty or so, and an older man with a bushy black beard much like Dr. Wont's sat around a scrubbed pine table, eating fish chowder out of thick white bowls. As Emma entered, they all stood up, Sandy first.

"Ooh! Mrs. Kelling, you look like a fairy godmother! See, Bern, didn't I say she was gorgeous?"

"That'll do, Sandy." Vincent wasn't annoyed with his daughter; he was seething nonetheless, though he wasn't showing it much. "Mind tellin' me who you are, mister, an' what you're up to?"

The bearded man shook his head. "I don't know."

"He can't remember his name, Dad," Neil piped up. "He can't remember anything."

"That so? How'd he get here?"

"I found him, Vince." That was the older fellow. "He was over on the rocks by Piney Point, wearin' a scuba suit with a big rip in it. I asked him where he'd come from and he just looked at me. I could tell the guy was all in, his hands were wrinkled and his lips were blue. He could hardly stand up. I yelled for Neil. Between us we got the wet suit off, rolled him in a blanket, and got some hot coffee into him. When he was able to walk, we brought him up here and gave him some of my clothes to put on. Bubbles said maybe after he gets a hot meal in him, his memory might come back, so that's where we're at."

"How come you called Neil instead of me?"

"Neil was within yelling distance and you were over at the cottages."

That wasn't going down with Vincent. "I'll talk to you later, Ted. Mrs. Kelling, I'd like to have you meet Bubbles Ryan, if he can spare the time to shake hands."

"Please don't let me interfere with your work, Mr. Ryan," said Emma.

"Pleathe call me Bubbleth, everyone elthe doth," the fat man replied. Emma could see why. Tiny bubbles formed at the corners of his pink little mouth, quite inoffensively, as he lisped out the words. He looked, she thought, like an overgrown version of the little chef in the Campbell's Soup ads she remembered from her childhood.

"Certainly, Bubbles, if you wish. What are you giving us tonight?"

"Lobthter bithque and thtuffed chicken with athparaguth. We alwayth keep thingth thimple the firtht night."

"Very sensible," said Emma. "I shall look forward to it. I mustn't keep you now, we'll talk tomorrow morning."

Bubbles said that would be nithe. She left him to his stirring and spoke to Sandy's friend.

"You must be Bernice." Bernice still had her puppy fat and was likely to have a good deal more of it after a summer in Bubbles's kitchen, Emma thought. Her cheeks were scarlet, her nose a pug, her eyes bright brown, her hair an even worse mess than Sandy's. Her Smurf sweatshirt was green. How could Bernice's mother have borne to let this little cuddlebug out of hugging distance? Perhaps she'd gone on the dig with Mrs. Vincent.

Neil had been sitting next to Bernice. He was going to be like his father. Emma could have sworn the boy grew another quarter inch even as he stood manfully to attention clutching the chowder spoon he'd been too flustered to put down. He and the older fellow, whom Vincent finally got around to introducing as Ted Sharpless, were both looking worried. Emma didn't blame them. No matter what sort of shape they'd found their alleged amnesiac in, they'd been incredibly stupid to bring him into a house like this without either her or Neil's father's permission.

She wasn't going to make an issue of it now. The kitchen clock said almost six, she must get back to the drawing room. She said something pleasant about hoping they'd all enjoy their summer together and went back the way she'd come, just in time to greet the cottagers.

Alding Fath, as the senior lady in their group, quite properly led the pack. She'd changed out of her sensible denim outfit into a sensible navy blue wash-and-wear shirtwaist sprigged all over with little red roosters and perked up with a string of red plastic beads. She had on navy blue nylon stockings and the sort of low-heeled navy blue sandals middle-aged ladies on sightseeing tours take along for dress-up; she carried a small red handbag. Her short gray hair was neatly dressed, her face discreetly touched up with a dusting of powder and a dab of lipstick. Absolutely nothing about her hinted of the arcane, much less of chicanery. Emma supposed it was all part of the stock-in-trade, still she felt mildly pleased to be with someone who looked much like some of the ladies in the Pleasaunce Garden Club.

Each in his own way, the guests had clearly made an effort to do her proud this first night on the island. Lisbet Quainley had done something really horrible to her hair and adorned her thin body in a long, baggy, olive-green skirt and a long, baggy, yellow-green sleeveless top. She must be depending on her jewelry to keep her warm; there was a great deal of it. The sort of chunks and blobs Little Em would go wild over; Emma rather wished she'd worn some of her own.

Joris Groot and Black John Sendick were presentable enough in slacks and sports jackets. No ties, but Emma hadn't expected a miracle. At least their shirts looked clean.

Count Radunov was naturally a hostess's dream come true in a white dinner jacket, navy blue trousers, and red bow tie. She must seat him opposite Mrs. Fath and the roosters, Emma decided. They'd balance her table if anyone could.

Everard Wont hadn't shown up yet, and that was fine with Emma. She was about to ask Radunov to help with the drinks—he might well have done a stretch as a waiter somewhere along the line—when she realized Vincent was back and coping.

"What can I get you, Mrs. Kelling?" he asked her.

"A very feeble gin and tonic, please, with lime."

She'd almost made the faux pas of adding, "If you have it," but caught herself in time. Of course Vincent would have fresh lime. He'd also have caught her hint about not mixing the drinks too strong, though it was most unlikely he'd have needed to be told. Emma was dying to know what he'd done about their mysterious stranger, but this was hardly the moment to ask. At least Vincent knew now she hadn't been dreaming about that man on the pier. How fortunate that she'd realized in time about the scuba suit! And how curious that the man bore so striking a resemblance to Everard Wont, though she supposed it was mostly the beard and the build.

Vincent handed her a glass complete with lime. "That about right, Mrs. Kelling?"

Emma took a sip and nodded. "Perfect. Thank you, Vincent."

Drink in hand, she circulated among the cottagers, making the sort of polite conversation one always made with a group of new acquaintances. She hoped they'd found their cottages comfortable. They had. She commented on the superb view. They approved of it, too. She wondered whether they were to enjoy a fine day tomorrow. They were, according to Alding Fath, who hadn't divined the forecast by mystic means but had heard it on a small transistor radio she'd brought with her. Mrs. Fath was having her tonic without the gin, she explained. Alcohol did things to her vibrations and she didn't want to disappoint Everard, since he'd been nice enough to pay her way.

Not knowing quite how to answer that, Emma asked her, "How soon do you think you'll be able to get in touch with the ghosts?"

"Oh, I don't expect to reach them at all. Most of this ghost stuff is poppycock, you know. It's not the entity who hangs around, as far as I've been able to make out, it's just some remnant of the earthly personality. Sort of like an old sock that's been left in the back corner of the closet, if you get what I mean."

"I must say I hadn't thought of it that way." Emma couldn't recall whether she'd ever thought of ghosts much at all. "Then can't they just be tidied out, so to speak?"

"Oh, they can. Ghosts are a cinch to get rid of, but you'd be surprised how many people won't let you. They hang on to their ghosts the way some folks collect old cigar boxes. There was an awful lot of that foolishness going around back during Queen Victoria's time, you know, her mooning around about poor Albert and the mass mind catching her vibes. Cluttering themselves up with their hair wreaths and mourning rings and all the rest of it.

Regular breeding ground for ghosts. Stirred up a lot of old ones that had been kicking around unnoticed, too."

Mrs. Fath took a sip of her tonic water. "I'm not trying to claim there's anything wrong with remembering our loved ones who've passed over, mind you. And it's only natural to want a few keepsakes. But that garbage about parking Aunt Minnie's ashes on the mantelpiece and Granny's teeth in the tumbler on the nightstand beside her deathbed so's a person would have something to go and weep over whenever they couldn't find anything better to do, that was carrying it too far, in my opinion."

"I couldn't agree with you more."

Emma thought of Cousin Mabel in that great ark of a house stuffed with dead relatives' portable assets. Mabel kept her parents' bedroom just the way they'd left it, though whether she ever went there to weep was something Emma didn't know and wouldn't have believed if anyone had told her, particularly Mabel. She wished she could get Mabel together with Alding Fath. Perhaps later on, after they were all back from the island—it dawned on her that she was actually thinking about inviting this fortune-teller out to Pleasaunce for a weekend. And that Mrs. Fath knew what she was thinking.

"Don't quite know what to make of me, do you, Mrs. Kelling? At least you're not scared of me, like some people. What gets 'em is that they think so-called psychic powers are something out of the ordinary. Actually, it's more like your appendix or the little tailbone at the end of your spine. Everybody's born with one but we don't use it for anything, and most of us can't even remember what we grew it for in the first place."

"If you say so." Emma still wasn't quite clear as to the relationship between the occult and the vermiform appendix.

Mrs. Fath was quite willing to enlighten her. "Back when a tribe had just one big mind among 'em, as you might say, and hadn't developed the concept of time as a kind of dressmaker's tape measure, all the ideas and experiences would be kind of mixed in together like a pot of stew: your thoughts, my thoughts, past, present, and future. When you needed a point of information, you just dipped into the common pot and hauled it out for yourself. As life began to get complicated, more and more stuff got thrown into the pot and it got harder to fish out the piece you wanted, so you got somebody who hadn't lost the knack to do it for you."

"Those would have been the oracles?"

"Or shamans or medicine men or whatever you want to call 'em. We've all got a bit of the shaman in us still, but most of us don't like to admit it to ourselves, so we squash it down and sit on it. You'd have been pretty good yourself, if you hadn't been so well educated."

"Do you think so?" Emma felt oddly pleased by this rather backhanded compliment, if such it was meant to be. "One does get hunches now and then."

"And I'll bet one's learned to trust one's hunches over one's so-called logical thinking. Right, Mrs. Kelling?"

"Well . . . ." Emma couldn't imagine what Cousin Mabel would think of this conversation. "I have to say I generally regret it if I don't. Is that how you got started, trusting your hunches?"

"Trouble with me was, I had 'em too often, and they were never wrong. My folks were real strict churchgoers and didn't hold with what they called Devil's work, so I had to either keep my mouth shut or darn well wish I had. They weren't mean people, but they thought it was their bounden duty not to spare the rod. I never did care much for getting walloped, even when I knew it was well intended."

SEVEN

I shouldn't think you would." Emma didn't know why Alding Fath was telling her all this, but how did one manage to turn the woman off? And did one honestly want to? "But when you got out on your own . . ." she prompted

"I didn't get out on my own. When I was fifteen, my parents were afraid I was getting worldly notions from too much schooling, so they took me out and married me off to the minister's nephew. We hadn't been hitched a week when I knew for a positive fact my new husband was having it off with his uncle's wife and only took me for a cover-up because he thought I was too young and stupid to know any better. I stuck it out for a while. Having my own place to keep was better than being home, and she kept him so busy he didn't bother me any about the married stuff. Finally, though, the hypocrisy began to get under my skin, so next time he told me he was going to choir practice, I told him a thing or two. He beat me up and threatened to kill me if I ever told on him."

"How dreadful! What did you do?"

"I waited till he'd gone off, then I took a little money he didn't know about that I'd made picking berries and went down to the bus station. There was just enough to buy me a ticket to Atlanta. My father had a sister there who didn't like him much, so I figured Aunt

Flossie'd be the one to go to, and she was. She put me up and got me a job clerking in a store. That meant I could pay my board and have a little over for myself, which was fine for a while. But then I got a feeling that my father had figured out I was with Aunt Flossie and was fixing to come after me. I lit out for Wilmington and slung hash in a diner till I could buy myself a few decent clothes and get a job in a bank. They had a training program and I was all set to go to night school and work my way up."

"That was ambitious of you."

"Sure, till I got one of my hunches that somebody was helping himself to the cash. Like a good little girl, I went to tell the manager. Just about half a second too late it hit me like a ton of bricks that he was the one with his hand in the till. So naturally he fired me."

"Oh dear."

"And that was how it went. I'd get a job and something would happen and I'd be out on my ear again. You'd have thought I'd learn, but I never could seem to keep my mouth shut. Finally, one day I happened to be eating at one of those sidewalk cafés and this woman came up and asked if she could share my table. I said sure, you know how you do, and the next thing I knew, she was telling me this big sob story.

"Her husband was a gambler. He'd joined some self-help group and was trying to quit, but a couple of days ago, a lovely antique clock that had been her grandmother's had disappeared out of the house. She knew her husband must have sold it for money to gamble with. He was swearing up and down that he hadn't, but he'd done the same thing before and lied to her about it. She didn't know what to do.

"So I told her. 'What you'd better do,' I said, 'is beg your husband's pardon and get rid of that sanctimonious young twerp who's living in your spare room. Tell him he'd better bring back your clock and get out of your house or you'll set the cops on him. The clock's in a pawnshop, and he's spent the money on a floozy.'

"I described the fellow right down to a hair. He was the son of somebody they'd met on a trip, passing himself off as a theological student, which he either wasn't or shouldn't have been. I could sense he was another one just like my husband."

"My goodness!" said Emma. "That must have given the woman a jolt."

"Oh, she wasn't having a bit of it. She started telling me what a lovely boy Ernest was. I said to her, 'You come with me right now to that pawnshop and I'll get your clock back.' So she finished her sandwich and paid her bill and we walked over to the shop. I'd never been there before, but my feet knew where to take me. Well, we looked all over the place, but the clock was nowhere to be seen. So I said to the pawnbroker, 'You've got a fine antique clock in your back room.' I told him just what it looked like and the name on the dial and all. 'You'd better trot it out here right quick,' I said, 'because it's stolen property and you'll be in big trouble if you don't.'

"I don't know what got into me that day, I guess I'd been stomped on once too often. I was bound and determined I was going to win this one, no matter what. I scared that man into believing I was an undercover cop, and by gum, he went and got the clock. Then I made him describe the person who'd brought it in and it was the young boarder, no doubt about that. He'd given the husband's name, the little sneak.

"So then the woman wanted to know how much the pawnbroker had lent on the clock. She meant to give it back to him so's he wouldn't lose out on the deal. He told her two hundred dollars, which was a lie. I said, 'Then how come you wrote down only fifty in your book? You knew perfectly well what that clock's worth, and you knew it wasn't that boy's to pawn or he wouldn't have settled for so little. You figured he'd never come back for it and you'd make a bundle on the deal. Don't waste any sympathy on this bird, lady. He's as big a crook as the other one.'

"So the upshot was, she gave me the fifty instead and told me I ought to go into the business. I decided that was the only way I'd ever be able to open my mouth and not get fired for it, so I did. And if I were you, Mrs. Kelling, I'd be darned wary of that man in the kitchen. I can't seem to get a handle on him yet, but he sure doesn't feel kosher to me."

EIGHT

This must be what her grandmother used to call the gypsy's warning, Emma thought. She didn't need it, she had qualms enough already. Emma wished she could have a little heart-to-heart with Vincent about what he intended to do with that unfortunate find of Ted's, but he'd disappeared. Into the kitchen, she supposed; it was getting on toward seven o'clock and she found herself eager for that lobster bisque.

Everard Wont still hadn't put in an appearance. Emma mentioned the fact to Joris Groot, who happened to be standing near her. He only shrugged.

"Don't worry about Ev. He'll show up when he feels like it."

"Then we must hope he won't show up feeling hungry after we've finished serving," Emma retorted. "Mrs. Sabine was quite clear that I mustn't let her employees work overtime to suit the whims of the guests. I believe there's a notice to that effect in each of the cottages."

Groot shuffled his feet uneasily. "Maybe Ev fell asleep or something. Want me to go see?"

"Certainly not. Why should you?"

Wont was more apt than not to be sulking in his cottage waiting for somebody to come and make a fuss over him. If Groot was fool enough to go now, he'd find himself stuck with the job for the rest of the summer. Alternatively, Wont had been at the wine jug again and drunk himself into a stupor, in which case Emma certainly did not want him at her dinner table.

"If he misses dinner, I expect the cook would let you take something to him afterward," she added so as not to seem too unfeeling. "I believe we're about to sit down."

Sandy had appeared in the door of the dining room. She'd changed into a fresh pink cotton dress and tied her snakes' nest into a net, Emma was relieved to notice.

"Bubbles says would you please come to the table now, Mrs. Kelling?"

"Thank you, Sandy. Shall we go in, everyone?"

Emma took her place at the head as a matter of course. Count Radunov pulled out her chair with a lovely bow, and she awarded him the place of honor at her right, putting Mrs. Fath next and the agreeable young Black John Sendick at the end. With Groot on her left and Lisbet Quainley next to him, she'd have her table balanced after all, assuming Wont showed up to take his place beside Miss Quainley.

Bernice appeared with two soup plates, sliding one foot carefully after the other and sticking out the tip of her tongue as an aid to balance. She was setting the first bowl in front of Emma with an air of triumphant relief when Wont lurched in and slumped without apology into the vacant seat.

He'd made no effort to clean himself up; he still wore the wilted shirt and too-tight jeans he'd sweated into during the ferry ride. Emma was grateful she'd given him the end seat. Too bad for Miss Quainley, but perhaps artists didn't mind so much. She gave Wont a cool nod and went on chatting with Count Radunov. Sandy came in with two more plates of bisque, more confidently than Bernice, thank goodness; then she brought two more and Bernice shuffled in with the last one, which she gave to Wont. He glared down at it and demanded loudly, "What's this stuff?"

"It's perfectly beautiful lobster bisque," Lisbet Quainley told him in an embarrassed half-whisper.

"I'm allergic to shellfish."

"Ev, you are not! You ate two lobster rolls when we stopped on the way up and they didn't bother you one bit."

"That was different."

"Sandy," said Emma, quite out of patience, "take away Dr. Wont's plate and bring him a glass of tomato juice. If any of you have other dietary problems you've neglected to mention, please tell me now so that I can speak to the cook in the morning."

Nobody did. Even Wont was momentarily silenced. He did rally enough to make a point of not drinking his tomato juice, but everybody else made a point of not noticing, so he went back to silent glowering. Emma noticed a bit later, however, that he took a double helping of chicken.

Radunov told a funny story about a grand duchess of his acquaintance. Black John Sendick capped it with one about his mother's cat, who sounded a lot like the duchess. Emma joked about her jewel robbery on the ferryboat, partly to keep the conversation moving but mainly to let everyone present know she'd brought nothing worth stealing.

She said nothing about being drugged. That was hardly amusing; besides, she still wasn't certain it had actually happened. She did notice Alding Fath giving her a couple of curious looks, though. If the woman was as psychic as she cracked herself up to be, Emma thought crossly, why didn't she finish the tale herself?

Mrs. Fath nodded as if she knew perfectly well what Emma was thinking and found it reasonable enough. "Oh my, yes," she said. "Lots of jewelry around here."

"What do you mean?" Lisbet Quainley was straining over the table, squinting through the candlelight, her voice quick and sharp. "Are you picking up anything about the treasure?"

"I'm picking up something, I can't tell what. Awful thick ether, too many cross-currents. Black and white, that's all I'm getting. Black and white."

"Black and white, huh?" Joris Groot wasn't looking at the dumpy seeress beside him. His light blue eyes were fixed on the candle flames. "Footsy-Wootsy put out a line of black-and-white spectators this year. They offered 'em in purple and white too, but the purple didn't sell. That can't be what Alding's talking about, can it? Black and white and cross-currents. Know what that makes me think of, John? Those big rocks sticking out of the water over at that place we walked to. Shiny black with the waves all swirling around them and those big white sea gulls sitting on top."

"Splashing their pretty white calling cards all over the rocks." Black John was amused.

Lisbet Quainley took umbrage. "Guano is not pretty! It's stark, lifeless, but not worthless. The end of the cycle and the beginning."

"That's right, Liz. In one end and out the other."

"Oh, shut up! Can't you see the symbolism? Life, death, fertility."

"Fertilizer," Black John corrected.

"Riches, you jerk! Riches from the earth. Ev, that's it! That's what we need for your book jacket."

Wont blinked. "Bird shit?"

This was almost certainly the first time that word had ever been used around Adelaide Sabine's table, Emma thought. Could she possibly keep her face straight?

Not with Count Radunov murmuring in her ear, "Miss Quainley is right. How deliciously appropriate!"

"Stop it, you dreadful man," Emma murmured behind her napkin. "I'm in agony."

She could have laughed, it wouldn't have mattered. The others were all too absorbed in the psychic to notice their elders misbehaving.

"So okay, Alding," Groot was coaxing. "What's in the water?"

"Water, yes. Water all around. Lots of water."

"She's right, you know." Another aside from Radunov. Emma committed the gross impropriety of kicking him lightly on the ankle.

Alding Fath was droning on, her face a perfect blank. "Shining stones coming out of the water. Black and white around the stones. And the dead in the water."

"The Spanish sailors!" Lisbet Quainley was fairly bouncing in her chair by now.

Sandy and Bernice, Emma noticed, were as enthralled as the artist. They'd come in to clear away the main course, but were standing spellbound by the buffet, their eyes popping out of their heads. Joris Groot was beaming.

"Well, there you are, Ev. Just wait till low tide, wade out in the mudflats, and dig up the swag."

Everard Wont reared up to make the most of his height and sneered down the whole length of his nose. "If it were that easy, Joris, I'm sure the treasure would have been found long ago. We're going to need diving equipment, dredges, air hoses, a boat—where's that caretaker? I want him now."

Emma turned to the two young maids. "Clear the table, girls. Sandy, if your father's not too busy, would you ask him to step into the dining room?"

"Yes'm."

Realizing they weren't getting paid to stand there eavesdropping, the two youngsters whizzed around the table grabbing up plates and silver and running to the kitchen. Before the swinging door had time to flap, they were back and Vincent was with them.

"You want me, Mrs. Kelling?"

Before she could answer, Everard Wont cut in. "I want you. I'm going to require the exclusive use of the boat until further notice. Where is it?"

"Depends on what boat you're talking about."

"I'll decide that when I see them. Where's the boathouse?"

"'Bout two miles from here, on the mainland, closest one I know of."

"Then where do you keep the boats?" Wont was almost screaming now. Vincent was taking it calmly.

"No boats."

"What do you mean, no boats?"

"I believe he means that there are no boats on the island or that guests aren't permitted to use them," Emma put in. "Am I right, Vincent?"

"Sure thing, Mrs. Kelling. We had too many people that wasn't s'posed to takin' out our boats an' gettin' in trouble 'cause they didn't know how to use 'em. So Mrs. Sabine told me to get rid of 'em, which I did. My two oldest boys swing by every mornin' with the mail an' whatever we need. Anybody needs to be picked up, we notify the ferry. That's how it's been, last ten years or so."

"But I can't work without a boat!" Wont really was screaming now.

"Might charter one." Vincent was getting a speculative gleam in his eye. "Cost you somethin'."

"How much?"

"Two hundred a day, more or less."

"Ridiculous!"

"Whatever you say. You want me any more, Mrs. Kelling?"

"Not just now, Vincent. When your sons come tomorrow morning, perhaps you'd be good enough to ask them who has a charter boat available and what the charge might be. In the meantime, Dr. Wont can be thinking of alternative possibilities. Please tell Bubbles the bisque was superb. I'll be out myself in a little while. What do we have for dessert, Sandy?"

"Lemon sponge pudding, and I'm s'posed to ask how many want whipped cream on it."

"Just bring the cream and pass it around."

"Hey, good thinking, Mrs. Kelling."

Sandy darted off behind her father, and Emma finally got to have her laugh. "Those adorable children! I can see we're going to have a lively summer. Dr. Wont, if those rocks are close to shore, why couldn't you anchor a raft out there and work from that?"

"And where am I supposed to get a raft?"

"Build it, I should think. There must be some expendable logs on the island; I've noticed a few dead trees from my bedroom window. If you like, I could speak to Vincent about having his helpers cut them down for you."

Emma didn't really care how Wont solved his problem, but she did want to keep the peace, and a raft seemed harmless enough. Dead pines were a fire hazard; it surely wouldn't hurt to take them down.

"A raft would look good in the illustrations," said Joris Groot. "Kind of a Robinson Crusoe touch."

"Provided we could get to it." Wont wasn't giving in to reason that easily.

"No problem." Black John Sendick was keen enough, that was obvious. "We could pole it back and forth, or rig a cable. Or wade or swim, or buy one of those little rubber boats you blow up with a hand pump. The rocks can't be more than about twenty feet out at high tide, for Pete's sake. We don't need any big Jacques Cousteau number, Ev."

Wont preferred to retain his ire. "I thought I was the one assigned to consider the alternative possibilities. Mrs. Kelling, would it be too much to ask why I was not informed that no boat would be available?"

"Could it be because you failed to tell Mrs. Sabine what you had in mind?"

"But this is outrageous! Out here by ourselves with no way of getting ashore. What if there's an emergency?"

"Like somebody getting punched out by the pirate ghosts," said Black John.

Wont was all set to explode, but Count Radunov defused him. "I have already asked Mr. Vincent what he would do in time of crisis. He said he would radio either his sons or the Coast Guard, depending on the circumstances. Should the radio be out of order, he would send up signal rockets, of which he has ample supply. As a last resort, we could always paddle ourselves ashore on this raft which it now appears should be built. We are in no danger of being marooned, Dr. Wont. I suggest we all relax and enjoy our pudding. It looks, I must say, remarkably good."

NINE

Coffee would be served in the drawing room, that was the way it had always been. Emma was glad to see that Vincent had got a driftwood fire going. At least the flames couldn't be forced to flicker within accustomed patterns or the salt-soaked wood to pop and crackle in a predetermined rhythm.

Sandy and Bernice had the coffee service already set out on a low table pulled up to the sofa. The demitasses were dainty things, pleated like opening hibiscus blossoms, each in a different shade, ranging from rose to orange to yellow to cream. A hostess gift, Emma supposed, from somebody who'd taken the trouble to find out what Adelaide would really like. She reserved the rose-colored one for herself and poured out for her guests. Adelaide Sabine's guests, rather. Still more specifically, Everard Wont's.

Dr. Wont hadn't become any more sociable as the meal progressed, but at least he'd stopped trying to throw his weight around. By now nobody was talking much. Even Count Radunov appeared to think he'd been charming enough for one evening, though he did throw Emma an *intime* little smile now and then when he happened to think of it. She'd put Groot and Sendick beside her on the sofa, but she didn't intend to stay with them any longer than she could decently avoid.

She was tired, desperately tired. She wished she might pack the lot of them off to their temporary dwellings, enjoy the fire by herself for a little while, then go back to that welcoming bedroom and sleep as long as she pleased, with nobody yodeling up and down the stairs.

Instead, she must get to the kitchen and find out what Vincent intended to do with their mysterious castaway. She was glad the caretaker hadn't known about the uninvited guest when he telephoned the Pences. He'd no doubt have felt duty-bound to tell, and they surely didn't need anything more to worry about just now. Emma wondered whether Adelaide would still be alive by the time this house party dispersed. As one grew older, one learned to recognize the look she'd seen on Adelaide's face in the tea tent, the look that meant, "I'm ready to go." On to whatever might happen next. Emma had felt a bit like that herself, on and off, ever since Bed had gone to find out.

More off than on, though; she'd adjusted to living with half of herself someplace where the rest of her couldn't reach. There was always something that had to be done before quitting time, and thank the Lord for that. As soon as she decently could, Emma set down her empty coffee cup and stood up. Without appreciable effort, she was happy to note. Firm sofa pillows were another blessing, though naturally Adelaide Sabine would never have been foolish enough to choose the kind of furniture anybody over forty had to be hauled out of by main force.

"Now if you people will excuse me, I must have that chat with the cook before he goes off duty. I hope you all sleep well during your first night on the island, and I shall look forward to seeing you tomorrow at breakfast. As you know, if you've read your notices, it's served buffet-style between half-past seven and half-past nine. Don't forget to ask for a packed lunch then if you're going to want one later. I'll send one of the girls for the coffee tray," Emma added because she had a psychic hunch Mrs. Fath was wondering whether the guests were supposed to help with the dishes.

Back in the kitchen, she found the company a bit livelier, even though Neil, Ted, and the amnesiac were all absent. Sandy and Bernice were washing dishes with much giggle and chatter and blowing bubbles. Vincent and the cook were having a companionable sit-down over the kitchen table, empty plates and half-full coffee mugs in front of them. When they saw her coming, the men stood up, not at all embarrassed at having been caught acting like normal human beings.

"Don't let me disturb you," Emma said quite redundantly. "I just wanted to let the girls know they can clear away in the drawing room and to ask what you've done with our mystery man. Has he shown any sign of recovering his memory?"

"I expect it'll come back when he takes a notion," Vincent grunted. "We got 'im bedded down for the night in the storeroom. Neil and Ted set up a cot an' done what was reas'nable. They've gone to check the cottages now. We always take a look around last thing before we go to bed. We all sleep in the ell, by the way, so you're not alone in the big house."

"I'm glad to hear it."

"We won't bother you none. Neither will he." Vincent jerked his head back toward where the storeroom was presumably located. "I locked the door."

"Very sensible," Emma approved. "I take it there are no windows in the storeroom."

"Ventilatin' slits high up in the walls. He'll do till my boys pick 'im up. I called and gave 'em the word. They're goin' to stop by an' take 'im ashore after they've finished haulin'. Can't ask 'em to give up a mornin's work."

"No, of course we can't." Emma felt a twinge of guilt at the mere notion of it, even though she wasn't altogether sure what Vincent was talking about. "And I must say I shouldn't mind having another try at getting some information out of him before we let him go."

"Me neither."

Vincent cast a glance down at his cooling coffee. Emma took the hint.

"Then we'll leave it till morning. Good night, everyone."

Emma dragged herself upstairs wondering whether she was going to fall asleep before she got to the top. Once inside her room, though, she found herself oddly reluctant to settle down. She made a lengthy business of getting undressed and parking her wig on its block. Emma had reasonably abundant hair of her own but wasn't one to fritter away time at the hairdresser's when it was so much more sensible to send the hair along without her. She wouldn't have access to a beauty shop for the rest of the summer, she supposed, unless she rode ashore with the lobsters. She'd have to manage the best she could.

Not that it mattered. She quit fiddling with the wig and started patting cream into her face with a tiny pink plastic paddle she'd never used before and couldn't imagine why she was bothering with now. She tossed the paddle in the wastebasket, retied the bow of her nightgown, kicked off her mules—pale green satin ones with pert little heels and marabou trimming; widowed or not, Emma was not yet ready to haul down the flag—and began wandering around the room in her bare feet.

Sandy had dutifully parked Emma's other luggage all arow in the big closet, but the old black Gladstone bag was still squatting on the bench at the foot of the bed. Emma sat down beside it and began sorting through the meretricious glitter that had raised such a fuss on the way here. She didn't know why she bothered; she certainly didn't intend to start glueing in rhinestones tonight.

It was immediately clear to her that the fairies' baubles had not been treated kindly during their brief pillage. Before starting on her journey, Emma had taken everything out and repacked the bag as neatly as the varied shapes and conditions allowed. Now the pieces were all one great jumble. The ferryboat snatcher must have taken them into the loo, she decided, and dumped them out to see what he'd got. When he'd found out he'd wasted his time, he'd stuffed them back any old way and ditched the bag where Radunov had found it. Or not, as the case might have been.

There was no earthly reason to take them out again now, but Emma did. They were, after all, old acquaintances. This was going to be the Pirates' fifth *Iolanthe*. No, their sixth, with all those others in between. Dear heaven, where had the years gone? She picked up the Fairy Queen's crown, the one with the big diamond butterfly on top, and perched it on her head for auld lang syne while she untangled the rest of the gauds. So it was five times, not four, that she'd tyrannized over her fairy court and nursed her secret passion for Private Willis before she'd faced the truth and called a halt.

"Leave 'em while you're lookin' good." Mae West had said that. Emma and Bed had sneaked off to Boston by train on their very first all-alone date to catch Mae's then-latest movie. They'd dined at the Copley Plaza on Bed's father's charge account, then gone on to the Tremont. Or was it the Majestic? She'd been too dazed with love and excitement to remember afterward, and she'd never thought in later years to ask.

One dressed in those days. She'd worn her coming-out gown with pink roses instead of white and that bottle green velvet wrap Bed had always loved her in, Emma remembered that well enough. Bed had been in tux, looking handsome enough to turn heads and pretending not to notice, the darling ham. And the movie palace had been a gorgeous welter of rococo swirls and painted ceilings and crimson plush draperies and sky-high gold-framed mirrors and chandeliers totally beyond the scope of reason or logic.

The last time her grandchildren had dragged her to a movie, they'd sat in a barren cube that might as well have been a lecture room in a teaching hospital, and the film had been about talking robots. Poor, glamour-starved children, little did they know how deprived they were. Emma took off the crown and looked in the satchel for the best place to stow it.

Over the years, the old Gladstone bag had taken a good many knocks. Even the thin calf lining was bubbled and ripped in places. One of the rips was longer than Emma remembered; something had got caught down inside. She fished out the bauble and thought she was going to faint.

Emma had enough diamonds of her own to know the true from the false. These were all too true. This was no mere necklace but what her mother would have called a dog collar: a band of diamonds fully an inch and a quarter wide, set in four solid rows, every single diamond as big as a baby pea. Dangling from it on diamond-studded platinum chains were three pear-shaped pendants, one with a blue diamond not more than half the size of the Hope, one with a yellow diamond of equal weight, and one great, dark blaze that could only be a rare black diamond, all of them framed in yet more diamonds—smaller ones these, of a paltry half-carat or so apiece.

Emma tried to think what such jewels might be worth on today's market and boggled. The women she knew didn't buy diamonds, they inherited them or got them from their lawfully wedded husbands. She herself had her grandmother's lovely sunburst, naturally, and her mother's modest parure, besides the ring Bed had put on her finger that fateful night going home from the Lambda Chi hop and the stud earrings he'd given her when Young Bed was born. All these were useful pieces a woman in Emma Kelling's position might reasonably have occasion to wear. Who on earth would dare to appear in a great lump of ostentation like this? A royal personage or a movie star, perhaps, surely not anyone from Pleasaunce.

As to the owner of the necklace, that was for the police to find out. As to what it was doing in Bed's uncle's Gladstone bag, that was no great enigma. Whoever stole the diamonds had had to get rid of them in a hurry. Emma Kelling's happening to show up on the ferry with a satchelful of fake jewels had offered a chance to work the old purloined-letter trick.

She'd read in the paper not long ago that there were more multi-millionaires in Maine than anywhere else in the United States, notwithstanding the fact that Maine was by no means a wealthy state by and large. They would be chiefly part-time residents like the Sabines, Emma surmised, weekenders and vacationers who came and went as the mood took them. It would not be too farfetched to visualize one of those super-rich women taking the ferry on a whim in the old Blue Train manner with a jewel case and a light-fingered maid or else with a husband whose millions were less multi than he was anxious to make his business associates keep on believing. This amazing discovery might be evidence of outright theft or of an insurance fraud in the making. Emma didn't care which; her sole concern just now was how to get rid of it.

Was this her only problem, as if it weren't enough? She laid the dog collar on the bed, fetched the long hatpin she'd worn on the boat to anchor her long-cherished panama, and began probing the bag's lining. To her relief, she failed to strike pay dirt again. To steady her nerves, she went back to sorting out the *Iolanthe* pieces. Some of the sets were incomplete, but that didn't surprise her. They'd been lent around so many times that it was a marvel the Pirates hadn't lost them all.

None of these blatant fakes could have functioned as a plausible substitute for that gold digger's dream. Emma supposed a couple might possibly have been stuffed into the jewel case, supposing there was one, in order to bring it back to the correct weight after the collar was taken out. For no special reason, she picked up the Fairy Queen's necklace she'd chosen for herself so many years ago, doubled it into a neat package, and stuffed it under the lining whence she'd drawn out the dog collar. Then, suddenly disgusted with the whole business, she jumbled the rest of the stuff in on top of it and closed the bag as best she could.

The plan, she assumed, had been for an accomplice to collect the bag from the men's room. Somebody might be feeling pretty sick about now because Count Radunov had got to it first. Unless, of course, Radunov himself was the accomplice. He could have made the pickup any time while she was asleep and decided only after that next-to-last stop that it would be safer to let her carry the Gladstone bag off the ferry herself. He'd have gambled on the assumption that a silly woman who'd let herself be drugged and temporarily robbed in full daylight aboard a busy ferryboat wouldn't have the brains to notice there'd been an addition to her imitation dragon's hoard before he found the chance to steal the necklace back again.

Well, Emma knew how to deal with that. Adelaide Sabine had confided to her the whereabouts of a wall safe that even Vincent was supposed not to know about. Emma thought he probably did, but he probably wouldn't know the combination; he wouldn't suppose Mrs. Kelling had anything special to put in it, and he wasn't likely to come snooping anyway. She put on her blue robe and found a pair of soft-soled slippers. It mightn't be wise to go clacking about in her mules.

Nor did she feel like turning on a light in Adelaide's bedroom, not even a flashlight. Ted and Neil might still be doing their rounds outside, or one of the cottagers could be taking a pre-bedtime stroll. The windows were large and the moon was close to full; she'd be able to see well enough. Emma turned off her own light, put the dog collar in the pocket of her robe, and went into the only other bedroom on the floor.

Hers was good-sized, but the one Adelaide and her late spouse had occupied was enormous. Mr. Sabine's bed had never been taken away; it stood complete with its nightstand and one of those high-backed wooden chairs with a coat hanger on top. There was a huge armoire; Emma supposed that was to compensate for inadequate closet space. There was a writing desk, and no puny one, either. There were a vanity table with a triple mirror, a cheval glass, a chiffonier, a semainier, assorted dressers, a slipper chair, an armchair, a spring rocker covered in faded tapestry, a television set in a walnut cabinet dating from the late fifties, if Emma was any judge. This must have been the Sabines' escape hatch when their never-ending duties as host and hostess got too overwhelming for them.

The safe was inside a small closet next to one of the beds. To Emma's relief, there was a bare bulb in the closet ceiling, with a long cord hanging from it. They'd left the light on to keep down the mildew, she surmised; dampness and mold were the penalties of living so close to the water. She let herself inside, closed the door, took down a woolen bathrobe that felt as if the moths had been at it—one of the late George Sabine's, probably, left hanging there partly for sentimental reasons—and found the knot in the cedar paneling exactly where Adelaide had said she would. She pushed.

A very neat job; her own carpenter couldn't have done better. Where no crack in the paneling had been visible, a tiny door flipped open. A small wall safe was revealed. Emma dialed the combination Adelaide had given her, opened the inner door, laid the necklace inside on top of some yellowed papers, which she naturally did not read, and closed the safe. She hung the bathrobe back on the hook over the knot and shut up the closet with a feeling of great relief.

Tomorrow she'd get in touch with Sarah's husband. One of Max Bittersohn's specialties was the discreet tracking down of stolen jewels; he'd know how to cope. For tonight, she'd done what she could. The sensible thing now would be to push that outrageous necklace to the back of her mind and try to get some sleep.

TEN

This was a heavenly room to wake up in. Emma lay watching the sunbeams dance across the old-fashioned lilac plissé blanket cover, pleased that her bed was so comfortable, that she wasn't feeling exhausted any longer, that the wood thrushes were in good voice, that from somewhere down below, a faint whiff of brewing coffee was being wafted up to her. She slid out of bed, put on her robe, for the sea breeze through the open windows had a morning nip to it, and went to the bathroom.

Now, back to bed or up and at it? Emma was debating the issue with one slipper on and one off when she heard a knock at her door. She put on the other slipper and called out, "Come in."

It was Sandy, bless the child, with a tray. "I heard the john flush, so I knew you must be up. Bubbles made the tea, and I picked the rose. There was a bug in it, but I chased him out. Go ahead and sniff if you want."

"How lovely. Thank you, Sandy."

The rose was a fluffy little pink one, the sort one always saw blooming in great clusters around old houses near the seashore at this time of year. Sandy had sorted out the prettiest, Emma supposed, and found that tiny silver vase for it somewhere in Adelaide's cupboards. So many charming things around here for the heirs to squabble over when the end came. Marcia wasn't the squabbling kind, but Emma wasn't so sure about those two sisters-in-law of hers. Perhaps Adelaide would have left lists of who was to get what, or perhaps she didn't care by now. Emma poured from the graceful silver pot into the dainty china cup and sipped. Perfect tea, of course. How could it be otherwise?

Sandy showed no disposition to leave. Emma didn't mind. "What sort of day are we going to have?" she asked the child.

"Mixed, I guess. The weather's okay, but Dad's blowing up a storm."

"Oh dear. What about?"

"You know the guy Ted found down at the point? He's gone."

"Sandy, no! I thought your father had him locked in the storeroom."

"He did, that's what Dad's so mad about. He thinks one of us let him out."

"Which one?" Emma hadn't meant to snap.

"Not me. And it couldn't have been Bernice because we sleep in the same room and she always stubs her toe on the bedpost and says 'ouch' when she gets up, so I'd have known. Anyway, she's scared of the dark."

"Then he suspects your brother or Ted?"

"Well, to begin with, Dad was none too pleased last night when Neil and Ted brought the guy into the house without asking him first. He likes to know what's going on. And Neil's mad because he thinks Dad was unfair. My mother says Neil's going through a phase, but I think it's just general cussedness. Parents never understand their children. You want more tea, Mrs. Kelling? There's still some in the pot. I could pour it for you."

"Just a touch, then. I don't like my cup too full."

Her cup was already running over, Emma thought gloomily. Why couldn't that beastly man stay put? At least he hadn't come roaming—or had he? She distinctly remembered leaving the Gladstone bag on the bench last night. It certainly wasn't there now. Emma set down her cup and began hunting around the room, to Sandy's expressed surprise.

"What's the matter, Mrs. Kelling? Did you lose something? Can I help?"

"Yes, you can. I'm missing that little black bag with the fairies' jewelry. Remember, you saw it yesterday when you helped me unpack. Take a quick look around the house. If you can't find it, go tell your father. I suspect that man may have taken it."

"Gosh! You mean he came in here while you were asleep?"

"He or somebody else, unless I walked in my sleep, which I've never done before. Sandy, I am very upset about this. Please hurry. I'm going to get dressed now."

The girl scurried away. Emma washed in a hurry, did her face, and put on a khaki cotton skirt, a beige-and-green striped shirt, and putty-colored espadrilles. With suitable underpinnings, of course. Time was when she'd have gone stockingless on a hot summer day, but never, never, braless. Emma could not imagine why any nubile female would ever have put herself to that particular discomfort just to make a political point. Didn't they know the brassiere as now worn was a modern invention designed to free women from the long, constraining, tight-laced corsets their bare-bosomed, unenfranchised grandmas and great-grandmothers had been forced to depend on for support where it was most needed?

No, they didn't. Nobody knew anything any more, they left it all to the computers. Emma squirted herself with Norell to show one's heart was loyal to the cause of femininity, put on her wig, and was ready for action by the time Vincent arrived at her bedroom door. He looked ready to bite somebody's head off, and she didn't blame him a bit.

"Sandy says you want to see me," he all but growled.

"Yes. She told me we've lost our amnesiac. Did she tell you he apparently didn't leave empty-handed?"

"Took your satchel with some jewelry in it, she says. Nothin' valuable, I hope?"

"No," Emma reassured him, "quite the contrary. Just some old costume jewelry I'd brought along to repair. But it's annoying to be robbed, just the same. Curiously enough, the stuff had already been stolen yesterday on the boat, then dumped in a washroom. Count Radunov rescued it for me. I'm beginning to wish he hadn't."

Should she tell Vincent about what she'd found in the bag last night, or should she not? Not, she decided; not yet, anyway. She'd known too many excellent amateur actors to take this Down East Admirable Crichton at face value. Besides, while Emma wasn't quite ready to come straight out and admit to herself that she didn't want somebody else running the show, the fact remained that she was used to being in charge. So was Vincent, obviously; he'd probably been running things pretty much his own way out here for years, especially since George Sabine died. Naturally Emma Kelling would not engage in anything so vulgar as a power struggle; it would never have occurred to her that she needed to. She'd told him about the bag, that was reason enough to expect some action.

"I've checked my handbag," she went on, "and nothing else appears to be missing. However, I do not relish the realization that somebody was prowling around my bedroom while I was asleep. If there's any sort of police force around here, I suggest we notify them."

"They know," said Vincent. "I got to thinkin' early this mornin' about you an' me having our chance for another go at 'im today before the boys come, an' decided to have a look at 'im. So I went to the storeroom to see if he showed any signs o' gettin' his memory back, an' he was gone, slick as a weasel. Cot hadn't even been slept in, far's I could tell. So I got on the phone to my brother Lowell—he's the harbor master—an' told 'im to notify the shore police an' start searchin' the harbor himself. I aim to comb the island, me an' the boys. I can't see how he could o' got off, but then I still don't know how he got on. Don't know how he got out o' that storeroom, neither, but I sure aim to find out."

Vincent had a jaw like a lobster trap, Emma thought irreverently, but much more solid. "Are you quite sure he didn't manage it by himself?" she asked.

"Door wasn't forced, lock wasn't broken, vents aren't big enough to squeeze a cat through, 'less it was a kitten. Stands to reason somebody let 'im out. Unless he had a key in his pocket when I put 'im in there. Which he didn't, because I frisked 'im pretty good with my own hands."

"But would it have been feasible for someone to let him out? How would they have got hold of the key? Didn't you keep it with you?"

Vincent wasn't precisely abashed, but he did look a trifle uncomfortable. "No, I didn't. See, the room where I sleep is down at the far end of the hall. I use that one because it's got an outside door to it so's I can get down to the boat or whatever without wakin' the rest. That means I'm quite a ways from the storeroom. Normally, like in the wintertime when there's nobody guardin' the place, I'd lock the deadbolt an' take the key with me when I left. But havin' a live human bein' inside was different. I couldn't help thinkin' what if there was a fire, or what if he done somethin' foolish an' needed to be got out in a hurry an' I didn't hear?"

"I see. Yes, of course."

"So, figurin' I could trust my own staff," he went on with some bitterness, "I hung the key back inside the key box where we usually keep it an' went to bed."

"The key box is in the kitchen?" Emma prompted.

"Next to the pantry door, where we can get at it easy. We never used to bother much about lockin' up in Mr. Sabine's day, but now with all these crazy writers an' what-not around, I'm scared not to. I never thought I'd have to worry about my own flesh and blood."

"Aren't you being a bit hasty in your judgment? Why couldn't it have been one of the cottagers who let him out?"

"They'd have to be pretty cagey to figure out how, seein' as they just got here yesterday afternoon. None of 'em so much as set foot in the kitchen last evenin', accordin' to Bubbles, so how'd they even know the man was here? I don't know what to say, Mrs. Kelling. Nothin' like this ever happened before, not since I been comin' to the island."

"Well, Vincent, it's not the end of the world."

Emma was less inclined by now to suppose the caretaker was other than sincere. He wasn't used to having his authority flouted, and he didn't know how to handle it. She could empathize with that. "I assume you have an inventory of the house's contents. If you like, I could start checking around after breakfast while you get on with your outside search. If our man's escaped with nothing more valuable than my old Gladstone bag, I'd say we're well rid of him. Since you say the cottagers don't know he was ever here, we don't have to tell them anything. If anybody starts asking questions, we'll know who to blame for letting him out. Now I'd better get down to breakfast. You've had yours, I expect?"

"Yes, Mrs. Kelling. I'll bring the inventory list up here an' leave it on the desk so's you can get goin' soon as you're ready. If you need me or the boys for anything, just give a whang on that big ship's bell outside the kitchen door. Any of the comp'ny want to know what we're up to, we'll tell 'em we're doin' an ecological survey."

They shared a much-needed laugh at that and went downstairs together. Emma had wanted to be first in the dining room, and she was. Bubbles was still fussing around a row of chafing dishes on the long buffet beside the table. He was delighted to see her.

"You thit right down, Mithith Kelling. I'll therve you a nithe plate ath thoon ath I get thethe disheth thet up."

"Please don't bother about me, Bubbles. I just wanted to make sure I'm here to greet the guests as they arrive. Thank you for the tea, by the way. You might send one of the girls up for the tray as soon as she can be spared."

Bubbles assured her in a fine cascade of misplaced sibilants that he could eathily thpare either Thandy or Bernithe any time she wanted them and went back to the kitchen murmuring of hot toatht and muffinth. Emma was beginning to think an inventory of the chafing dishes might be interesting when Black John Sendick bounced into the room, wearing almost invisible jogging shorts and a baggy sweatshirt with a picture of Tycho Brahe on it.

"Hi, Mrs. Kelling, been swimming yet? I have, for about thirteen and a half seconds. I tell you, Maine water is cold! What smells so good?"

Emma smiled. He reminded her of her grandson Wally except that, mercifully, he wasn't yodeling. "I was just about to find out. Shall we?"

They'd got nicely settled with their plates when Joris Groot joined them. Groot announced that he'd slept like a log and expressed his considered opinion that there was nothing like sea air to give a person an appetite. He then helped himself to a good deal of everything and proceeded to eat it all.

Lisbet Quainley showed up with Everard Wont in tow while Emma was finishing her second cup of coffee and wondering whether she'd be more usefully employed starting the inventory than staying there to see whether anybody was going to mention the man in the kitchen. That was how Mrs. Fath had referred to him last night.

Or had she? There'd been, Emma reminded herself, four men in the kitchen at the time, five if one counted Neil. She might have meant any one of them, or have simply been talking for effect, knowing there was bound to be somebody she could pinpoint as her intended target should anything happen that might lend any weight to her vague prediction.

Anyway, nobody was saying anything about a man; they were all too busy telling her how well they'd slept. Even Everard Wont was admitting to an undisturbed night, not that Emma believed him. Lisbet Quainley had been clutching his arm in a proprietary sort of way, looking rather wan about the eyes, when they came in. It was more likely they'd bedded down together, though what either could have seen in the other was a mystery to her. At least Wont had shaved and showered and put on a clean red jersey with his blue jeans. Was that for Lisbet? More probably he'd decided he'd better start trying to mend fences with Mrs. Sabine's representative. So far, at least, he hadn't made a single attempt this morning to throw his weight around.

Emma was surprised Alding Fath hadn't yet manifested herself. She'd thought the psychic would be an early riser and an enthusiastic breakfaster, considering her alleged country upbringing. It was nine o'clock by now, according to Emma's wristwatch, and still no Mrs. Fath.

There was, however, Count Radunov, fresh as a daisy and twice as ornamental in pale gray slacks, blue shirt, red ascot, and a madras plaid cotton blazer in navy, red, and gray. Emma had guessed he'd show up about now. She'd been right on one of them, at any rate. The count did not tell her he'd slept well, he said it was obvious Mrs. Kelling had slept well. He made flattering allusions to morning dew and the blush of the rosa rugosa, but he said nothing about a missing stranger.

Emma decided she had in fact been wasting her time here, and furthermore that she shouldn't have eaten that last muffin. She pushed back her chair. "Don't forget to ask for your luncheon baskets; you know we shan't be serving again until dinnertime. I do hope Mrs. Fath remembers breakfast is over at half-past nine. Perhaps I'd better nip out to her cottage and make sure she's aware of the time."

Nobody volunteered to go in her place. Count Radunov had made a well-pondered selection from the chafing dishes and was giving his chosen viands the serious consideration they deserved. Wont and his fellow treasure-seekers were deep in a discussion of the raft they either were or weren't going to build. Emma left them to it, took a faded straw sun hat that must have been Adelaide's from a rack by the door, and went out into the sunlight.

Except for that short walk up from the dock yesterday, this was the first chance she'd had to stretch her legs on the island soil. It was good to feel the springy pine mold under her canvas shoes, to sniff the piny scent she kicked up at each step. Emma remembered the path to the cottages well enough; nothing much had changed since that long-ago time when she and Bed had walked here. Island trees never grew big, they got too much buffeting from the sea winds. Acid rain hadn't done much harm yet to the island granite as far as Emma could tell, but then she felt no great affinity with rocks. They were too sedentary for a woman of her temperament.

Now, which cottage was Alding Fath's? Ah yes, the one down by the cove, the same one Emma and Bed had slept in that time. The inner door was open; Emma could see clearly enough into the one good-size room. Mrs. Fath was lying in the single bed, her head on the pillow, the rest of her hidden by a pale blue blanket. She was awake, but showed no inclination to rise even when Emma went up on the porch and tapped on the wooden frame around the screen door.

"Mrs. Fath, are you all right?"

That roused her enough to raise her head a little. She stared at the door as though she couldn't remember where she was. "Oh, Mrs. Kelling." Her voice was somewhat between a drawl and a croak, nothing like last night's brisk, cheerful prattle. "I don't know. I just don't feel right. Wait a minute."

Mrs. Fath fumbled the blanket away from her body, revealing a great deal of peach-colored tricot. Her nightgown had got hiked up around her hips, and she spent quite a time tugging it down while Emma gazed steadfastly out to sea. At last the seeress got herself decently covered in a garish Japanese kimono, the slimpsy kind made of a cheap synthetic Emma had only seen before hanging in touristy souvenir shops. She stuck her bare feet into straw scuffs and slipslopped over to the door.

"Sorry to keep you waiting, Mrs. Kelling. I left the screen door hooked. Afraid the skunks would come in and get me, I guess, though I can't think what they'd want me for. It was too stuffy with the door shut. I couldn't get my breath."

"Oh dear, didn't you sleep well?"

"I don't know. Seems to me I'd drop off and then wake up feeling smothered, don't ask me why. I'm usually a great sleeper. I can't think what's the matter with me. I just don't feel right."

"In what way don't you feel right, Mrs. Fath? Is it your stomach?"

"Not specially. It's—well, there's this funny feeling in my head, and I'm kind of woozy standing up. I'm not sick exactly; I just don't feel right."

She didn't look right, either, though Emma couldn't quite figure out why. "I do hope you're not coming down with something, Mrs. Fath. You don't suppose it could simply be that you got too much sun yesterday on the boat?" Emma couldn't imagine how a person might get a delayed reaction from sunstroke, but it was the least contagious thing she could think of. "It couldn't have been dinner; everybody else feels fine. They're finishing breakfast now; I came to see if you wanted any. We stop serving in about fifteen minutes."

Mrs. Fath didn't say anything.

"I could send one of the girls over with some tea and toast."

This was stretching the rules, but surely Adelaide wouldn't mind Emma's making an exception for somebody who didn't feel right. Mrs. Fath finally managed a pathetic attempt at pretending to be grateful.

"That's nice of you, Mrs. Kelling, but I—I don't know. It seems like such an effort."

"Maybe you're simply tired out. Have you been working awfully hard lately? You haven't had any—er—psychic intimations that you ought to take a good rest?"

"I never get messages for myself, just about other people. And when I'm not feeling right, I can't get anything at all. Ev's going to be awful mad if it turns out he's paid my fare up here for nothing."

ELEVEN

The seeress didn't sound unduly worried at the prospect. Emma began to have a psychic intimation of her own. Could this be how Mrs. Fath intended to wangle herself a pleasant vacation with all expenses paid while getting around the problem of not being able to locate Pocapuk's imaginary treasure? Emma knew she ought to be affronted, but she found herself rather amused and wholly sympathetic.

"You'd better get back to bed, then. I'll have somebody look in on you after a while. Here, let me help you."

For a second there, she'd thought the woman was going to faint. Maybe it was part of the act, but Emma didn't dare take any chances. She steered Mrs. Fath over to the bed, helped her out of her kimono, and got her safely tucked in. Her pulse was a trifle slow—Emma had done enough home nursing on her own family to know—but lots of people had slow pulses for no special reason. Her skin felt chilly and clammy, but why shouldn't it if she'd been there for some time with the sea breeze blowing in through that open door? Emma decided the sensible thing would be to let the woman rest a while longer and see what happened.

She went back to the house, spoke to Bubbles about taking Mrs. Fath a light snack in a little while, and got to work on the inventory.

Rather than go down the entire list, which would take the rest of the summer from the look of it, she decided to check out the more obvious possibilities, starting with the one thing that wasn't listed.

The necklace was exactly as she'd left it in the wall safe. It really was an impossibly gorgeous thing, she had to admit. Could she be wrong about the diamonds being genuine? Emma picked up the tumbler that went with Adelaide's bedside carafe and tried an experimental scratch or two. Sharp and clear, no doubt whatsoever. She got a bit carried away and began doodling little ducks and fishes on the glass with various stones, realized what she was doing, and put the necklace back in the safe.

She oughtn't to have handled it so freely; there might have been fingerprints. Could fingerprints be got off diamond necklaces? One wouldn't think so, but police laboratories did manage incredible technical feats these days. She'd better switch this glass with the one in her bedroom and accidentally drop it on the bathroom floor. Too bad to break up the set, but those clear glass carafes were nothing that couldn't be replaced, assuming there'd be any point in doing so. She went on to Adelaide's dresser.

Silver filigree perfume bottles, silver-backed brushes, combs, buttonhooks, silver pin tray, silver picture frames, silver thisses, silver thats, all present and accounted for. Wedding presents, birthday presents, silver anniversary presents, Emma supposed. Guests would have noticed the plethora of silver gewgaws, decided the Sabines must be collecting them, and sent some more. That was a penalty of being rich; one kept on accumulating stuff that had to be taken care of. These knickknacks were rather badly in need of polish; she'd turn Sandy and Bernice loose on them some rainy afternoon.

Not that they'd ever be at a loss for chores; there was a great deal of work here for two young girls. Vincent might have been better advised to get somebody more grown up, but perhaps an older girl wouldn't have wanted to be stuck out on an island all summer. Or perhaps Vincent had shied away from starting something that might lead to a sticky finish. That fellow Ted had what Emma's mother would have called an eye; Mama wouldn't have trusted any housemaid of hers within a mile of him.

Enough of this. Nothing was missing up here that Emma could see. The dining room must have been put to rights by now, she'd better go count the silver there. She was exploring the buffet for some triple-plated serving pieces when Vincent burst through from the kitchen, soaking wet, dripping on the carpet and not even noticing.

"Vincent, what is it?" she exclaimed. "Can't you see what—"

"I got to get to the phone."

When a man spoke in that tone, a woman knew better than to ask him why. Emma stood aside and let him pass. The proper thing then would have been to stay here and keep on counting silver. Emma followed him into the living room.

Vincent didn't pay any attention to her. He got the phone out of its box and dialed a number he didn't have to look up.

"Lowell there? Hell! Then get ahold of him fast as you can an' tell 'im the bugger's found. Over the cliff in five feet o' water, dead as a mackerel with 'is head stove in. Hit the rocks runnin', looks like. Tell Lowell I said he better get out here quick as the Lord'll let 'im."

He slammed down the receiver without waiting for an answer and turned to Emma, taking it for granted she'd been listening.

"We got 'im up on George's Rock."

"Where is that, Vincent?"

"High end o' the island, over beyond the pine grove. Drops off pretty steep there. He must o' went over in the dark an' got caught down among the rocks an' mud with the tide makin'. Good thing it was comin' in 'stead o' goin' out or we might never o' known what become of 'im. Ted spied that ol' black bag o' yours floatin' upside down, is how we happened to look there. Must o' got air trapped inside when it fell. So we clambered down an' fished around some an' there he was."

"What a shock it must have been for you!"

"It was a worse one for him, I reckon. Must o' lost 'is bearin's an' thought he was headin' for the dock. Or somewheres. Anyways, that's where he got to." Vincent was being garrulous, for him. Shock took some people that way.

"Ted's blowing up the rubber boat we keep for emergencies. We wasn't goin' to let on we got one for fear that loudmouth who thinks he's going to find Pocapuk's treasure'd get 'is paws on it an' tear it to pieces on the rocks. Didn't seem sensible to haul the poor bugger up over the cliff on a rope an' have to carry 'im out o' the woods on a stretcher, though. We figure to load 'im aboard off the rock an' float 'im around to the dock so's Lowell can pick 'im up easy in the patrol boat."

"Much the best plan," said Emma. Not that she knew, but what did it matter? "Vincent, hadn't you better get yourself a tot of brandy and put on some dry clothes?"

"Mug o' coffee'll do me. No sense changin' now when I'm just goin' to get wet again. We picked up a few o' your pieces. The bag must o' come open when he fell. Neil's still huntin' for the rest of 'em."

"Yes, the clasp was broken. Please tell Neil not to bother. I'm ashamed to think a man lost his life over so paltry a theft."

It hadn't been something paltry, it had been the diamond necklace he'd thought he was stealing. And that probably meant he had an accomplice who'd not only let him out of the storeroom but also told him where to look. She ought to tell Vincent right now. But Vincent was in no mood to listen.

"I got to get back. You goin' to tell the rest of 'em?"

"We'll have to, shouldn't you think, if we're going to have a corpse laid out on the dock till the boat shows up? In any event, this should make an exciting addition to Dr. Wont's book," Emma added dryly.

Vincent grunted. "One man's foul weather's another one's fair. You wasn't plannin' to put it off too long?"

"No, I'll do it right now. I don't suppose there's much point in going on with this inventory now that we know he didn't take anything except my bag."

"We don't know," Vincent contradicted. "Might be somethin' we haven't found yet."

"Then it will turn up when the tide goes out, won't it? Are the rocks bare then?"

"Just about, but that ain't sayin' the stuff mightn't get washed out on the ebb tide. She's just about on the turn now. Don't leave us much time to look."

"I'll hurry," Emma promised. "Where are the cottagers, do you know?"

"Last I seen of 'em, they was over lookin' out at Shag Rock an' wishin' pretty loud for somebody to build 'em a raft. You take that path from the side door over there an' keep on it till you come to either them or the ocean, dependin'."

Vincent squelched off to the kitchen. Emma put Adelaide's sun hat back on and went out the side door. Actually she wasn't going to need the hat, she realized. The sun, which had been so bright when she'd gone to check on Mrs. Fath, was now all but obscured by great clouds. So much for the forecast. Well, she wasn't going to bother taking the hat back, not now.

She hurried on. Once down from the knoll, she could hear a distant yapping that sounded like a dog but was more probably Everard Wont laying down the law about something or other. She couldn't make out any words, but that didn't bother her.

Sounds must carry remarkably well on the island, Emma decided after she'd been walking for a while. She still didn't seem to be near the end of the path; she hadn't caught so much as a glimpse of the ocean. She didn't mind; she wasn't looking forward to telling the cottagers about the dead man, and she was enjoying the exercise in spite of her conscience. Wont had stopped orating, thank goodness; she was able to pick out the birds' various tweets, chirps, honks, and quacks over the less obtrusive voices of his companions.

Emma herself must have been making no noise at all; Count Radunov was even more startled than she when she rounded a particularly large boulder and ran smack into him.

"Oh, sorry," she gasped. "I was hurrying."

The count must keep his aplomb within easy reach at all times. He replied suavely, "And why should one hurry on so glorious a day? Dear madame, can I not persuade you to linger with me in this enchanted spot?"

This was no glorious day, the wind was picking up and those clouds were growing blacker and thicker by the second. Nor was there anything particularly enchanting about the spot that Emma could see. Furthermore, that was surely poison ivy growing up the rock he'd been lounging against.

Or had he been lounging? Radunov was giving the impression of having lounged, but Emma had used the same bit of business once when she was playing Buttercup in *Pinafore*. And carried it off, she thought, a good deal more convincingly.

"I haven't time to linger," she all but snarled back, "and you'd better get away from that poison ivy or you'll be sorry you didn't."

That fetched him, and he fell into step with her. They walked the rest of the path together without saying much of anything. In fact, the end was just over a short rise. As Vincent had told her, Everard Wont, Groot, Sendick, and Lisbet Quainley were clustered on the shore, staring out at some rocks shaggy with bladderwort, scaly with mussels, black with the splashing of the increasingly high waves. One rock was taller than the rest, shaped like a stela, and capped with white. Miss Quainley's phallic symbol, no doubt. Emma suppressed a wholly unsuitable giggle. Radunov was trying not to look too amused; she preferred not to speculate on what he might be thinking.

Black John's sweatshirt lay on the beach, if such the narrow strip of rocks and dried seaweed could be called. His trunks were wet and his skin looked a trifle blue; he must have been braving the cold water again. Groot had a camera slung around his neck but wasn't taking any pictures. Lisbet Quainley was making a few absent-minded squiggles with a stick of charcoal on a drawing pad she held in the crook of her left arm. None of them seemed to mind being interrupted in whatever conclave they might have been holding, though Wont's greeting was less than cordial.

"Oh, it's you. Where's Alding?"

"In bed," Emma told him. "She's not feeling well."

Of course he took her answer as a personal affront. "What do you mean, she's not feeling well? What's wrong with her?"

"I have no idea. Neither does she. We're hoping it's simply that she's exhausted from traveling and feeling the change in climate. Anyway, she's going to take it easy today and the chances are she'll be fine by tomorrow. But that's not what I'm here to tell you," Emma went on before Wont could start his hectoring again. "I'm sorry to say that something dreadful has happened. I should explain first that it's not any of our staff, not even anybody they know. Apparently the man himself didn't know who he was."

She had them now. Emma explained the whole business: Ted's finding a stranger in a torn wet suit who claimed not to remember anything about himself or how he'd got to Pocapuk, the man's escaping from the storeroom, his being found dead in the water at the foot of the cliff with her Gladstone bag floating above him and her false jewels scattered around him.

"Might be able to use it." Joris Groot was fingering his camera. "Is he still there?"

"No." Emma supposed she couldn't blame an illustrator for focusing on the graphic possibilities, but she was repelled nevertheless. Wont at least was having the grace to keep his mouth shut, though she did notice the nod he gave Groot. One for the book.

Lisbet Quainley's reaction was at least appropriate. "Oh, Mrs. Kelling, I am so sorry. Thank goodness he didn't hurt you! But how did he know you had the jewelry? You don't suppose one of the staff—but they wouldn't, would they? I mean, Mrs. Sabine wouldn't have anybody around who—" She realized she was on shaky ground. "And besides, there's no telephone. Is there?"

Emma wasn't about to open up any schism between the cottagers and the staff. "What I think, Miss Quainley, is that this man must have fallen for a ridiculous yarn my cabdriver was spreading around the dock after he'd let me off at the ferry. You see, when he picked up my bag to put it in the cab, the clasp let go. He noticed the glitter inside and started talking about Pocapuk's treasure. It dawned on me that he must think I was carrying real stones, so I told him they were only costume jewelry and I was Mrs. Sabine's new housekeeper. But he quite obviously didn't believe me."

"Who would?" murmured Count Radunov. "Dear lady, your housekeeping abilities are no doubt without parallel, but never, never could you fool anyone into thinking you were somebody else's servant."

"I could if I'd had time to develop the part," Emma insisted. "You should have seen me as Hannah in *Ruddigore*."

"To my dying day, I shall regret having missed that performance. But this, what you tell us, is most remarkable. It is, if I may say so, hard to credit that this unfortunate man obtained a wet suit at a moment's notice and swam behind the ferryboat all the way to Pocapuk. That he rode the ferry with us and jumped overboard only when we were coming into the dock is possible, one may suppose, but why did none of us see him do it?"

"If he waited till we were all down in the gangway waiting to come ashore and jumped off the stern, he could have done it, I'll bet," said Black John Sendick, "but what's to say he didn't come in another boat? He could have driven along the coast until he was near Pocapuk, then got some pal of his to bring him as close as he could come in the boat without being spotted and swum the rest of the way. That's what I'd do if I were writing the story."

"If you wrote the story, you'd have no trouble providing the pal," grunted Joris Groot. "What if this guy didn't know anybody with a boat?"

"He could have hired somebody, couldn't he? And they didn't come back last night to pick him up the way they were supposed to, which is how he drowned."

"I don't see where that follows."

"Maybe I'll have to work on the plot a little," Black John conceded. "Anyway, he must have got here somehow, or he wouldn't be dead now. Dead on Pocapuk, I mean. So what's going to happen next, Mrs. Kelling?"

"Vincent has made arrangements for his brother, who's the harbor master, to come and pick up the body in his boat. I'm not sure when the boat will get here. In the meantime, Vincent and his helpers were planning to float the body around to the dock, since bringing it up over the cliff would be too difficult. So I'd suggest we all stay away from there."

"You mean we can't even go see him?" protested the young writer.

"John, you ghoul!" cried Lisbet Quainley.

"I was just thinking that if he was on the ferry, maybe some of us could identify him."

Sendick was either blushing or getting badly sunburned, Emma thought, despite the low overcast. She couldn't tell whether he was really being ghoulish or merely helpful. A combination of the two, most likely; the corpse of a mysterious stranger must be a powerful temptation to a budding crime writer.

"I don't know what the protocol will be," she told him. "You'd have to ask Vincent. As for myself, I just hope whoever's to deal with this horrible affair will come along soon. Mysteries are all very well in books, but I loathe them in real life."

"What a rotten time for Alding to get sick. She'd have everything solved in no time flat." That was Lisbet Quainley again; Emma realized she was jeering. Miss Quainley didn't believe in Alding Fath's psychic powers any more than Emma herself did.

Then which of these people did take Mrs. Fath seriously? Everard Wont, presumably, since he was evidently basing his entire summer's work on the premise that Mrs. Fath could and would lead him to Pocapuk's buried treasure. Unless he was planning to fudge or fake his denouement; Emma couldn't believe he'd have gone to all this fuss without first sliding an ace up his sleeve. But if he'd trusted the Comrades of the Convivial Codfish not to pull his leg, he must be gullible enough to believe anything. Or had he simply been lazy enough? Annoying man! Why couldn't he be pigeonholed?

Black John Sendick either believed or wanted to; Emma was fairly sure of that. Beddoes Kelling had told her long ago that the best salesmen made the most gullible customers; therefore, it ought to follow that writers of sensational fiction would be the readiest to embrace the fabulous.

Joris Groot? Maybe yes, maybe no. Emma wished she knew whether he was doing his illustrations on speculation or whether he'd been clever enough to wrest an advance payment and a firm contract out of Wont. A person could believe whatever his employer wanted him to, she supposed, so long as he knew his money was safe.

TWELVE

And what about Count Radunov? Did that dapper gentleman believe in anything at all, other than the irresistibility of his Old World charm? At least the count was showing a streak of common sense now.

"If I may suggest, it would be well for us to return to shelter before those clouds grow any blacker. Already I think I feel a drop."

He felt a good many drops; they were all well sprinkled before they reached the main house. Nobody was wet enough to bother changing, though, and none of these allegedly dedicated creative artists seemed inclined to go back to his cottage and get on with his work. Groot and Sendick built up a fresh blaze on the ashes of last night's fire. They all stood around drying themselves while Emma hunted out cards and chips. She found plenty of other games: Scrabble, Monopoly, Chinese Checkers, all the devices by which vacationers in bad weather drive off the ennui of having nothing to do but enjoy themselves. However, they opted for poker.

There was plenty of room for the six of them around Adelaide Sabine's round gaming table, but Emma excused herself. "Go ahead without me; I want to see whether anybody's taken Mrs. Fath her breakfast."

She could have mentioned that other matter of the body, but that would not have been courteous. A hostess tried not to subject her guests to domestic unpleasantnesses even while admitting the possibility that one, two, or all of them might be at the root of her problems.

The rain was coming down in dogged earnest by now; the wind was beginning to pick up. "When the wind's before the rain, soon you may set sail again. When the rain's before the wind, topsails lower and halyards mind." Emma remembered that bit of weather wisdom from her long-ago yachting days, and it worked every time. They were in for an all-day soak, if nothing worse, and quite possibly a gale to go with it.

Whoever he'd been, whatever he'd done, they couldn't in common humanity leave that wretched man's body out on the open dock in such a storm. Perhaps it was absurd to accord dead bodies a deference they might not have received while their occupants were still using them, but there it was and Emma would have to make Vincent understand.

Vincent, of course, was several jumps ahead of her. She found him in the kitchen, changed into dry clothes and boots, standing beside the big black iron wood stove, drinking another mug of coffee. The stove was alight; Emma could see yellow flames licking behind the open slits in the front damper. He lowered his mug and gave her a nod. "Want something, Mrs. Kelling?"

"I was wondering whether anybody'd taken some food out to Mrs. Fath and also what you've done with the stranger." She couldn't bring herself to say the body, it sounded too callous. "To leave him out there on the dock, in the rain—" She didn't quite know how to finish.

Vincent did. "Wouldn't be fittin'. Wouldn't be safe, neither, if the waves out there got much higher. We brought 'im up on the 'lectric cart an' put 'im in the old stable. Laid 'im on a couple o' planks over a pair o' sawhorses an' covered 'im with a horse blanket left over from when we had the pony. It's clean," he added somewhat defensively. "Wasn't no place else but the storeroom, an' you wouldn't o' wanted 'im in there with the food, would you?"

Emma shuddered. "Hardly. Do you think there's any real chance of his being picked up today? It's getting awfully rough out there, don't you think?"

"Be worse before it gets better, like as not," Vincent agreed.

"They said somethin' about that tropical storm blowin' up the coast later on, but she must o' picked up a dern sight faster'n they expected. Blow 'erself out before mornin' if we're lucky. I was figurin' on Lowell bein' here before noontime, but he's likely got a harbor full of overturned boats to worry about right now. He'll figure our feller can wait till mornin'. 'Tisn't like there's anything could be done for 'im."

He took his last sip of coffee and set the cup on the shelf behind the stove. "Mrs. Fath, now, Bubbles has kind o' taken her under 'is wing. He's already been over there with a cup o' tea an' a piece o' toast; now he's fixin' to bake 'er a custard. He's down cellar now gettin' the eggs an' cream."

"Down cellar? I didn't know this place had one," said Emma.

"It's just a root cellar, really." Vincent pronounced "root" to rhyme with "foot" and "cellar" to rhyme with "mullah." "Underneath the pantry. Food stays cool down there, saves us runnin' two refrigerators. Want to see?"

"Not just now, thank you," Emma replied. "Did Bubbles say how Mrs. Fath is feeling?"

"So-so, I guess. She drunk the tea an' kep' it down. Leastways it was still with 'er when Bubbles left."

"That's a healthy sign. Are the girls back from doing the cottages yet? I hope they didn't get soaked."

"Take more'n a little rain to melt them two. They better be back, if not I'll go get 'em. I figured it was safe enough to send 'em over there while the professor an' his crew was out diggin' up Pocapuk's treasure, but I don't want 'em in the cottages if the guests are back."

"Don't worry," said Emma. "They're all in the living room playing poker at the moment. I expect they'll stay there pretty much."

"Good a place as any on a day like this. I better light a fire for you then. Should o' thought of it sooner."

"A couple of the men have already taken care of that, thank you. It won't kill them to wait on themselves, Vincent. You have far more important things to think about just now. What are Neil and Ted doing?"

"Workin' outside, where I ought to be. Can't stop for a little rain. Lots to be done on a place the size o' this."

"Then I mustn't keep you. There is just one thing more, Vincent.

Mr. Sendick brought up the question of taking a look at the body on the chance some of the group might recognize him. It's a question of whether the man might have been on the ferry with us," she felt called upon to explain, however disingenuously.

Vincent shrugged. "Give 'em a little entertainment for a dull day, I s'pose, if that's the way their minds run. I don't see what harm it would do. The corpse ain't goin' to mind, that's for sure. Send 'em along any time you want to get rid of 'em. I'll be in the stable anyway, overhaulin' the cart. Meant to do it last week, but I never got the time. Too many other things needed doin' first. Tell 'em to come through the kitchen so's they won't track the whole house up goin' back. There's some slickers hangin' in the back entry."

"Thank you, I'll remember."

Emma went back to the living room and amused herself for a while watching the poker game. Count Radunov was doing rather badly; she laid a private bet with herself he'd improve fast enough when the stakes went higher. Joris Groot was a good, steady player. Black John was a wild man, taking outrageous risks and getting away with them as often as not. Lisbet Quinley was so timid Emma wondered whether she really understood the game. Everard Wont evidently fancied himself an expert but wasn't doing much better than Radunov. He was, as Emma had suspected, an ungracious loser. After a while she pulled up a chair between Sendick and Radunov and allowed herself to be dealt in.

Emma was an old hand at poker; she and Bed had played with a group of old friends almost every Saturday night for years and years. When she picked up her hand and detected a few tiny nicks along the edges of her cards, she knew what they meant. Were these marks a holdover from the Sabine era or had today's group started with a fresh deck? Out of curiosity she added a few infinitesimal nicks of her own to the hand she held and continued marking her cards round after round until somebody's private code was effectively scrambled.

Half an hour later, Emma was holding more chips than the rest of them put together. Black John Sendick was stunned and subdued. Joris Groot's steady game had gone to pieces. Radunov's had improved, but not enough. Lisbet Quainley was playing no better but looking much happier; she seemed to feel Emma was striking a blow for women's liberation. Everard Wont made it plain without coming straight out and saying so that he thought Emma was cheating. He insisted they play dealer's choice and started inventing wild variations. Black John Sendick grew even more reckless, almost manic. Lisbet Quainley became hopelessly confused. Emma stuck to plain five card stud and kept scooping the pots.

Groot was the first to fade. He quietly laid down the hand Emma had just dealt him, walked over to the fire and hurled on a fresh log so hard that sparks flew out on the hearthrug, then settled down on the sofa with his sketchbook. Contrite, Emma folded, too, and went to sit beside him. Almost immediately Count Radunov was there, as well.

"Ah, dear lady," he murmured, "what a pity the days of the great transatlantic luxury liners are no more."

The implication was that he and Emma would have made a fine pair of international card sharps. She laughed at him and asked Groot if she might see some of his sketches.

That perked him up. He willingly turned over page after page, starting with a pair of hunting boots among the autumn leaves and working his way past feet in rubber boots splashing through puddles, feet in overshoes wading through slush, women's feet in evening pumps and men's in dress shoes at a New Year's party, or so Emma judged from the meticulously drawn noisemaker an elegant high-heeled sandal with rhinestone straps was about to squash. Off in one corner was one incongruous left foot in a black sneaker with white stripes on the side and a small hole in the toe, resting on what was probably a bar rail.

"I suppose you meant this as a bit of social commentary," Emma remarked. Groot shrugged and flipped to a pair of plastic ski boots dangling from somebody's mittened hand.

This was the only drawing so far that indicated Groot did in fact realize the human form didn't begin at the knees and go down from there. Like all the rest, it was accurately drawn, carefully shaded, and showed not a glimmer of originality. Emma wondered what sort of illustrations he was planning to do for Wont's book. She also wondered how much longer Radunov was going to keep on reciting Kipling's poem about "boots—boots—boots—boots" in her ear sotto voce.

He did stop, but only to ask in ever so innocent a tone whether Groot was a shoe fetishist. Groot replied quite calmly that, no, he didn't have any hang-ups about shoes, he just liked to draw them. He was all set to move from winter to spring. Emma was deeply grateful when the last round was played out at the card table and Black John came dashing over.

"Say, Mrs. Kelling, did you ask about the guy who was drowned?"

Emma couldn't understand why he was so eager, but she answered readily enough. "Yes, Vincent says it's all right to go out to the shed and look at him if you have the stomach for it. He wishes somebody could come up with an identification, but I don't suppose there's any hope of that. Does anybody else want to come?"

"Ugh, no thanks. I'll stay here" was Lisbet Quainley's reaction, and an entirely proper one, in Emma's opinion. Emma didn't want to see him either, but she did have a hankering to observe the viewers' reactions.

Everard Wont and Joris Groot said they might as well go for want of anything better to do. Radunov shrugged, cast a rueful glance at his elderly custom-made brogues, which had already suffered a bit of a banging on the path to Shag Rock, and joined the party. Bubbles was in the kitchen putting a club sandwich together as they passed through.

"Thinthe nobody'th going anywhere in thith thtorm, I thought you might like to eat your lunch with the otherth, Mithith Kelling. I'll make you thome freth coffee."

"That's a splendid idea, Bubbles," Emma replied. "Tea for me, please, and perhaps a little sherry for everyone first. We'll be back in just a few minutes; we're only going to the stable."

"Ah, yeth."

Bubbles heaved a dutiful sigh and went on assembling the sandwich. Emma sorted out raincoats for size and handed them to the men, wishing they weren't all the same somber black. Adelaide must have bought out a volunteer fire department sometime or other, she thought. Old-fashioned yellow oilskins would be more appropriate for Pocapuk, but of course they did smell a bit. She found a hooded black raincape for herself, at least it was appropriate for a call on a dead man. Count Radunov helped her into the cape, adjusted the hood for her, and bowed her out the door.

It was still teeming. Those sou'wester hats the men had put on were demonstrating their usefulness, sending solid streams of water down the backs of the antique rubber raincoats. They were all glistening like wet seals by the time they got to the stable.

Even with that horse-blanket-covered bundle on the improvised trestle, the interior was a cheerful refuge from the outside. Vincent, his clothes protected by a greasy overall suit, was kneeling under a two-hundred-watt bulb that hung on a cord from a cobwebbed beam. Bits and pieces of the electric go-cart were spread around him on a tarpaulin. He stood up for Emma quick as a cat, she noticed a bit ruefully, with no creaking or popping of the joints.

"Come to view the remains?" He led them over to the trestle, drew the blanket away from the face, and folded it deftly over the chest.

"God, Ev, he looks like you!" was Sendick's first reaction.

"He does not!" was Wont's immediate and quite understandable response.

"Ev's right," said Joris Groot.

The illustrator went on to point out a few anatomical discrepancies, not particularly to Wont's advantage. Emma didn't see that they added up to much and didn't really care. Her chief concern just now was to find out how the man had died. She wished she knew how a drowned person was supposed to look. Of course he could have hit his head as he fell; there was certainly no dearth of rocks to land on out there. She did so wish the storm hadn't kept the harbor master away, but he'd have been crazy to risk the trip for a dead man.

The wind was really howling now, even the short walk from the house had been a struggle. As they stood looking down at the blanched face in its tangle of wet beard, a limb snapped off a nearby pine tree and struck the stable roof with a thump loud enough to startle even Vincent.

"Damn that kid!" he surprised them all by exclaiming. "I better go see what's happenin'."

Without stopping to put on a raincoat, he charged out into the storm. Not knowing what else to do, the rest stood around exchanging shrugs and blank looks, telling each other they'd never set eyes on the dead man before and wondering which kid was in trouble.

They didn't have to wonder long. Vincent came back, herding before him a wet, shivering boy wearing nothing but bathing trunks and rubber thong sandals. Neil had a white towel that he was carrying bundled up like a sack. He looked pleased with himself even if his father wasn't.

"Anyway, Pop, I got 'em," he was yelling against the wind.

"Huh." The father shoved him into the stable, not roughly. "Here, for God's sake put somethin' around you before you freeze to death."

He wrapped his son in another of those black slickers, one he'd most likely brought along for himself, and hustled Neil along to the kitchen. Without his burly presence, the stable wasn't cozy any more. Emma set out after him and the others followed her.

On a counter just inside the kitchen door, Neil was spreading out his white towel. On the towel lay the Fairy Queen's tiara and several more pieces of Emma's stolen stage jewelry.

"I knew they'd be buried or washed away if I didn't get 'em before low tide," Neil was bragging, "so I did. It wasn't too bad down under the cliff, Pop. I was in the lee of the wind, you know. But, boy, she's sure picking up outside. I hope to heck Ches and Wal got in all right before that wind really hit."

Appalled by the risk Neil had taken over her worthless junk, Emma started to say, "I'm deeply grateful for the trouble you've taken, Neil." Before she could get to the "but," though, she was interrupted by a shriek. Lisbet Quainley stood in the doorway from the butler's pantry, pointing at a huddle of black-coated figures, at the white draped counter, and the wet, glistening paste diamonds.

"That's it! Just as Alding said. Black and white, and the dead man in the water and the shining stones coming up. Right on the button. Only . . ." Lisbet started to laugh, so hard she had to pull out a chair and sit down. "Only she wasn't talking about Pocapuk's treasure. Tough luck, Ev."

"I can't imagine what you find so hilarious, Liz," was Wont's cold reply. "I thought we had a definite lead; now we've got to start over and Alding's out of commission. I don't see why in hell she had to go and get food poisoning just at the crucial time." He glared at Bubbles, blaming the cook.

Bubbles wasn't taking that. "It'th not food poithoning! She'th got a bug."

"How do you know? You're not a doctor."

"No, but I'm a regithtered nurthe."

"That's right," said Vincent. He was rubbing Neil down with a kitchen towel and quietly enjoying Wont's frustration. "Bubbles specializes in male geriatrics. He comes here every summer for a change."

"I get deprethed," Bubbles explained to Emma. "I work at a hothpithe and all my patientth die. But thomebody hath to look after them."

"You must be a brave and kind man," said Emma. "And how is Mrs. Fath? Have you been out there since breakfast?"

"I took her thome thoup about half-patht eleven. She took a few thipth and fell athleep. That'th good, you know. She needth retht more than anything elthe. I expect she'll be okay in a few dayth."

"I can't wait that long," yelped Wont. "Can't you give her some pills or something?"

"I'll do whatever ith nethetharry," Bubbles replied with quiet dignity. "Mithith Kelling, when do you want uth to therve lunch?"

"In about twenty minutes, if that's convenient," Emma told him. "I expect we'd all like to wash up first, and have some sherry to take the chill off."

"Sounds good to me," said Black John Sendick.

The men could use the downstairs washrooms; Lisbet Quainley might do as she pleased. Emma went upstairs to her own room for a moment's respite. The room had been tidied to a fare-thee-well, and Sandy was treating Bernice to a clandestine peek at Emma's wardrobe.

"Oops! Caught in the act." Sandy was blushing even redder than Bernice. "I'm sorry, Mrs. Kelling. It's just that your things are all so beautiful. And they smell so nice."

"Yes, well, I think you'd better run along downstairs now. Bubbles needs you to help serve luncheon. You've done a lovely job on my room," Emma added out of compassion, not that the little minxes deserved any. "Oh, and you might bring up the rest of the jewelry that I left in the kitchen. Neil went out and fished it up, which was very brave and extremely foolish of him. Please remind him for me that children are far more precious than diamonds, even real ones. Now scoot."

They scooted. Emma repaired her face, straightened her wig, and changed into a pair of soft-soled, brown leather house shoes. After a moment's thought, she also changed her blouse and skirt for a favorite lounging-about dress of a snuggly mouse gray material, and added a string of what looked to her like brown, beige, and gray tiddlywinks interspersed with chunks of glass that had perhaps been cut from the necks of discarded beer bottles.

Loopy beige-and-gray earrings went with the necklace. They hung almost to her shoulders and made her feel like an illustration out of the *National Geographic*. Count Radunov would probably get a chuckle out of them.

Not that she cared whether he did or not; she was merely getting herself comfortable for what promised to be a long and quite possibly dreary afternoon. She did hope Everard Wont wouldn't go into a full-scale sulk because Alding Fath was not in shape for fresh prognostications. That business about black and white and the stones and the dead man was a trifle eerie, Emma had to admit. How could Mrs. Fath have predicted all that?

Of course the Gladstone bag was black, and there'd have had to be something white around it, even if it was only a white pebble on the shore or a white man with a black beard. She'd have known about the bagful of false diamonds if she'd been planning to give them to the man herself. She'd have known about the death if she'd intended to trail him to the cliff with his booty and shove him over herself. Maybe Alding Fath had good reason to be feeling poorly.

Maybe Emma Kelling had better quit telling herself horror stories and go pour the sherry so that Everard Wont wouldn't hog it all for himself.

THIRTEEN

The impromptu picnic around the fireplace was pleasant enough. Emma put some Rachmaninoff and Moussorgsky recordings on the phonograph as a slightly left-handed gesture to Count Radunov, then switched to Broadway show tunes. Adelaide proved to own a surprisingly large collection, some of them dating back half a century or so. More house gifts, Emma supposed.

A good many of the shows had opened in Boston before going on to Broadway. She'd never lost the thrill of going in on the train, getting off at Back Bay, and checking into the Copley Plaza for a night on the town. The manager himself had always come out to greet them; Emma doubted whether there was a single waiter left at the Copley who'd recognize Mrs. Beddoes Kelling nowadays.

What a dismal Desdemona she was turning herself into! Emma shut off the record player and sat down at the piano. Like it or lump it, this lot were going to hear Little Buttercup sing her swan song.

Her voice was a far squeak from what it used to be, but here she had no great hall to fill. The piano, as Adelaide had promised, was in tune. The rain drumming on the house and the wind howling around the eaves made a wild orchestral accompaniment. Mad Margaret's first solo from *Ruddigore* would be just the thing on a day like this. "Cheerily carols the lark over the cot. Merrily whistles the clerk, scratching a blot." Emma didn't think she sounded too bad, all things considered. "And why? Who am I? . . . Mad Margaret! Poor Peg!" She'd be Buttercup next and to heck with the high notes.

Radunov came over to sing with her. He knew the lyrics to every one of the patter songs and most of what Emma still thought of as the Darrell Fancourt parts. The rest of the cottagers had gone back to playing cards; Emma couldn't have cared less. For upward of an hour her cure for the mulligrubs worked like a charm. But then her throat got sore, her fingers began to stumble on the keys. Radunov was down to a croak. Time for old swans to crawl back up on the bank.

The card players had switched from poker to bridge, a game Emma had always loathed. She and Radunov sat down to the cribbage board for a while, but they were both feeling the effects of their sing-along, the sherry, the fire's warmth, and the monotonous pounding of the rain. When the count asked halfheartedly, "Would you like to play another round?" Emma shook her head.

"What I'd really like is to take a nap, but I suppose I'd better check on Mrs. Fath."

"I'll do it if you wish. It's time I went to my cottage anyway."

"But then you'd have to come back here and tell me how she's doing. I'll ask Bubbles to go instead."

"You're a kind woman, Mrs. Kelling."

Relieved of the duty to be charming, Radunov went to borrow a raincoat and brave the storm, which in fact seemed to have slackened off for the moment. Emma tidied away the cards and the cribbage board and wandered into the kitchen.

From somewhere back in the ell, she could hear muffled sounds of rock music and high-pitched giggles. The youngsters were enjoying themselves in their own unfathomable way; she was glad they were doing it out of earshot of the main house. Vincent must still be in the stable. Bubbles was dozing in a chair by the wood-burning stove with his feet propped up on the little shelf in front of the oven. He had a big pot of something simmering on the back burners and, from the smell, a crock of beans baking inside.

He'd earned his rest; she wouldn't disturb him. Emma put on the old rubber cape and a pair of rubber boots that didn't fit her too badly and slogged down the path to Mrs. Fath's cottage. The air was bracing but the walking on wet pine needles in clumsy boots left something to be desired. An alpenstock, for instance. She congratulated herself on making it to Mrs. Fath's cottage without so much as a sprained ankle, rapped lightly on the door, got no answer, and went in.

Mrs. Fath was asleep. Her color was good, her breathing regular, she didn't need any Florence Nightingale hovering about her. Emma slipped and slithered back to the house, went up to her room and lay down on the chaise.

After all, she couldn't sleep. She tried reading and couldn't get her mind on her book. She switched on the radio and found nothing she cared to hear. Emma supposed she ought to get started on her repairing job, now that she had the fairy jewels back, but the thought of handling once more those worthless trinkets Neil had risked his neck to retrieve and that unknown thief had evidently lost his life trying to steal was revolting to her. She couldn't even find solace in tidying her dresser drawers; Sandy already had them so neatly arranged that Emma felt guilty taking anything out. Whatever had possessed her to volunteer for this crazy venture? She might have known there'd be a catch in it somewhere.

Emma went to the windows and stared out with a feeling of personal grievance. She could barely make out the pier, there was nothing to see but a welter of foaming, surging grayness. If only this storm had held off, Brother Lowell would have been here hours ago. The dead man would be gone from the island, and so would that wretched necklace. She felt a compulsion to go to the safe once more and make sure the diamonds were still there but told herself not to be a fool. Whoever was dummy right now in that interminable bridge game might be on his or her way upstairs to spy around after it. They must all be assuming she was asleep; she'd yawned enough over the cribbage board. Which of the cottagers was it who'd sneaked back into the main house last night and let that man out of the storeroom?

Or had it in fact been one of the staff? Why had Vincent been so quick to lay the blame on his own son? Why hadn't he picked on that cheeky fellow Ted? It occurred to Emma that Ted was the one person on the island whom she hadn't laid eyes on once today. Why hadn't he been with Neil when the boy came back with the stage jewelry? Neil hadn't mentioned Ted's having been with him; it must have been dreadfully risky for a young boy alone, rooting around those treacherous rocks in weather as bad as this.

Vincent had known what Neil was up to. He'd been worried; why hadn't he stopped his son from going? Was it because he'd expected more than fairy necklaces to have fallen out of the bag they'd found floating above the body? Had Vincent himself been out there this afternoon, groping around in the mud? Was he still at it now that the tide was back in?

It ought to be a two-man job, Emma thought, one to do the hunting and one to hold the lifeline without which nobody in his right mind should even think of trusting himself to that churning, leaping ocean. Was she putting other lives in danger by keeping the necklace hidden? Would it be wiser to carry the diamond necklace downstairs right this minute, toss it in the middle of the table, and say, "Look what I found. Would anyone care to claim it?"

No, it would not be wiser. It would be cowardly, stupid, and quite likely dangerous. Emma picked up a book of crossword puzzles she'd brought along for a rainy day, took it back to the chaise, and began doggedly shoving in words. After a while, without meaning to, she did fall asleep.

She woke with a stiff neck, feeling logy and cross. The room was all but dark now, the storm still howling and crashing. For goodness' sake, what time was it? Ten minutes to six, she ought to be getting downstairs. She dashed cold water on her face, did what she could with powder and lipstick, and hurried downstairs to be charming.

Radunov was back, looking a good deal fresher than she. No doubt realizing nobody else was going to dress, he'd settled for his gray slacks and tweed jacket. As far as Emma could see, the rest of the cottagers hadn't moved. The card table was still strewn with score sheets, loose playing cards, and the poker chips nobody had bothered to put away. The hearth was messy with bits of bark and ashes from inexpert fire-tending; the whole room had an air of dishevelment that Emma found fully as annoying as its usual frozen impeccability. Why hadn't Vincent told the girls to tidy up? Why hadn't he brought the drinks? Where on earth was he?

He'd been out getting wood, naturally, because this pack of louts had burned up every stick in the woodbox and been too lazy to go out for more. Even as Emma stood fuming, Vincent came in with a canvas carrier full of dry logs, swept up the hearth, and tended the fire practically in one motion. Sandy dashed in with a trayful of hot stuffed mushroom caps, set it by the fire to keep warm, and went to deal with the card table. Vincent opened the drinks cabinet and began setting out glasses. Bernice rushed an ice bucket and a plate of garnishes up to the bar, rushed out again, and whizzed back carrying a round of cheese and a basket of crackers. Sandy flipped the last poker chip into the rack, plumped the last sofa pillow, snatched up the tray of mushrooms and began passing them around just as the cuckoo clock on the wall, another house gift, no doubt, chirped the hour.

Back in business, right on the dot. Emma took one of the mushrooms Sandy was proffering and bit into it. Delicious, naturally; she swallowed the bite with a feeling that she was being manipulated. She switched on the television to see whether she could find a weather report on the storm and ran into a commercial for drain cleaner. She went over to ask Vincent for Scotch and water, discovered he'd already fixed her a gin and tonic, and took it so as not to hurt his feelings even though gin was not her notion of a drink for a stormy night.

All in all, this was not a satisfactory evening. Nobody, not even Count Radunov, had anything interesting or entertaining to say. They were all patently sick of each other's company, sick of being penned in here, probably sick of what they'd seen in the stable, although not one of them had uttered a word about that afterward, at least not in Emma's presence.

Nobody tried very hard to hide his relief when the ritual of coffee was over and they were free to go their separate ways. Vincent insisted on lighting the cottagers out to their abodes with a big battery lantern. Emma decided to go along with them and pay Alding Fath a good-night visit even though the caretaker assured her that Bubbles had already been out with a light but sustaining supper.

She found the invalid awake but not disposed for conversation. All Emma could get out of Mrs. Fath was that she wasn't really sick, she just felt poorly. She didn't want a drink of water; she didn't want a book to read. She didn't want anything except, quite plainly, for Mrs. Kelling to go away and leave her alone.

Vincent was waiting on the porch with his lantern. Emma supposed she ought to be grateful for such devoted attention, but she wasn't. If he were all that caring a person, how could he have spent his day fiddling around with the electric cart not ten feet away from a dead man?

That was unfair, she told herself. Vincent had had a job that needed doing and nowhere else to do it. The unknown departed had been nothing to him, a body was only an outworn shell. The caretaker had shown what respect was appropriate; he'd got the cadaver in from the storm, arranged such a bier as he could manage, and made sure the horse blanket was perfectly clean. Why fault a man for refusing to be superstitious about the dead? Nevertheless, Emma didn't like it much when Vincent took her arm quite respectfully and impersonally to help her over a slippery patch.

The one bright spot on her horizon was that the storm showed signs of letting up. About the only remark Vincent made on the way back, aside from things like "Watch your step here," was "Goin' to blow 'erself out. My brother'll be here by mid-mornin'."

"That will be an immense relief," Emma replied. "I wonder what that unfortunate man will be found to have died of."

"Hit 'is head fallin' over the cliff an' drowned while unconscious."

"You sound awfully sure." Emma found Vincent's matter-of-fact omniscience was getting under her skin.

"The examinin' doctor'll be my brother Franklin."

And Pocapuk was not going to have a scandal. That was the way it had always been and would always be as long as Vincent remained the power behind the Sabines. Another Vincent, the Maine poet Edna St. Vincent Millay, had written a line that fitted Emma's mood better: "I know. But I do not approve. And I am not resigned."

She kicked off the muddy boots and hung up the streaming rubber cape, went to her room, took a hot bath, and put on her nightclothes. Then she picked up the crossword-puzzle book again, settled herself on the chaise, and waited for the house to quiet down. As soon as she was reasonably sure she wouldn't be caught prowling below, she pocketed the key to the telephone box, went to the extension in the pantry, shut herself in there to muffle the sound of her voice, and dialed a Boston number.

The Bittersohns were at their Beacon Hill residence. Sarah still owned the historic brownstone she'd inherited from Alexander Kelling and still hadn't got around to turning the ground-floor bedroom back into a drawing room. Thus she had an ideal place to park a husband with a badly smashed leg and an assortment of cracked ribs who'd just been released from Massachusetts General Hospital and would be going back there for therapy as soon as a battery of doctors said he could.

Son Davy's crib had been set up in Theonia Kelling's boudoir on the second floor. His doting aunt was only too happy to have him near her, particularly now that her husband Brooks was having to do Max's legwork. Brooks was out of town now, hot on the trail of an Audubon Elephant Folio, three Mary Cassatt pastels, and a rare cockatoo named Barnaby, which had been stolen from a private estate in Cape May, New Jersey. Cockatoos were not generally within the province of the Bittersohn-Kelling detective agency, but Barnaby happened to be a personal acquaintance of Brooks, who was also an expert ornithologist, and was an assignment he could not have refused.

Sarah was sharing the double bed with Max, offering what small wifely comfort was possible in the circumstances and trying to get used to sleeping with a husband much of whom was rigidly encased in gauze and plaster. Max still had one arm whole and free; it was with this he reached for the telephone.

"Max," came a familiar voice, sounding oddly agitated. "Is that you?"

"Oui, c'est moi, je t'Emma." Max, an opera buff when he got the chance, had been listening to *Faust* that afternoon. "What's up? We thought you'd run away to sea."

"I'm on Pocapuk Island and I'm in a jam, Max. Is Sarah there?"

"Right beside me. Just a second, I'll put us on the speaker phone so we can all hear. Okay, shoot. What flavor's your jam?"

"Actually, I don't know that it's so much a jam as a dilemma. And, please, no more puns, I'm not up to them. So far, I've been drugged and had my fairies' jewelry snatched on the ferry, got it back and discovered I'd acquired something I don't dare talk about, and been robbed again while I was asleep last night, which probably means I was also drugged again, though that detail hadn't occurred to me until just this minute. The robber was dragged out of the sea this morning, dead either by accident or otherwise. Vincent, the caretaker, has him out in the stable now waiting for the storm to let up so his brother Lowell can come and take the body to his brother

Franklin to be autopsied. Vincent's already decided what Franklin's report will be, though I don't know whether he's told Franklin yet. And the psychic is feeling poorly."

"Whoa, Emma. You lost me on that last sentence. Would you care to elucidate?"

Emma elucidated. It took her quite a while, starting with the taxi driver and working her way through the roster of cottagers, on to Vincent and his somewhat frighteningly efficient management of the Sabine demesne and messuage. "So the gist of it is, I'm in a bit of a flap and I don't know what to do. I was hoping you two might have some suggestions."

"My suggestion is that you pack them all off to wherever they came from and let us lend you our house at Ireson's Landing till the yodelers go home," said Sarah. "I don't expect you'll take it."

"Thank you, dear. I couldn't possibly, not after promising Adelaide Sabine I'd cope. She's tottering on the brink already, poor sweetie. All I want from you is—oh, dear!—somebody to hold my hand, I suppose. But you can't leave Max and Davy."

"No, I really can't. And Brooks is hopelessly tied up, and Uncle Fred's off on a cruise with Martha and a bunch of paraplegic children from that school he supports, and Cousin Dolph's busy with his senior citizens, and Uncle Jem's utterly hopeless, as you know. But we'll think of something. Tell us a little more about Alding Fath, Aunt Emma. She intrigues me."

"She does me, too. I know she must be a charlatan, but I can't quite see how she manages some of her effects. Of course one's not supposed to, is one? Anyway, absurd as it may sound, I like Mrs. Fath the best of the lot and I do wish she hadn't come down with whatever it is she's got. I thought at first she was just manufacturing an excuse for not being able to locate that preposterous pirate treasure in her crystal ball or whatever, but now I do think there's something the matter. It's—this is going to sound totally insane—it's almost as though she were under a spell."

"Why shouldn't she be?" said Max. "I should think spells might rank as a natural occupational hazard of her profession. Cousin Theonia will know, we'll check it out with her. Now what about Radunov? He doesn't by any chance wear a monocle and carry a long cigarette holder?"

"No, but he rather looks as if he'd like to. The monocle, at any rate. I'm sure he wouldn't stoop to the cigarette holder. He is a bit on the dapper side, I grant you, but it's the right kind of dapper. Do you follow me?"

"At a short distance, yes. And you say Radunov knows me?"

"He certainly gave every indication of knowing you when I happened to mention your name, and he didn't sound any too pleased about it. He was quite enthusiastic about Sarah, though. He said he'd met her at an embassy party in Washington and she was the best-dressed woman there."

"Then he's either nearsighted or full of hot air," said Sarah. "The name doesn't ring a bell with me offhand. Can you describe him a little more closely?"

Emma did her best. Sarah was still in the dark, but Max wasn't. "I think I know the guy," he snarled. "Tell him Bittersohn says to keep his hands to himself."

"Max! Count Radunov is barely an acquaintance; I shall tell him no such thing. What do you mean, keep his hands to himself? Adelaide has nothing of real value out here, of course, but there are some nice bits of silver and a few rather good Orientals. He's not a petty thief, is he?"

"Oh, there's nothing petty about Radunov. Okay, Emma. You need a secret agent, we'll send you one. What's the layout there?"

Houses were easier to describe than people. Emma went quickly through the salient features, alluding to the wall safe in guarded terms as "a closet built like yours." Max seemed satisfied.

"Good. In the morning, have those kids make up the bed in Mrs. Sabine's room and set an extra place for lunch. Now go to bed yourself and don't worry about a thing."

He waited till Emma had hung up before adding, "We'll do the worrying for you. Damn it, Sarah, why can't your relatives stay out of trouble?"

FOURTEEN

The storm had blown itself out. Emma woke to bright sunlight, a sparkling sea, though by no means a calm one, and a feeling of immense relief. By noontime she'd have a helper. Max hadn't told her who he'd be or how he'd arrive; no doubt it was a matter of whom they could get and how they could manage at such short notice; but Emma didn't care. She'd soon have someone on the premises whom she knew she could trust, and she'd be rid of that ghastly necklace. All she needed now was to get it ready to hand over in some appropriate disguise.

The only thing she could think of on such short notice was to choose an empty jewelry box roughly the size and shape of a book, lay the necklace inside well muffled in facial tissues, stuff it inside a padded bag she'd brought along to return a library book she'd borrowed and hadn't yet finished reading, and address the bag to Sarah. A couple of letters she'd written were lying around waiting to be sent off; she could pass them along with the package. She was wondering whether she ought to write another note or two when Sandy blew in with her tea.

"Bernice wanted to bring up your tray, but I said she could have a turn tomorrow. Want me to get you a shawl or something, Mrs. Kelling? How about if I turn up the heat?"

"Just hand me that mohair throw off the chaise, dear. The air is a bit nippy, but isn't it lovely! Tell Bernice I have a special job for you both this morning. I want you to strip one of the beds in Mrs. Sabine's room and make it up fresh. Clear all the brushes and things off the dresser and put them very carefully in one of the drawers. We're going to have another guest and there's nowhere else to put anyone. You might also air the room and pick a few roses for the night table, the way you did for me. Run along and start my tub while I drink my tea." Emma wasn't about to let Sandy get in a question for which she had no answer.

"Then you can lay out my green skirt and blouse and tidy my room before you begin on Mrs. Sabine's. I'm not sure how soon it will be needed and we want to be ready. I'll explain to your father when I go down."

"Okay, Mrs. Kelling, if you say so. Bernice is going to be scared stiff if she has to serve breakfast all by herself."

"There's not that much to do. Bubbles can help her. I'll help her myself, if necessary." Or one of the cottagers could and serve them right. This was surely not the way things had always been done, but Emma was past caring. "Now, fetch me my robe and slippers, like a good girl. Has your uncle been here yet?"

"Nope. Ches and Wal were here about an hour ago. Wal says something happened to Uncle Lowell's boat, and they don't know how long it'll take him to get it fixed. Pop's madder'n a hornet. I guess Uncle Lowell's none too pleased, either. This the blouse you want, Mrs. Kelling?"

"No, dear, the cotton one with the leaf pattern. How's my bath coming?"

One way and another, she managed to get downstairs before Sandy could satisfy her curiosity. Vincent was not in the kitchen; Bubbles said he was outdoors checking for storm damage. Emma was relieved at that, she'd as soon not tell him about the extra guest until she knew who that guest was to be. Bubbles wasn't at all perturbed by the news, and even Bernice didn't appear cowed by the thought of having to manage without Sandy. Emma told them how nice it was to have such a competent staff and went into the dining room to pour herself another cup of tea and wait for the cottagers to appear.

Again, Black John was first on the scene. No bare legs today; he had on baggy red running pants with his Tycho Brahe sweatshirt. The noted astronomer's copper nose was displayed to fullest advantage on so manly a chest; Sendick did seem awfully athletic for a writer, Emma thought. He'd skipped his morning swim because the undertow was still pretty fierce, he told her, but he'd had a great run clear around the island. Vincent was out with the two young guys, cutting up some fallen trees. They said the guy who was supposed to come for the body had got his boat busted in the storm; did Mrs. Kelling know that?

Emma replied that she'd heard something to that effect and could she pour Mr. Sendick some coffee?

Mr. Sendick said he thought he'd have milk, thanks, and could Mrs. Kelling please not call him Mr. Sendick? It made him feel too serious, and he was already sort of down about that poor stiff out in the barn. What did Mrs. Kelling think?

Mrs. Kelling thought she'd prefer to talk about something else at the breakfast table. Conversation rather languished after that until Joris Groot showed up, closely followed, to Emma's surprise, by Count Radunov in flannel slacks and a bulky Aran fisherman's sweater. Groot had stopped by Alding Fath's cottage and peeked through the window. She'd looked to be asleep, so he hadn't knocked. Radunov had in fact knocked, or so he said, but had got no answer. He hadn't tried her door because it didn't seem quite the thing. Emma said she'd go herself in a little while and hoped everyone had slept well.

They got through breakfast on polite generalities. Everard Wont slouched in at about a quarter past nine, reasonably kempt but not in the mood for chat. Lisbet Quainley showed up ten minutes later, just under the wire. She'd stopped to see Alding Fath, she explained by way of apology. Alding had been drowsy and still feeling poorly, so Lisbet had come away.

Emma decided it was time she, too, went away. She ought to go out to Alding Fath; she'd better go up and see what the girls were making of Adelaide's bedroom. But then she heard the sound of a motorboat above the waves and decided she'd stroll out to the dock first. This might be, and she fervently hoped it was, Brother Lowell in his mended boat coming to get the stranger.

Vincent was on the pier now, nailing down a board that had worked loose. Suddenly he laid down his hammer and jumped in surprise, as well he might. The motorboat Emma had expected was actually a seaplane, bobbing around now on the choppy water and taxiing up to dock. As Emma hustled down to meet it, clutching the package she'd slipped into the capacious pocket of her full skirt, she saw a door open and a line thrown to Vincent.

The plane was made fast to the pier. A portable gangplank was poked out; a passenger stepped on it and reached for Vincent's extended hand.

This was a woman, tall and queenly, clad in a figured black-and-white dress with a white jacket. Her black straw boater hat had a crimson scarf tied around it with the ends blowing jauntily out behind. Only one middle-aged woman of Emma's acquaintance, other than Emma herself, could look so magnificently poised climbing out of a dinky little plane in a choppy sea.

"Cousin Theonia!" Emma fairly flew the length of the pier. "How dear of you to come!"

And how right for her to be here. Why on earth hadn't Emma thought of Theonia in the first place? Mrs. Brooks Kelling had worked with her husband as well as Max and Sarah on several cases requiring her unusual areas of expertise. She was bright, resourceful, and a great deal tougher than she looked. And who else would be able to deal with Alding Fath on her own plane? The daughter of a beautiful young gypsy and a cultural anthropologist who'd got a little too zealous in his fieldwork, Theonia had learned all the angles of the fortune-telling trade before she was into her teens.

The two women hugged and rubbed cheeks with that exquisite balance of sincere affection and respect for each other's maquillage that is so endearing to watch and so pleasant to experience. Vincent gazed upon them goggle-eyed. This was obviously not how it had always been done. Emma took pity on him.

"Mrs. Brooks Kelling, you must meet Vincent, the real master of Pocapuk. Mrs. Brooks will be spending a few days with us, Vincent; we talked on the phone last evening. However did you get here so quickly, Theonia?"

"I happened to remember that Brooks's friend Tweeters Arbuthnot was flying Maineward today to take a puffin count, so I rang him up and hitched a ride. My husband is also an ornithologist, Vincent, though he hasn't become seriously involved with puffins. Right now he's up to his ears in grebes. I spoke with dear Adelaide, by the way,

Emma. She's feeling a wee bit stronger and sends her love. I'm to give her particular regards to Vincent," Theonia added, with a smile that rocked the lord of the isle back on his L. L. Bean heels.

"And I must give mine to Tweeters," said Emma. "I haven't seen him since that day he took us to visit the kittiwakes."

Before Vincent could come out of the daze that was any male's inevitable reaction to meeting Theonia for the first time, Emma nipped over the gangplank and into the seaplane; greeted the pilot like a long-lost friend, notwithstanding the fact that she'd never laid eyes on him in her life; thrust her package into his hand; babbled an inanity or two about puffins; and ran back to play hostess.

"Vincent's daughter has your room all ready, Theonia. Don't tell me that's all the luggage you've brought, just one little case?"

"This is all Tweeters would let me bring. He's got the plane crammed full of herring for the puffins. Since you and I are about the same size, I have every intention of raiding your wardrobe without scruple to supply my deficiencies. You're looking marvelous, Emma. Island life must be agreeing with you. No, really, Vincent, you mustn't let me take you from your work. If you could just help Mr. Arbuthnot get away from the dock without denting his pontoons? Tweet-tweet, Tweeters! Toss the puffins a herring for me."

With cooings and waves of a plump and shapely hand, Theonia got herself and Emma away from the men and up to the house. Sandy was on the doorstep hopping with impatience to unpack the unexpected guest's bag and see what she had.

"Oh, wow! Two Mrs. Kellings. Now Bernice and I won't have to fight about who gets to take up the morning tea. Let me take your bag, Mrs. Kelling. Where's the rest of your stuff? Is Daddy going to bring it?"

"Mrs. Brooks had to come off in a hurry so she's going to share with me," said Emma. "And you'd better remember to call her Mrs. Brooks so you won't be forever getting us mixed up. Has breakfast been cleared away yet?"

"Nope. Miss Quainley and Mr. Wont are still in there pigging out. You want some breakfast, Mrs. Brooks? I can bring it to you on a tray. Bubbles won't mind making fresh coffee; he does it all the time for Pop. My father hates warmed-over coffee."

"Thank you, Sandy, I'll have coffee in my room. Black, please, with no sugar." Theonia was always dieting, up to a point. "And a muffin or something of that sort if you have one. With just a smidgen of jam."

"Sure, you bet. Bubbles makes great muffins, if those guys haven't scoffed them all up. Boy, can they eat! Want me to take your bag up first?"

"We'll manage," said Emma. "Run along, Sandy."

Theonia was trying not to laugh. "So that's your upper-parlor housemaid. What a darling."

"Isn't she though. There are two of them, as you may have gathered. Sandy brought a friend along. Bernice is a trifle shy as yet, but I'm afraid she'll soon get over that. Vincent also has a young son working here. The mother's away on a field trip for the summer. She's an archaeologist, he tells me."

"An interesting family," Theonia cooed. "Is that all the staff? Who's this Bubbles?"

"He's the cook. Ryan's his last name; I don't know the first. Everyone calls him Bubbles. You'll see why. He told me he's a registered nurse by profession and works at a hospice during the winter. He comes out here in the summertime because he gets depressed at all his patients' dying, which sounds plausible enough. All I know for sure is that he's always cheerful when I've seen him, speaks with a rather engaging lisp, and cooks divinely. Bubbles is more or less taking care of Mrs. Fath, who's one of the reasons I'm so glad you're here. Did Max fill you in?"

"Mostly on what's been happening to you personally. I must say you've been having a time of it, my dear. I didn't want him to tell me too much about the cottagers, as you call them, because I think one's own first impressions can be helpful. How are you enjoying the house, Emma?"

"I was about to ask you the same question. My personal feeling is that it's absolutely perfect and if I were given carte blanche, I'd burn it down."

Theonia didn't try to hold back her laughter this time. "What a typical Emma Kelling remark! I think I'd content myself with painting the outside screaming chartreuse and setting plastic gnomes under all the pine trees. I can see why Vincent felt the need to bring his children with him; he's trying to persuade himself that the place is still alive. That's a badly shaken man, in case you hadn't noticed."

"Do you honestly think so? He seems to me such a Rock of Gibraltar."

"Even a rock may crumble, my dear, if the pressure's kept up too long. Or crack, if it gets a hard-enough jolt."

Emma thought this over a moment, then nodded. "You're more perceptive than I, Theonia. I suppose Vincent's worried about what's going to happen when Adelaide Sabine dies. And we already have an unknown dead man in the pony stable. Did Max tell you that?"

"Yes, and I shouldn't mind getting a look at him, if it can be done without making waves. But why hasn't he been taken away? Max was under the impression the body was to be picked up first thing this morning."

"So was I, but Vincent's brother's boat was damaged in the storm last night, so he couldn't come."

"Vincent's brother?"

"Lowell. He's the harbor master. Brother Franklin is the medical examiner or whatever they call him up here. Vincent has given me to understand that Franklin will be cooperative about the verdict."

"Has he indeed? Quite a local dynasty. What size are your feet, Emma?"

Taking the hint, Emma gave Theonia the run of her wardrobe. By the time Sandy came back with fresh coffee, a cranberry muffin the size of a soccer ball, homemade jam, and a little pat of butter formed in a mold that had a cow on top, Theonia had changed into one of Emma's full skirts, a blue cotton blouse, and low-heeled sandals with crepe soles.

"You'll want something around you," said Emma. "The air's really nippy. Here, take this."

On impulse she handed Theonia the wool challis shawl with the giant peonies on it. With the long, full skirt and her black hair in its heavy chignon, the shawl suited her almost too well. Theonia looked at the half-gypsy woman in the cheval mirror and chuckled.

"All I need are a pair of hoop earrings and a dancing bear. Perhaps I'll be able to pick up a little extra money dukkering."

"I daresay you could, if you really felt the urge," said Emma.

"The expedition's official seeress is feeling poorly. Max did tell you about Alding Fath?"

"Yes, but I want you to tell me. What do you really think of the woman, Emma?"

"I know she must be a fake, but I think she's a dear."

Emma explained what had happened on the first night while Theonia drank her coffee and worked her way through Bubbles's giant muffin. "So what do you make of that?"

"I shall know better after I've met her." Theonia set down her empty cup and made careful dabs with her napkin. "Now, just give me a moment to wash the jam off my face, and we'll make a quick dash to the barn before Vincent finishes putting the dock back together. Which way?"

"Out the side, I think. We can slip around behind the house. It's not far."

"I need a walk anyway, after having been folded up inside that puddle-jumper all the way from Lake Cochituate. Tweeters practically had to butter my hips to squeeze me in."

Discussing the state of Max Bittersohn's multiple fractures for the benefit of anyone who might be listening, the two majestic ladies strolled down through the house and out across the spongy pine-needled path. That stiff breeze was still blowing off the water, so their choosing to walk in the lee of the house was a perfectly natural thing to do. To their relief they saw nobody around the old pony shed. The door was padlocked, but Theonia had a feeling Vincent would keep the key hidden up under the eaves and of course she was right.

The dead man was still there, stretched out on the planks, covered by the clean horse blanket, just as Emma had last seen him. She'd read somewhere that gypsies have religious scruples against touching corpses; she'd never thought of her cousin Brooks's wife as a gypsy before, but that shawl was just a tad too appropriate. She stepped forward and turned back the blanket just enough to reveal the wax-white face. The beard was still damp from the seawater. The effect was not lovely, but Theonia did not flinch.

"So that's what became of him," she said. "I can't say I'm greatly surprised."

FIFTEEN

Do you actually know who he was?" Emma exclaimed.

"Yes." Theonia caught a sound of footsteps on the little patch of gravel that had been laid down outside the barn door, presumably for better drainage. She tossed Emma a look that from a less stately dame might have been called impish and raised her voice a decibel or two.

"I see a definite look of the Pences about the ears. You know that knack of mine about spotting resemblances, and ears are so distinctive, don't you think? I have a strong hunch this might be that third cousin of Peter's, the one dear Adelaide was telling us about."

Theonia's total acquaintance with dear Adelaide had run to a chat of perhaps six minutes' duration a couple of years ago at one of Emma's lawn parties. Dear Adelaide, moreover, would have been the last person in the world to gossip about her son-in-law's relative to a casual acquaintance, even one bearing the Kelling name. These minor details were beside the point. That footstep was most likely either Vincent's or one of his helpers', and now was an excellent chance to straighten him out on that matter of the autopsy. Emma understood perfectly and couldn't have agreed more.

"Theonia, how perceptive of you! I'd quite forgotten about Polydore Spence. Such a gifted young man, Adelaide said, till he had that terrible encounter with the giant clam while diving off—Osaka, was it? Anyway, I understand that ever since then he'd had delusions of being a seal."

"A walrus, I believe," Theonia contradicted. Boston ladies liked to get their facts straight, even when they were making them up as they went along. "It's the walruses that have those big mustaches."

"But not beards," Emma argued back.

"I expect the beard was intended to hide his lack of tusks. Or else Polydore simply forgot to trim the mustache and it got out of hand. He became dreadfully forgetful, Adelaide said."

"Subject to fits of total amnesia," Emma shoved in promptly. "The walrus delusion was only a part-time occupation, so to speak. He'd put on a black wet suit and lounge around on beaches slapping his swim fins against the rocks. I don't believe he ever went so far as to eat raw fish."

"But he practically lived on sardines," said Theonia. "And sometimes Polydore would get to thinking he was a merman. On the whole, I gathered the Pences wished he'd stick to being a walrus. He'd slap around in nothing but his swim fins, looking in the unlikeliest places for treasure. Polydore didn't realize the effect this had on people. He was visualizing himself with scales from the waist down, you know. Still, it could be terribly embarrassing when he showed up around two A.M. in some woman's bedroom, as he was apt to do."

"Really?" said Emma. "Then that would account for his having taken my bagful of junk jewelry. I'm glad I didn't wake up. A merman in one's bedroom would be a somewhat unnerving spectacle, shouldn't you think?"

"Ghastly," Theonia agreed. "And what if the poor man came out of his merman phase just at the wrong time? Was that when he'd have amnesia attacks, do you suppose?"

"I think it was mostly when he'd been a walrus. He'd suddenly realize he wasn't amphibious and be all at sea. Theonia, this is dreadful. One gathers Polydore's been quite a pet among the Pences. Not everybody has an aquatic mammal showing up at the family birthday parties. Do you think I should let Adelaide know?"

"Heavens, no! Not in her fragile condition. We mustn't breathe a word to anyone until we find out whether this is really Polydore. I don't wish to be an alarmist, but it seems most unlikely he'd have died by accident. According to Adelaide, Polydore was surefooted and totally at home in the water, no matter how cold it got. Just pushed aside the ice cakes and plunged right in."

"I do think I'd better drop a word to Vincent," said Emma. "You know how litigious some of those Pences are. They're sure to insist on a second opinion, no matter who does the autopsy. One little slip and Brother Franklin could get slapped with a malpractice suit."

It was about time to discover they were being overheard. Emma stepped to the door.

"Oh, Vincent, come in. Mrs. Brooks thinks we may have a new problem here."

"I was listenin'. I'll tell my brothers." He appeared strangely uninterested in the mythical Polydore. "You happen to know where Sandy went to? Bernice's been lookin' for 'er all over the place an' can't find hide nor hair."

"Did Bernice check the upstairs bedrooms?" Emma asked him. "The last we've seen of Sandy was when she took Mrs. Brooks up some coffee. She may have gone back for the tray and stayed to tidy around."

To try on Theonia's hat, more likely. "Or perhaps she's gone to the cabins."

Vincent shook his head. "Bernice looked upstairs. An' Sandy ain't in the cabins, leastways she better not be. Them two girls have strict orders never to go into any of the cabins without each other an' never while anybody's inside. Not that I don't trust 'em, but there's too damn many nuts around these days." He rubbed his chin and glanced down at the man under the blanket. "So you think this might be one o' the Pences, Miz Brooks?"

"We have to consider every possibility," Theonia replied. "I hope I'm wrong, but since we're all in the dark, it behooves us to take every precaution. I don't suppose either you or Cousin Emma will care to approach the Pences on the question of Polydore until an effort's been made to find out whether this might, as I'm sure we all hope, be somebody else. I assume the police will know how to arrange for an identity check. Doesn't the FBI have some kind of computerized fingerprint file?"

Emma half expected Vincent to say he had another brother in the FBI, but he didn't. Perhaps he'd been as badly shaken earlier as

Theonia thought; he was visibly upset now, and she couldn't say she blamed him.

"I'll go and check the house again," she said. If the minx had gone so far as to try on Emma's clothing, she might have got scared and popped into a closet when she heard Bernice coming. "What about you, Theonia?"

"Well, I can't say I care for staying here with poor Polydore, if in fact it is Polydore. Of course I'll help you hunt for the child. Please don't worry, Vincent. I expect she's just mooning about somewhere, as youngsters are so apt to do."

"Sandy don't moon."

Vincent was already out the door as he spoke. The two women left him to relock the shed and walked back to the house.

"My guess is that Sandy's shut in your bathroom sniffing your perfume and trying on your makeup," said Emma. "Still, one can't blame a father for being concerned."

"She wouldn't have gone off somewhere with her brother?" Theonia suggested.

"I shouldn't think so, but one never knows." Telling herself she wasn't worried, Emma was nevertheless walking faster.

She took Theonia in through the kitchen door because it was nearest. Bubbles wasn't there; maybe he was out carrying a custard to Mrs. Fath. Or checking the servants' wing to see whether Sandy was in her room, though surely Vincent would have done that himself. The work hadn't been slacked, anyway; the dishes were out of the way, the dining room cleared, the big living room back to its petrified elegance. She led the way upstairs. The door to Theonia's room was open. They walked in. Over behind the bed that had been made up for Theonia, in front of the closet that held the hidden safe, Sandy was sitting on the floor, the overturned breakfast tray beside her.

"Sandy!" cried Emma. "Your father's having fits. Why aren't you with Bernice?"

"I don't know."

Sandy wasn't effervescing now, she sounded dazed. "Why am I sitting here?"

"I haven't the faintest idea." Emma knelt and slipped her fingers through the spiky mess on Sandy's head. "Does it hurt when I press?"

"Ouch! Yes, right beside my ear. Maybe I've got amnesia."

"What's your name?"

"Sandy. Alexandria, I mean."

"And what's mine?"

"Mrs. Kelling."

"You don't have amnesia. It's possible you have a mild concussion. Do you remember banging your head on anything?"

"Such as this closet door," Theonia suggested. The door was open now, she didn't add that it had been shut when she left the room. Her traveling dress, the sailor hat, an opulent mauve satin negligee dripping with lace, and an equally sumptuous nightgown were hanging inside. "Sandy, do you remember Bernice coming to look for you?"

"No."

The two women exchanged shrugs. "I suppose if Bernice merely poked her head in, she wouldn't have seen Sandy because the bed was in the way," said Emma.

The antique four-poster sat high and its voluminous counterpane swept the floor, an effective screen for a young girl sitting or, more probably, lying on the floor. Sandy might, then, have been unconscious for some little while. How could she have given herself such a whack?

Anyway, the important thing now was to let Vincent know his daughter had been found. Together, Emma and Theonia boosted Sandy up on the bed, took off her sneakers, and pulled a comforter over her.

"Now, Sandy," Emma told her, "I want you to lie still till we say you can get up. You're probably going to be dizzy for a while yet, and you surely don't want to fall and bang your head again. I'm going to find your father and let him know where you are. In the meantime, you mustn't be left alone. Theonia, would you mind staying with her?"

"Not a bit. Go right along."

Theonia pulled up a chair to the bedside and settled herself to be temporary ministering angel. Emma wished she'd thought to ask whether Max had told Theonia about the wall safe in the closet. She didn't want to be an alarmist, but this was rather too much of a coincidence. Maybe it would have been possible in that rather unlikely spot for Sandy to whack her head hard enough to knock herself out, but Emma couldn't quite see how.

Anyway, she sincerely hoped Uncle Franklin could be got out here fairly soon to have a look at the child. If not, Sandy would have to be sent ashore in the lobster boat as soon as she was able to travel. A head injury severe enough to have stunned her this badly was nothing to be trifled with. Vincent must know at once. She picked the scattered dishes up off the carpet, set them on the tray, and carried them to the kitchen. Then she stepped outside and rang the big ship's bell beside the door.

Naturally she got more of a response than she'd bargained for. Bubbles was first, chugging up the path from the cottages, carrying what had presumably been Mrs. Fath's breakfast tray.

"What'th the matter, Mithith Kelling? We're not therving lunch in the houthe today."

"I know. I have to get hold of Vincent. He told me to ring the bell if ever I needed him in a hurry. Ah, here he comes now."

And here he came indeed on the dead run, with Neil and Ted close behind him. "What's the matter?" he panted.

"It's all right, Vincent, we've found Sandy. She apparently gave her head a whack on a closet door while she was picking up Mrs. Brooks's breakfast tray. She was down on the floor behind the bed, still dazed. It looked to me as though she may actually have been unconscious for a while. That would explain why she didn't respond when Bernice came looking for her. We've put her to bed in Mrs. Sabine's room. Mrs. Brooks is with her now, but I do think we ought to get the doctor's opinion before we let her up. One can't be too careful about a head injury, you know."

"My God, what next?" groaned the father. "All right, boys, you might as well go back an' finish clearin' away them broken limbs. For God's sake, be careful with the chain saw. We got trouble enough already. Come on, Bubbles, you better take a look at Sandy."

By now others were gathering to see what the commotion was about, and Emma was regretting her impromptu performance on the gong. She had to stay and keep explaining to startled cottagers and a dithering Bernice when she'd much rather be upstairs trying to find out whether an attempt had been made to open the safe. How she'd manage that without letting Vincent and Bubbles in on the secret Adelaide Sabine had kept, or at least thought she'd kept, all these years was something Emma hadn't yet figured out.

Yet it had to be done, for her own peace of mind if nothing more. Why couldn't she have left that necklace where she'd found it? Then the man who wasn't Polydore Pence might have lived to carry it away from Pocapuk, and Sandy would have escaped a knock on the head. Or not, as the case might be.

Emma was not used to crying over spilled milk, mainly because she'd never spilled any to speak of. She'd often acted on impulse, but she'd always known pretty much who'd be holding the net when she jumped. There'd been darling Bed and the unflappable Heath-erstones, there'd been the Kelling clan, her many friends and neighbors, and latterly her own grown-up children to support her in whatever scheme happened to grab her fancy. She was used to being the general but not to having to operate without her army. Theonia was a capable woman, but was Theonia enough?

Emma suddenly remembered that Theonia still hadn't had a chance to tell her who the man in the shed really was. She must find out, for whatever good the information might do her. She ought also to be questioning cottagers, getting a line on which of them might have been lurking inside Adelaide's wardrobe when Sandy tried to sneak a peek at Theonia's elegant nightwear.

What made her think they were going to tell her? And what kind of sense would it make to let them know she suspected Sandy's bang on the head was no accident? She was reassuring Black John Sendick that the house wasn't on fire and nobody needed to be rescued when Vincent came downstairs with his daughter in his arms.

"She's stayin' down here where I can keep an eye on 'er," he told Emma. He wasn't bothering to be amiable about it, and Emma couldn't blame him.

"Certainly, Vincent. If Sandy were my child, I shouldn't trust her to strangers either. I expect Bubbles and Bernice can manage between them till the doctor gets here. My cousin and I'll be on call if we're needed. Bubbles, were you planning to serve lunch in a while, or shall I fix something for Mrs. Brooks and myself?"

The cook was openly horrified. "Oh no, Mithith Kelling, you muthn't! I alwayth therve Mithith Thabine at half-patht twelve on the thun porch. Ith that all right for you?"

"That will be fine." Emma had quite forgotten there was one, a small glassed-in veranda off the dining room. She'd been too fagged to go out there the afternoon she arrived and yesterday had hardly been sun-porch weather. Now that she'd been put in her place, she might as well not rock the boat. At least, with Sandy out of the upstairs bedroom, she was free to go and check out the wall safe.

No, she wasn't. Here came Count Radunov at a gentle canter.

"Mrs. Kelling, may I have the boldness to inquire whether the bell has tolled for me?"

"Why not?" she replied. "Everyone else has. What took you so long?"

"My advanced state of decrepitude and the fact that I have actually begun to outline my magnum opus. I was pondering whether to allow Grigori Rasputin a brief flirtation with Queen Victoria."

"Do you think he was really her type?"

Radunov shrugged. "There were Disraeli and John Brown. One born Jewish, one Protestant; therefore we may assume her tastes were somewhat catholic. Getting back to the subject of the bell—"

"I merely wanted to get hold of Vincent in a hurry and the bell seemed the fastest way. I'll know better next time. Though I hope to goodness there won't be a next time."

He didn't ask why there had been need for haste this time. Such restraint deserved its reward, Emma decided.

"His daughter got a bad bang on her head and I thought he'd better know."

"But of course. He is, one observes, a devoted father. I hope the child is not seriously hurt."

"So do I. Sandy's such a darling."

"Is she? That, I confess, I had not observed. I prefer my darlings to be more mature."

He spoke with some empressement, Emma couldn't tell whether he was trying to flirt with her. Perhaps he was envisioning himself as Rasputin and her as Victoria Regina and seizing the chance to get in a spot of literary research. More likely it was just that Theonia had now joined them on the doorstep.

SIXTEEN

"Oh, Theonia," said Emma, "may I present Count Alexei Radunov, one of our cottagers? Count Radunov, this is Mrs. Brooks Kelling, my cousin's wife. Mrs. Brooks has just arrived unexpectedly for a short visit."

"And how glad I am to be here." Theonia extended a shapely hand, which the count, quite naturally, kissed. "How do you do, Count Radunov? Emma tells me you're here to write a novel. Are you making satisfactory progress?"

"I find it satisfactory to be in the presence of two so beautiful ladies, Mrs. Brooks. As to my novel, one can but hope. And how, if I may ask, did you get to Pocapuk? Not by the ferry, I surmise, for I heard no hoot. Not in your own yacht, by chance? If so, I must warn you that our zealous Professor Wont will attempt to commandeer the vessel for his treasure hunt."

Theonia's laugh was like the ringing of tiny silver bells. She favored the gallant Russian with a short peal, causing him to reel slightly and lose his grip on the hand he'd been reluctant to let go. "Professor Wont is in for a sad disappointment then. I merely hitched a ride with an old friend of my husband's who was flying up to look at the puffins. You don't happen to know Tweeters

Arbuthnot, by chance? He lives on that long, winding road over near the Kittiwakes."

Count Radunov didn't seem to recognize the name, though he was a trifle slow in shaking his head. "I regret that I have not the pleasure of Mr. Arbuthnot's acquaintance. But how fortunate for you and for us that he was able to fly you directly to Pocapuk. How ever did he manage to land on so small an island? Was he flying a helicopter? Or did you jump out with a parachute, as your intrepid cousin would no doubt have done?"

"I'm not that intrepid," said Emma.

"Nor I," Theonia obliged with another argent chuckle. "Tweeters flies a seaplane, of course. He landed on the water and taxied me up to the dock."

The count struck his brow with a fine melodramatic flourish. "Ah, how disappointingly prosaic! Instead of a death-defying leap, you merely entrusted your invaluable life to the ill-tempered ocean out there. Brhh! Rather you than I, madam. Did you take a horrible bouncing around?"

"Oh, I wasn't worried. Tweeters is always setting down in impossible places and never gets into the tiniest bit of trouble. My husband flies with him quite often; Brooks wouldn't have let me come if he'd thought there was any risk."

Brooks had let Theonia come because he wasn't around to stop her, Emma amended silently. Did Radunov have to keep ogling her quite so blatantly? He was shaking his head from side to side now, putting on a show of bemusement.

"Your husband flies off with this Tweeters to look at puffins when he might otherwise stay home and look at you? Truly, I find the ways of American men strange and wonderful."

"All men are strange, though not always wonderful." Emma decided she'd been left out of this conversation quite long enough. "Shall we walk you back to your cottage, Count Radunov? We're about to pay a sympathy call on Mrs. Fath."

"Ah, I am reminded. Mrs. Fath has sent a message. As I passed her cottage just now, she called out to me, 'Ask my guardian angel to bring me some orange juice.' She didn't explain who her guardian angel might be, so I thought I might as well just get some from the cook and take it to her myself."

"That was kind of you. I expect she was in fact referring to the cook. Bubbles has been plying Mrs. Fath with invalid goodies, Vincent tells me. We'll tend to the juice; you'd better nip on back to Queen Victoria while the fires of inspiration are still blazing nicely."

Emma hoped she'd managed to jog Radunov's memory. Cottagers were supposed to stay clear of the kitchen and not bother the cook. She could hardly have said so point-blank when he'd come on an errand of mercy. Anyway, it was a relief to hear that Alding Fath was awake and clamoring for nourishment.

Theonia, always adept at covering small awkwardnesses, stepped out on the path to show Radunov a brown creeper that was making its industrious way up and down a tree trunk, poking its curved beak into bark crevices like an avian Everard Wont searching for hidden treasure. The bird, at least, appeared to be having some success. Emma turned her attention to the orange juice. Would she be flying in the face of protocol if she simply opened the fridge and took some out? Apparently she would. She wasn't halfway across the kitchen before Bubbles charged in from the ell.

"Thomething I can do for you, Mithith Kelling?"

"Yes, thank you, Bubbles. Count Radunov has stopped by to say that Mrs. Fath wants some orange juice. If you'll get it out, I'll take it to her. Mrs. Brooks and I were just on our way there anyway."

"But I took her a whole pitcherful thith morning with her breakfatht," Bubbles protested. "She can't pothibly have drunk it all up tho thoon."

"Maybe she upset the pitcher."

Or maybe she was pining for another visit from her guardian angel. Emma wouldn't have dreamed of saying so in front of him.

Bubbles didn't see how Mrs. Fath could have spilled the juice. He'd put it into a plastic container with a screw-on lid and a lever you had to hold your thumb on when you poured. He'd shown her how to work the lever; she must have forgotten. He'd better go himself and show her again.

This small errand was turning into a major project. Emma was not about to have a wrangling match with Adelaide Sabine's cook.

"Very well then, Bubbles, if you think best. But you're not going to leave Sandy alone, surely? I know Vincent's depending on you to look after her."

"Bernithe ith with Thandy. She'll be all right for a few minuteth."

"If you're quite sure then."

Emma didn't suggest to the cook that they walk to the cottage together, that was surely not the way things had always been done. She merely nodded and went ahead to join Theonia. The count, to her surprise, had taken her suggestion and gone back to his writing, so she and her cousin-in-law went by themselves after all.

Emma was itching to ask Theonia who the man in the pony shed really was but prudence forbade. It was entirely possible there might be something besides a brown creeper lurking among the pines. Theonia would tell her soon enough. For the moment, it was safer to stick to the beauties of nature.

When they got to Mrs. Fath's cottage, they found the seeress lying in bed sound asleep, with a half-full glass of orange juice sitting on the bamboo nightstand beside her. One of those complicated plastic thermos jugs that turn up in expensive mail-order catalogs stood nearby.

Emma picked up the jug and sloshed it around. "It feels to be about half-full," she said. "Theonia, what do you make of this?"

Instead of replying, Theonia picked up the glass, sniffed at it, and took a tiny, careful sip. She then took a small plastic container with a bright red lid out of the straw tote bag she was carrying, poured about a third of the juice into it, made sure the red top was secured, and stashed it away in her bag. She did the same with a blue-topped container and some juice straight out of the pitcher. For a moment, Emma thought Theonia must have lost her mind, then she caught on.

"Theonia, do you actually believe—"

"Sh-h!"

Bubbles was coming up the porch steps with a duplicate plastic jug in his hand. Emma stepped to the cottage door.

"Mrs. Fath's sound asleep again, Bubbles, she must have gone back to bed after she spoke with Count Radunov. And look, there's juice in her glass and still some in the pitcher. She must have been confused when she asked for more. You don't suppose she's taking something?"

The man's friendly blue eyes narrowed to unamiable slits. "Thuch ath what?"

Emma shrugged. "Not liquor, or we'd smell it on her. Pills of some kind, wouldn't you think?"

Bubbles shook his head so hard that his fat cheeks flip-flopped. "Mithith Fath would never take pillth! She thayth they dithturb the vibrationth. There'th nothing the matter with her. It'th jutht the thea air. It affecth thome people that way when they firtht come, they thleep and thleep. A thenthitive perthon like her ith naturally more thutheptible than the otherth."

"So that's why I've been feeling drowsy ever since I got here?" said Theonia. "I thought it was from having had to get up so early this morning. Then you don't think Mrs. Kelling should ask the doctor to look at Mrs. Fath when he comes to see Sandy?"

His reaction was almost violent. "That would thcare her thilly! Mithith Fath ith my patient; I know what'th betht for her. Believe me, all she needth ith retht."

"Then the best we can do is leave her to it." In fact, as far as Emma could see, this was the only thing they could do without having a fight on their hands. "Come along, then, Theonia, let's pop over to Shag Rock Point and see what the treasure hunters are up to. We'll be back for luncheon at half-past twelve then, Bubbles. If you should happen to catch Mrs. Fath awake anytime soon, tell her we stopped by to say hello."

Radunov was holed up with his muse; they could see him through his open screen door, writing at a small table. He didn't look up as they passed. Nobody else appeared to be around; they must all have gone together. There was another path from here that led along the cliffs, high, bare, and private. Emma elected to take it. As soon as they were well away from the cottages, she took advantage of the privacy it afforded to murmur, "Theonia, what do you make of that? Did Mrs. Fath actually send Count Radunov for orange juice or was he lying to us? And why?"

"Your guess is as good as mine, my dear, and I expect we're both guessing along the same lines. Anyway, we should know by this time tomorrow."

"Tomorrow? Are you planning to run some kind of test on the sample you took? How can you?"

"I can't, but Tweeters can. Perhaps I forgot to mention that he'll be stopping back here later on. I told him drinks about five, is that all right?"

"Yes, of course. That will give us time to talk before the cottagers arrive. Will he be staying to dinner? And the night? Not to seem inhospitable, Theonia, but we really have no place to put him."

"Don't worry, Emma, I'm not about to drop another cuckoo in your nest. Tweeters will have one double martini and a piece of cheese or whatever because he'll have forgotten to eat his lunch, and then he'll buzz along back to Boston with the juice and the films."

"What films?"

"The ones I've been taking with my little Dick Tracy camera, as Max calls it. Haven't you noticed my bracelet?"

Emma smiled. "How could I not?"

The trinket Theonia wore on her left arm was fully two inches wide and fairly bulgy, one of those arty clunkers Little Em would go mad for. Emma had assumed the bracelet must have come from India; it was fashioned of narrow, dark red silk ribbon wound around some kind of core and starred with tiny rounds of mirrorlike polished metal, such as one often saw on articles of East Indian manufacture. Emma herself would have felt a bit overloaded wearing such a bauble, but Theonia could get away with anything and so often did that Emma hadn't paid any attention until now.

"Do you mean one of those mirrors is a lens?"

"Precisely, my dear. This was one of Brooks's clever ideas. You may recall that he built his first midget camera into a belt buckle so that he could take pictures of ospreys' nests and still have both hands free to beat off the mother birds with if they attacked. He made this one for me. I wore it once before hidden inside a pair of fancy plastic sunglasses, but they were really too hideous and made it hard to focus, so he came up with the bracelet. It's rather attractive in its way, don't you think?"

"Charming," Emma agreed, "but how does it work?"

Theonia explained. "There's a tiny squeeze bulb inside. I just squeeze it with my fingers or press my arm against whatever comes handy. I still cut off a good many heads and feet, but I take multiple exposures and one's bound to be on target. Tweeters knows how to develop the films; Brooks made him one, too. For the puffins, you know. Tweeters's is built into that old-fashioned aviator's helmet he wears; he activates the shutter by pulling on the chinstrap. With his teeth, often as not. I noticed the strap's getting a bit chewed up around the edges."

"Aren't we all?" said Emma. "Brooks never ceases to amaze me.

And now what about that man in the pony shed? You spoke as if you knew him."

"I did, to my sorrow, though fortunately I never had to spend much time with him. His name was Jimmy Sorpende."

"Sorpende? But wasn't that your—" Emma wasn't quite sure how to go on.

Theonia shrugged. "Sorpende was the name of my late and decidedly unlamented first husband, yes. Jimmy was allegedly Francis's nephew; I always thought he was more likely a son by some casual encounter. Women were one of Francis's hobbies, though swindling fat cats was his first and only real love. Jimmy resembled Francis in every respect, unfortunately, except that he wasn't so good-looking. Hence the beard, perhaps. I can't tell you what he was doing here on Pocapuk other than stealing your jewelry, but you may rest assured it was nothing good. Goodness, what a view from here! And there are your treasure seekers down on the beach. I assume that's a beach, though there's not much of it. They appear to be building a raft."

"Or trying to."

Emma couldn't see any real progress, though a good many logs and boards were strewn around much too close to the high-water mark. She and Theonia had reached the spot where the path began to drop off down to Shag Rock Point; they stood a moment watching the scene below them.

Everard Wont appeared to be acting as foreman, with no visible result. Joris Groot was arguing with him about something, waving a large hammer around in a totally irresponsible manner. Emma was surprised to see the usually phlegmatic illustrator so excited; Wont must be making himself even more obnoxious than usual. Black John Sendick was tugging at a log much too big for one person to handle, yowling for help and not getting any. Lisbet Quainley was clearly out of sorts with the lot of them but wasn't raising a hand to put things right.

"A clear case of much ado about nothing," Theonia observed. "Shall we go down there and add to the confusion?"

"By all means," said Emma. "Watch your step here. These little rocks have a nasty habit of rolling under one's feet."

The going was ticklish; Emma rather wished she had Count Radunov to lean on. However, they weren't halfway down before all three men were rushing to assist them. Emma got Sendick. Theonia got Wont and Groot, as might have been expected.

It was clear that the advent of Mrs. Kelling and her guest came as a welcome interruption. Wont tried hard to twist his lips into an ingratiating smile, with fairly hideous results. He should stick to his usual supercilious sneer, Emma thought; he looked more natural that way. Joris Groot, once he'd made sure Theonia was safe on level ground, snatched his pad and began making a sketch of her. His model affected not to notice, nevertheless Emma observed that Theonia happened to have struck a particularly graceful attitude.

Not to be outdone in diligence, Lisbet Quainley also began sketching. Since Everard Wont was treating Theonia to a lecture on the pirate Pocapuk and the treasure he was confident of recovering, Emma had the choice of helping Black John Sendick move his log or fading gently into the background. She chose to fade, which gave her a chance to watch the two artists at work.

Groot's drawing, she saw, was crisp and professional but not particularly interesting except around the feet. He really did have a knack for shoes, no doubt about that. As for Lisbet Qainley's, the only adjective Emma could think of was nasty. Had the woman any talent or just a dirty mind?

Emma Kelling was no philistine. She'd had a solid grounding in art history at her excellent private school. She'd been looking at pictures all her life; she possessed some good ones herself. She was usually willing to give even the more inscrutable moderns the benefit of the doubt, but finding merit where none existed was not something she'd ever been good at. She was relieved when young Sendick started casting sheep's eyes at his luncheon basket and she could remind Theonia that it was time they started back to the house.

Theonia must have heard enough verbiage from Wont to last her a while. She seemed indisposed for conversation on the walk back and Emma didn't try to push her. When they got to the house, they found the glass-topped table on the sun porch set with yellow place mats and napkins as well as yellow-bordered dishes Emma hadn't seen before. No doubt this particular set of china had always been reserved for luncheon on the porch.

Bubbles had done them proud. There were lidded yellow pottery cups of hot consommé. There were avocado halves stuffed with fresh crabmeat salad. There were hot rolls that tasted fresh from the oven even though they'd more probably come out in the lobster boat with Ches and Wal. There were tiny wild strawberries for dessert, with cream so heavy it practically had to be dug out of the pitcher with a spoon. There was, of course, perfect coffee.

Bubbles waited on them himself; he said Bernice was keeping Sandy company. Other than that, he didn't say much of anything. Emma didn't try to coax any more out of him, especially on the subject of Mrs. Fath. She did mention that Mr. Arbuthnot would be stopping by in his seaplane for a drink about five o'clock but would not be staying for dinner. Bubbles replied, "Yeth'm," and went away with the empty dessert plates.

"What's bothering that man, I wonder?" Emma fretted. "I hope Sandy isn't worse. Perhaps he's more concerned about Mrs. Fath than he's letting on. And perhaps he has reason to be. I gather you think so."

"I try not to think too much, my dear. It makes wrinkles." Theonia held out her cup for Emma to refill. "Ah, I believe we're about to have company."

A fast motorboat was zooming up to the dock. Vincent was running to meet it. After a flurry of docking, two men who could only be Vincent's brothers jumped ashore. The sunburned one in the yachting cap with the big folded plastic sheet over his arm must be Lowell; the paler one with the old-fashioned black doctor's satchel in his hand would of course be Franklin. Emma was debating whether she should walk out to meet them when Vincent solved her dilemma by herding them straight toward the pony shed.

The two women were still in the yellow-painted wicker chairs sipping coffee when Vincent and Lowell came around the house and headed toward the dock again. They were both aboard the electric cart, Vincent driving, Lowell keeping a weather eye on a long plastic-wrapped bundle stretched out on the long luggage carrier that trundled behind. Emma grimaced and set down her cup.

"What a way to end a meal!"

She didn't want to watch. She tried to keep her eyes focused on the clematis vine that was growing up the side of the porch on an old-fashioned wrought-iron trellis. A sturdy trellis and a sturdy vine, loaded with long, tapering buds ready to burst into bloom. Emma coaxed herself to wonder what shade the flowers would be:

white, pink, delicate lavender, that heavy deep purple that always made her think of funerals? Oh, what was the use? Her eyes kept straying to the dock. She felt astonishingly relieved once they'd got the bundle safely aboard the harbor master's boat and stowed somewhere out of her sight.

Lowell stayed with the boat; Vincent drove the cart back alone. Not more than a couple of minutes after the women had seen him pass the porch a second time, he came in to make his report.

"Franklin's takin' a look at Sandy," he told Emma without preamble. "He'll be out in a minute."

"You must be greatly relieved to have him here," Emma replied, "and we're anxious to hear what he has to say. Would your brothers care for some refreshment?"

"They et before they come." Vincent was clearly in no mood for the amenities. "Been too damn much time wasted today already. You want more coffee or anything?"

"Not I, thank you. You, Theonia?"

"Gracious, no, I couldn't possibly. That was a scrumptious luncheon and I've eaten far too much. I do hope your brother finds your daughter to be recovering satisfactorily, Vincent."

"I better go see."

Without further ado, he went. Theonia stood up and set her empty cup on the yellow tray beside the yellow coffeepot. "I'll carry these out to the kitchen."

"Don't you dare!" cried Emma. "That's not the way it's always been done. One keeps to one's own side of the fence here; I'm surprised you hadn't noticed. I've already committed a few infractions and been firmly put back in my place."

"Then I shall try not to embarrass you further." Theonia left the tray alone and came back to her chair. "This is an extremely interesting situation, Emma."

"I'm glad you find it so." *Interesting* was not the adjective Emma herself would have chosen, but perhaps Theonia knew best. She most fervently hoped so.

SEVENTEEN

The word *interesting* could also apply to the local fauna when it came from the lips of an ornithologist's wife. In case somebody might be listening, Emma decided it better had. She was asking Theonia what the chances were of spotting any pied grebes on Pocapuk when Vincent came back to the porch with his brother in tow.

Franklin looked a great deal like Vincent except for one detail. Whereas Vincent wasn't a bad-looking man, Franklin was out-and-out handsome. Why this should be so when there was so little difference in their features, Emma couldn't quite decide. Not that it mattered, of course. She gave the doctor a courteous but impersonal greeting, in keeping with her position as temporary doyenne, and asked what he thought about his niece's condition.

"I think I'd like to see that closet door you claim she struck her head on," was his brusque and not altogether courteous reply.

"I don't recall having made such a claim." One could carry courtesy just so far, Emma decided. "I mentioned the door as a possibility because when my cousin and I found her sitting on the floor in front of the closet, the door was standing open. By all means come and see for yourself. This way, please. Theonia, perhaps you'd better come too, and make sure I don't get the facts twisted."

The four of them went upstairs, the two women in front, the two men behind, nobody saying a word. Emma led them into the big, cluttered bedroom, around behind the bed Theonia would sleep in tonight, and pointed out the spot where they'd discovered the missing Sandy.

"She was here and the door was about the way it is now. I don't recall having touched it. Did I, Theonia?"

"No, I don't believe either of us did. The hinges are rather stiff. I noticed that when I went to hang up my things. One would have had to give it a firm push to change the angle."

"And Sandy was how?" demanded Franklin.

Emma promptly plunked herself down on the floor. "Like this, with her back resting against the bed."

The doctor shook his head. "She couldn't have hurt herself that way."

"Of course she couldn't," Emma replied somewhat testily. "If I may venture another conjecture, I assumed at the time Sandy must have pulled herself up and braced herself against the bed because she still felt dizzy. She'd been missing for quite a while when we found her, you know. She could well have been knocked unconscious and had time to come out of it."

"But she was definitely still groggy?"

"Oh yes, no question about that. I raised two accident-prone sons of my own, Doctor. I can tell when a youngster's putting it on and when he's really hurt. In any event, I shouldn't think Sandy would be much good at faking an injury."

Vincent emitted a little snort. "Not her. Sandy's so consarned truthful it gets embarrassin' sometimes. An' you can't get around that jeezledy great lump on 'er head, Frank."

"Just so, Vince. Let me in there, will you, Mrs. Kelling?"

Emma made way for the doctor. He examined the edge of the door up, down, and sideways; he even went into some peculiar gymnastics of his own. At last he shook his head again.

"No way I can see she did that to herself, Vince. I'd say Sandy was standing in front of the open closet when somebody came around behind her and beaned her one."

Vincent didn't like that one bit. "Jesus H. Christ!" he exploded. "Then there's two of 'em."

"Two what?"

"Hell, Frank, look at the facts. That bugger who stole Mrs. Kelling's fake diamonds was already dead by then. That means there's got to be another crook still runnin' loose on the island."

"But why should he have hit Sandy, and why here?"

"Damned if I know. Nothin' like this ever happened till now."

He was glaring at Emma as if it were all her fault. She decided she'd better take the bull by the horns.

"I think it must have been a case of Sandy's happening to be in this room at the wrong time. Am I to gather, Vincent, that the Sabines never told you about the safe?"

"What safe? Mean to say you know somethin' about this house that I don't?" He was furious and no wonder.

"I'm sure it's not that they didn't trust you, Vincent. I expect they were trying to shield you from suspicion in the event of a theft," Emma improvised. It would have been unkind to say, Why should they? After all, you are only a servant.

"Anyway," she went on, "since it's unlikely Mrs. Sabine will ever set foot in this house again and I don't suppose her heirs will care one way or the other, I see no reason to keep the secret any longer. There is in fact a small wall safe hidden behind the cedar paneling in this closet. Mrs. Sabine told me about it in case I was bringing any money or valuables with me that I didn't want to leave lying around loose. She was a bit concerned, since she knew nothing about any of the crowd who'd be using the cottages."

That rocked the handsome doctor. "Do you mean Mrs. Sabine has invited a bunch of people to stay here whom she doesn't know from a hole in the ground?"

"As I understand it, she didn't even invite them herself. She let Dr. Wont, whom she'd never met, invite them for her. I know that sounds totally irresponsible, but I think it was mainly that she didn't much care. She's been sick so long, and she's so old. Mrs. Sabine was simply going through the motions, trying to carry on the way she always had so that her children wouldn't feel she'd given up on life. Somebody she knew told her Dr. Wont wanted to bring a party of artists and writers here for the summer; it was a way of coping, so she simply let him organize the whole business sight unseen."

This must have been something else Vincent hadn't been aware of. "By Godfrey, if I'd o' known that—"

"You'd have done exactly what you're doing now," his brother finished for him. "What else could you have done, Vince? It's still Mrs. Sabine's place; she's still paying your wages. You'd no call to question her judgment unless she'd asked you to do something illegal or downright crazy. Would you care to show us that safe, Mrs. Kelling?"

"Yes, why not?" said Emma. "If this bulb were stronger, you could all see better."

Vincent, naturally, produced a flashlight on the spot. Emma pushed the knothole and popped the cover. The safe was shut; she couldn't see any sign that anybody had tried to force it. She twirled the combination and opened the little round metal door. The empty jewelry boxes and the papers she'd left in one neat stack were toppled into such disarray as the limited space allowed.

Emma hesitated. Should she mention the necklace? Theonia wasn't offering any hint, but her lips were more tightly pressed together than they normally would be. No necklace, then. But she had to say something.

"Yes, somebody's definitely been in here. I opened the safe last night myself, partly out of curiosity and partly to make sure Mrs. Sabine hadn't left anything of value that ought to be sent along to her in Pleasaunce. I couldn't quite bring myself to examine the papers because that would really have been prying, but I did look inside the boxes and found them all empty. I put them back precisely as I'd found them, not jumbled around like this. Somebody searched through them in a big hurry, don't you think?"

"As though they wanted to get out of the room while Sandy was still unconscious," Theonia offered.

"We ought to be thankful she didn't come to at the wrong time," said the doctor. "I suppose it would be hopeless to try to get fingerprints off those velvet covers. You didn't put anything of your own in here, Mrs. Kelling?"

"I didn't bring anything worth locking up except for my engagement ring, which I never take off, and some traveler's checks, which would be hard for a thief to cash. They're still in my purse, by the way."

"Good for you. I suppose we should have a look at these papers, just in case. Here, Vince, you do it."

They turned out to be nothing more earth-shaking than plans for the island's septic system. Vincent studied them with some interest, then carefully stowed them back in the safe. "What beats me is why Mrs. Sabine left these boxes here with nothin' in 'em."

Emma shrugged. "Why shouldn't she? That's the sort of thing anybody might do. When they first started coming to Pocapuk, I expect the Sabines used to travel with steamer trunks. There'd have been plenty of room for this sort of thing in a trunk. Later, when they only brought suitcases, Mrs. Sabine would have used a jewelry roll of soft leather that would pack easily. She might have been in the habit of transferring her jewels to these cases when she unpacked, or the cases might simply have been left in the safe for the same reason you yourself probably have a couple of old cuff-link boxes or whatever stuck somewhere at the back of a dresser drawer. Vincent, do you think perhaps we ought to call your brother Lowell up here?"

"Dunno what for. He's not a policeman. County sheriff's the one to handle it, far's I know. We never had any trouble out here before, not in all the years the Sabines kept comin'. Why'd it have to happen now?"

"Perhaps because somebody formed the mistaken impression that because Mrs. Sabine is too old and ill to travel, things on Pocapuk had got out of control and they could do as they please without getting caught," Theonia suggested quietly. "Vincent, would it have been possible for anybody to get into this house long enough to discover the safe during the off-season? You don't stay here in the wintertime, I don't suppose."

"No, I don't, and yes, it would be possible. When I leave for the winter, I board up all the windows and double-lock the doors, but that's not to say somebody couldn't come along and take one of the boards off. They'd have had to put it back just the way I had it or I'd have noticed when I came to make my inspection, which I do faithfully once a week, all winter long. Unless the weather's so bad I can't get here," he conceded, "in which case nobody else could, neither."

"Do you always come on the same day?" Theonia asked him.

"Either Saturday or Sunday. Only time I have. I work five days a week at the college."

As president, no doubt, Emma thought. One could hardly envision Vincent in a lesser post.

"So all a person would have to do would be to show up on

Monday or Tuesday," Franklin grunted. "You know as well as I do, Vince, anybody can get in anywhere if he wants to badly enough. How's Ted making out?"

"All right, I guess. Cocky bugger, considerin'."

"Think I'd better have a talk with him?"

"Wouldn't hurt."

"I'll be back in a day or so, then. I expect Lowe's about ready to be getting along. You keep Sandy quiet the rest of today and see how she feels in the morning. I'll call later and tell you how I made out with your man there. I understand you ladies think he might be one of the Pences."

"We sincerely hope he isn't," Theonia replied. "We've neither of us ever met Polydore alive, you see; it's just that we shouldn't like to see you run into trouble because of a misconception. If it is Polydore, his fingerprints are no doubt on file somewhere. He's been picked up by the police at various times because of his bouts of amnesia and his unfortunate habit of collecting other people's jewelry. Polydore doesn't think of it as stealing but naturally the owners do. You do understand how awkward the situation could be."

"One does have to wonder." Emma decided that if Theonia could tell fairy tales, she might try her hand at it, too. "A member of the family might have had a better chance than an outsider to learn about this safe. The Pences are a clannish lot, like the Kellings. And like your own family, one gathers. But we really mustn't keep you here chatting while your brother's down there waiting. Then you think you may have the results of the autopsy by this evening?"

"With any luck, yes. I'll get hold of the county sheriff's office as soon as we get him ashore. Ready, Vince?" With the minimum allowable degree of courtesy, Dr. Franklin made his good-byes to the two women and followed his brother out of the room.

"Well," said Emma. "Poor little Sandy! What a beastly thing to find out, but I can't say I'm surprised. You really are the most charmingly plausible liar, Theonia."

"Practice, my dear, practice. What about this fellow Ted?"

"An excellent question. Do you know, I hardly think I've spoken more than two words to that young man since I've been here. The only time I've been in Ted's company, Vincent was ripping him and

Neil to shreds for having brought your step-whatever into the house without permission."

"For which one could hardly blame him," said Theonia. "Where do you suppose Ted is right now?"

"The last I knew, Vincent had sent him out to clear up some of the damage from yesterday's storm. Broken trees and all that."

"Then let's go find him."

"Is it safe for us to be prowling the woods by ourselves?"

"My dear Emma, this from you? I didn't think the word *safe* was in your vocabulary. You know, statistically it would appear we'd be safer out there than in here. I don't suppose there's any hope Sandy managed to get a look at whoever coshed her."

"I don't suppose we have a prayer of getting near enough to ask her," said Emma. "Vincent's going to guard her like a wolf with its cub. I had the impression he was more angry than surprised at what his brother told us, didn't you?"

"Oh yes, decidedly so. One can hardly blame him. What a spot for a caretaker to be in!"

Emma thought it was rather a spot for an acting hostess to be in, but all she said was, "Just let me get my hat." The sun was hot now and she wasn't about to appear in that faded relic of Adelaide's alongside Theonia's fetching black boater. Not that one should be thinking of such things at a time like this, but old habits die hard. She adjusted her brim to its most becoming angle and led the way out toward the pine grove at the western side of the house.

The whine of a chain saw told her she'd guessed right. It didn't take more than a couple of minutes to track the noise to its source. Ted was working by himself, cutting the branches off a pine tree he'd felled. He was clearly only too pleased at an excuse to shut off the saw's motor.

"Something I can do for you, Mrs. Kelling?"

"I'm just showing Mrs. Brooks around the island. Where's Neil?"

"Down at the dock talking to his uncle."

"Isn't Lowell your uncle, too?" Emma remarked innocently. "I had the impression you people were all related."

"Huh! Better not let Vincent hear you say that."

"Why, Ted?" Theonia spoke as though she'd known this young stranger all his life. "What were you in for?"

That rocked him. He jerked the saw toward her in an ugly, tentative gesture. "What are you talking about? In where? What for?"

"You tell me, Ted. You've violated your parole, haven't you?"

He looked down at the saw, then slowly, carefully, laid it down on the fallen tree trunk. "You're not a parole officer?"

"No," said Theonia, "but you'd better come clean with me anyway. It's all right, Ted; I won't run you in if you tell us the truth."

"How do I know you won't?"

"You'll just have to trust me. The way you trusted Jimmy Sorpende."

"Jimmy?" Now he was totally demoralized. "Who the hell are you?"

"My name is Theonia Kelling, and I'm married to Mrs. Kelling's cousin Brooks. That's why she called me Mrs. Brooks, merely to avoid confusion. You may, too, if it makes you feel any better. What did they bust you for? As a guess, I'd say aggravated assault while under the influence."

"The bastard had it coming," he growled. "How'd I know his aunt was a cop?"

"Life is full of surprises, Ted. This was your first serious offense, I suppose, or you'd still be inside. You're from around here somewhere. Your parents are respectable people and friends of Dr. Franklin. They think you got a bum rap, and you behaved in jail or you wouldn't be here now. Vincent doesn't know you're only out on parole, though, does he? That was the hook Jimmy used to make you let him into the house, right?"

Ted swallowed. "What was I supposed to do?"

"You might have stayed where you were supposed to be and got a job there."

"Like how? Who's going to hire a con?"

"The labor situation being what it is, I should think you could have found something."

"Yeah. Minimum wage for cleaning out sewers."

"Sewers would have been better than violating your parole and risking more time, Ted. But that's your mess, not mine. All I want to know is whom Jimmy was working with. Not you, surely. Even Jimmy would know enough not to pick an accomplice who can't control his temper. Come on, Ted, what did he tell you? And do get away from that saw. You might cut yourself with it."

"I might do something else with it," he blustered.

Theonia shook her head. "Not you, Ted. You've been acting like a fool, but I don't think you're quite a damned fool. What did Jimmy say?"

"He said I'd better go along with his act or he'd blow the whistle about my breaking parole. My folks think I've been released early for good behavior. Which is true, sort of."

"Or was, till you fouled up. So that's why they asked Dr. Franklin for help and why he put in a word for you with Vincent. What would Vincent do if he found out the truth?"

"Ship me back to Boston in handcuffs, I guess. He's so law-abiding it's pathetic."

Theonia remained serene. "I shan't comment on that. Did Neil overhear what Jimmy said to you?"

"No. See, Jimmy came dragging himself ashore in this old torn wet suit. He acted as if he was all in and claimed not to know his own name or how he got here. As soon as I realized who he was, I figured it must be a put-on, so I sent Neil back to the house for a blanket and some hot coffee. So then Jimmy told me what I had to do and I did it."

"He didn't say what he was here for?"

"No."

"Or whom he'd come to see?"

"He didn't have time, for God's sake! Neil came running back with the stuff as if the devil was after him. That kid can move! Then we got Jimmy out of the wet suit and up to the kitchen, and that's all I know. Honest to God!"

He was probably telling the truth, Emma thought. Too bad. "Were you the one who let Jimmy out of the storeroom?" she asked him.

"No, I wasn't." He was sulkier with her than he'd dared to be with Theonia. "Once I'm in my bedroom, I stay there."

"Why? Is Neil a light sleeper?"

"Neil sleeps in his father's room. Do you think Vincent would trust his son with a great big nasty criminal like me? He doesn't trust me with his daughter either, which is why I damned well stay put even if it means I have to pee out the window in the middle of the night. Look, I've got work to do if it's okay with you. Vincent'll be wondering why he isn't hearing my chain saw. I've caught enough hell already."

"Then we must make very sure you don't catch any more," said Theonia sweetly. "Don't you want to change your mind about how Jimmy escaped from the storeroom? You wouldn't, for instance, have palmed the key after Vincent locked him in, then gone for a bedtime stroll and chucked it in through one of the ventilating slits with a note telling Jimmy to hang the key back in the pantry after he was through with it? You may think that's not the same thing as letting him out, but I doubt whether either Vincent or a judge would agree with you. You'd better go straight from now on, Ted. You just haven't the brains to be a successful crook."

EIGHTEEN

"You know, Theonia, you can be a trifle spooky sometimes. How in the world did you learn all that?"

"Elementary, my dear Emma. Any good tea-leaf reader learns to size up her customers at a glance. Ted's the absolute prototype of the arrogant young troublemaker who swaggers around drinking in sleazy bars and looking for a punch-up. They're apt to get picked up by the police for being drunk and disorderly or driving under the influence, if not something worse. Some of them are decent enough otherwise, I suppose, but Ted struck me as being completely self-centered. I couldn't see him performing a Good Samaritan act unless he was forced into it, so I deduced that Jimmy must have had a handle on him. The only places he'd have been likely to meet Jimmy would have been at a bar or in jail. I plumped for the latter and made a leading remark. Ted gave the response I was looking for, and it went along quite smoothly from there. Standard fortune-telling technique. I'm sure you could have done as well if you hadn't led such a respectable life."

"Don't be a snob, Theonia. If you don't mind, I prefer to go on thinking of you as omniscient. It makes me feel somewhat less uncomfortable about the spot I'm in."

"Then by all means revere me as much as you like. I don't mind a bit."

"Do you think Ted knew what Jimmy came for?"

"The necklace? That's a ticklish question, Emma. We have to assume your bag was stolen on the ferryboat for the express purpose of getting the necklace to Pocapuk. The man who hid it might even have gone ashore at the next-to-last stop, assuming that whoever picked it up would be staying aboard till the end of the run."

"Wouldn't that have been an awfully chancy way to treat an object of such value?" Emma argued. "What if nobody used the rest room before they docked? What if the person who found the bag was also going ashore at that stop? What if he was a crew member instead of a passenger?"

"The crew probably have their own rest room. Anyway, I expect whoever stole your bag would have hidden in one of the cubicles until he'd made sure the right person got hold of it."

"But how would he know?"

"Because he'd watched when the passengers went aboard to see what color tickets they were holding. Tweeters and I checked with the ferryboat office on the way up and found they give out different colors for the various stops because they charge different fares depending on how far you go. You show your ticket when you get on and turn it in when you get off to prove you haven't gone farther than you paid for. Isn't that what you did?"

"Yes, that's right," said Emma. "Mine was a garish salmon color, as I recall."

Theonia nodded. "Easy to spot, you see. And there weren't that many going to Pocapuk, so you'd have been easy to remember. But I'll grant your point that it would have been chancy. The more probable alternative, as I see it, is that the person who was carrying the necklace to Pocapuk got nervous about having it on his person and chose you as an errand girl because your bagful of junk jewelry provided an excellent camouflage."

"Why do you say the 'person'?" Emma argued. "It must have been a man if he went to the men's room."

"We mustn't be too sure. Blue jeans, running shoes, and a baggy sweatshirt sometimes make it hard to tell whether the person inside is a he or a she. And of course hair styles are no help whatever nowadays."

"All right, I'll grant you the ambiguity. But why should he or she have been nervous?"

"Well, my dear, if it's one of Dr. Wont's crowd, I should say the reason might be Alding Fath. Tell me a little more about her, can you?"

Emma told Theonia as much as she could remember. Her long experience at memorizing Gilbert and Sullivan roles had made her a quick study; she was able to quote verbatim a good deal of the conversation they'd had on the ferry and at the dinner table. She even managed a fair imitation of the country woman's delivery.

Theonia didn't miss a syllable or an inflection. "And you say you liked her the best of the lot even though you were sure she must be faking?"

"She had to be, didn't she?"

"Not on the strength of your evidence, Emma. I don't say she mightn't have romanced it a bit in spots, even the best of them do that when it's a case of not disappointing a patron. Quite frankly, if I were carrying a hot diamond necklace and found myself in the company of somebody like her, I'd want to ditch the thing as fast as I possibly could. You may find this hard to believe, but if those stones are as big as you describe, they must carry some awfully strong vibrations. A real psychic couldn't help picking up something."

"Could you?"

"Possibly, though I don't consider myself a real psychic. It wouldn't be just the necklace itself, you know. There'd be little clues from the carrier himself, no matter how good an actor he was: signs of unusual tension, fear, suspicion. I might not understand what I was picking up, but I'd sense things were happening so I'd start feeling around, the way I did with Ted. I might not be able to identify the object itself, but I'd come up with something. Alding Fath sounds to me like a really gifted lady. She'd quite possibly have been able to get a clairvoyant picture of the necklace and would have blurted out what she was seeing because she's obviously proud of her talent and likes to show it off. That could be a real disaster for the one holding the necklace."

"But if it was Alding Fath who alarmed the carrier, then it must have been one of the other cottagers who drugged me and took the bag," said Emma. "Mrs. Fath told me Wont had paid her way, and his group appeared to be the only ones she was talking to."

Theonia shrugged. "We mustn't jump to conclusions. Shall we stroll back and see whether I can pick up anything from the treasure hunters?"

"By all means. What did you sense about Dr. Franklin, by the way?"

"That he probably has to beat off his women patients with a stick."

Emma laughed. "Even I could have deduced that. I wonder whether he might even have been a tad put out because neither you nor I leaped to the attack? Though of course that would have been a totally ridiculous thing for a woman of my age to do."

"Humbug, Emma! You're charming, intelligent, quite indecently attractive, and have pots of money. Don't try to tell me you couldn't still draw the men like flies if you cared to flash the green light."

"Well," Emma admitted, "there have been a few overtures since Bed died, but I've always assumed it was not so much my charm as Bed's money."

"Very well, then, let's put you in a room with Cousin Mabel and six eligible men and see which of you two all six of them go for."

Emma was amused. "Mabel isn't exactly stiff competition."

"Why shouldn't she be?" Theonia argued. "She's no uglier than some of the other Kelling women and a great deal richer than most."

"A great deal richer than I, certainly. All right, Theonia, I'll concede you, Mabel. Though I'm not sure Count Radunov might not find her a temptation."

"I can't imagine he's that hard up for a meal ticket, but one never knows. Invite them both to one of your musical evenings when you get back to Pleasaunce and see what happens. Isn't it funny how one's tastes in men can change, Emma? Radunov is the perfect picture of the man I once dreamed of being swept off my feet by. Now that I've met him, he doesn't budge me an inch."

"You certainly budged him, though." Emma spoke a trifle more tartly than she'd meant to.

"Hardly a budge," Theonia replied modestly. "I'd call it merely an involuntary reflex. Radunov's much too sharp to let himself be swept off his feet by a superannuated adventuress, which is what I suspect he thinks I am."

"Then he can't be clever, after all."

"Don't judge him so harshly, Emma. After all, I'm not your typical Boston matron, no matter how hard I try to make people think I am."

"If you were, Brooks would have shunned you like the plague."

"What would have happened to me then, I wonder? Do people actually die of broken hearts?"

Brooks Kelling, it might be said, was several inches shorter than his statuesque wife, somewhat older, and a good deal plainer. He reminded some people of a chipmunk and others of former Massachusetts governor (and later president) Calvin Coolidge, more remembered for his Puritan rectitude than for his charisma. It may also be noted that Coolidge himself married a tall, beautiful, and charming woman.

"What I'm wondering is which of our guests or staff could have been heartless enough to bash poor little Sandy," said Emma. "I'd prefer to think Jimmy had another accomplice somewhere on the island, but I can't think where the person could be hiding. I've been over most of the place myself, except for the servants' wing and the cottages. Good heavens, Theonia! You don't think that's why Mrs. Fath is staging her lie-in, because she's got somebody hiding under her bed and doesn't want us in there poking around?"

"Anything's possible, I suppose. That would be one way of keeping the person fed. He or she could share the meals Bubbles takes out there. It would mean rather slim pickings for two of them, though."

"Not if Mrs. Fath's asleep all the time," Emma insisted. "Even if she's only pretending to sleep, she can't get very hungry. She's not doing anything to work up an appetite. Or maybe the rest of Wont's crowd are in on it, too, and donating food out of their picnic lunches. The men all eat huge breakfasts, so one might think they could each spare a sandwich. Or Lisbet Quainley might be giving up hers, she only eats about enough to sustain a good-sized sparrow."

"A fox sparrow, that would be," said Theonia. "They're the biggest."

"So they are, now that you mention it. And Lisbet Quainley is a foxy doxy if ever I've seen one. If she's a genuine artist, I'm Whistler's mother, though of course she may fancy she is. Apparently she's managed to make Dr. Wont think so."

"That's common enough," said Theonia. "I can understand the self-delusion of some artists; what beats me is how they manage to persuade others to share their fantasies. But then I'm a fusty old traditionalist myself."

"That's because you're a living Titian," said Emma.

"Ah, but you should have seen me when I was a Boucher!"

The two of them were still laughing when they got to the beach. By now the men had managed to cobble together a ramshackle assortment of logs and timbers. If they were lucky it might hold together long enough to maroon Dr. Wont on Shag Rock, Emma thought.

The moment he caught sight of Theonia, Joris Groot dropped the hammer with which he'd begun pounding nails into the logs for no apparent purpose and reached for his sketchpad. Black John Sendick took time enough to finish whatever it was he thought he was accomplishing, then snapped to attention.

Everard Wont had evidently been dictating to Lisbet Quainley. She must be acting as his secretary, Emma decided, along with whatever other services she might be providing. He stopped talking and gave the two Kelling women an oddly furtive look. Miss Quainley stopped scribbling on the pad of yellow paper resting against her sketching block and gave them a look, too.

Miss Quainley's was not the sort of look Emma was accustomed to receive from a reasonably personable woman many years her junior; she naturally assumed it was directed at Theonia. Then again, perhaps it wasn't. Did that skinny snip actually imagine that the widow of Beddoes Kelling might conceivably be interested in attaching to herself a boorish poseur like Everard Wont? It was to laugh, as Emma's long-ago French governess would have been apt to say.

However, Emma had had her laugh for today. She'd have to tell them. They'd know anyway, as soon as the police arrived. Black John gave her the opening.

"Come to see how we're making out, Mrs. Kelling?"

"No," Emma replied. "We've come to give you a report on what's been happening at the house. I'm sure you're anxious to know."

Wont naturally took the remark to himself. "Why should I be? It has nothing to do with me."

"I sincerely hope it has nothing to do with any of us, Dr. Wont. However, it appears we're all going to have to prove that as soon as the police get here."

That started a babble which Emma quickly overrode. "Listen to me, please. Dr. Franklin, who's the medical examiner for this area, has been here and gone back with the body of our mysterious stranger. He expects to have the autopsy report back to us one way or another this evening. We may also have an identification by then. What's more upsetting is that he's examined Sandy. I've told you how Mrs. Brooks and I found her upstairs in the main house, sitting on the floor in a dazed condition. Dr. Franklin's determined that Sandy hadn't accidentally hit her head on a closet door as we'd assumed but had been struck from behind. The blow nearly fractured her skull and did in fact knock her unconscious for some time."

"My gosh!" cried Sendick. "Is she going to be okay?"

"We don't know yet. Sandy's conscious and rational but doesn't remember how she got hurt. As of now, all the doctor can do is keep her in bed and hope for the best."

"Can you beat that?" Joris Groot managed to divert his attention from drawing Theonia's feet. "She has no idea why it happened?"

"No, but the reason is perfectly obvious," Emma replied. "Whoever hit her was trying to rob a small wall safe hidden inside the closet where we found her. It's in the bedroom where Mrs. Brooks was planning to sleep tonight."

"And still am, if you'll let me," Theonia put in. "You might mention, Emma, that the safe has been very carefully examined and found to contain nothing except for a few empty boxes and some diagrams of the septic system. Which can't possibly be pirates' treasure maps in disguise, in case any of you may start wondering," she added with an arch sidelong glance at Dr. Wont.

"I might also mention that I'd already opened the wall safe yesterday evening out of curiosity and found nothing else in it then, either," Emma added. That was true. She hadn't found, she'd put.

"So the poor kid got bopped for nothing." Black John was really taking the news to heart. "Gosh, I don't know. It's one thing to write about some character in a book getting conked on the head but when it happens to a cute kid in a Smurf suit who brings you a hot muffin at breakfast, it's enough to make a guy switch to writing Westerns."

"But then you'd have to brand the poor little dogies, and I'm sure you'd hate that, even on paper," Theonia cooed sympathetically. "One does have to suffer for one's art, Mr. Sendick."

"And a bookmaker should stick to his . . . oh dear, that's not coming out the way I meant it to," said Emma. "I just hope that, regardless of what we feel, we can all prove where we were during the time Sandy was attacked. I'm sure whoever questions us will want to know."

"But it can't have been any of us," cried Black John.

"It has to have been somebody, Mr. Sendick. And there aren't that many people here on Pocapuk."

"But why couldn't that guy who got drowned have had an accomplice hiding under the dock or someplace?"

"Good thinking, John," said Lisbet Quainley. "Would you care to go and look?"

"Well, sure, I guess I could. If Mrs. Kelling really wants me to."

"I want you to do no such thing," Emma protested. "We've had one death and a potentially deadly assault here already; this is no time to go playing hero. I want you all to keep your heads, stay together, and not try anything that might get you or anybody else in trouble. Vincent is going to organize a search. If he wants your help, he'll ask for it and tell you precisely what he wants you to do."

Everard Wont exploded. "Mrs. Kelling, do you seriously believe I came here to be ordered around by your hired help? Since you're so obviously intent on sabotaging my entire project, it looks to me as if I may as well give up in despair right now. If I may be allowed one last request, would you kindly summon a boat by whatever arcane method may be available and get me out of here as soon as possible?"

"I'd be more than happy to oblige you, Dr. Wont," Emma replied in all sincerity, "but I very much doubt whether we could get the ferry here on short notice, and I'm absolutely certain you wouldn't be allowed to leave in any event without official permission. When that will come depends, I suppose, mainly on what the autopsy reveals."

"The autopsy will show that the man drowned. What else could it show?"

"I have no idea. After that brutal attack on Sandy, we can't be sure of anything. Of course we might be able to oblige Dr. Wont by speeding up his departure if one of you would care to confess right now."

She hadn't expected any takers and she didn't get one. Wont's face was bright purple by now, Groot's an absolute blank. Black John appeared more interested than alarmed. Lisbet Quainley began to giggle. "You three look like a bowl of goldfish. Mrs. Kelling, you can't really believe one of us slugged that kid."

"I should certainly prefer not to," Emma told her. "I understand you and Dr. Wont were the last to finish breakfast this morning, Miss Quainley. Could you tell us what you did after you left the dining room?"

"Me? I went back to my cottage and brushed my teeth. Then I came over here with the others and haven't left since. Have I, anybody?"

It had been a mistake for her to start asking questions, Emma realized. Naturally this lot would back each other up. Wont was revving up for another blast, which she didn't want to hear. She glanced at Theonia. Theonia shrugged. Emma back-pedaled.

"What a shame. I suppose I was hoping you might tell me you ran into another mysterious stranger slinking up the stairs as you left the house. But since none of you has anything helpful to offer, I believe I'll go back to my room and lie down for a while. I don't know whether it's from the sun or the suspense, but I seem to be developing a ferocious headache."

NINETEEN

Theonia didn't want Emma to walk back alone. Joris Groot didn't want to lose sight of his model. Black John wanted to find Vincent and volunteer for the search party. Everard Wont wanted to stand there and fulminate, but nobody wanted to listen, not even Lisbet Quainley.

"Oh, shut up, Ev," Emma heard her snarl. "Can't you see what an advantage you've got here? Those dead Spanish sailors have put a curse on the expedition and made it impossible for us to go on. Write your book from that angle. That'll be a damned sight less work than digging around in the mud."

"And anybody dumb enough to read you would swallow one bunch of garbage as well as another," Black John added, mainly for Emma's benefit. She gave him a grateful look and wondered briefly whether he'd care to be adopted.

Her head was really splitting; the men had to help her over the path. Theonia led her upstairs, bathed her face, took off her shoes, and got her tucked up on the chaise. Emma fell asleep almost at once and didn't wake up until Theonia came to ask whether she felt well enough to go down and meet Tweeters Arbuthnot. She took inventory and decided she did.

"My headache's quite gone, thank goodness. Is Mr. Arbuthnot here?"

"Not quite, he's circling for a landing, and do call him Tweeters or you'll scare him to death. See the plane out there?"

"Then you'd better go down. I'll be along as soon as I can pull myself together. Did you find something to wear? Oh, you did. Good."

Theonia had changed into one of Emma's long skirts, deep eggplant color, with a mauve silk blouse. The colors were a bit subdued for Theonia, but perhaps she'd felt some atavistic urge to put on mourning of a sort for her former nephew-in-law. Or stepson, as the case might have been. Emma decided on gray as being equally suitable under the circumstances. She dashed cold water over her face, did a quick makeup, put on her spare wig and pearls, and picked up an amethyst satin stole. She didn't feel chilly as yet, but she might later on. Besides, the rich purple did more for her complexion than the dove gray silk shirt that went with the skirt.

"Vanity of vanities," she murmured, "all is vanity. Silly old woman!" She stuck out her tongue at the mirror, fluffed her wig, swept the flattering strip of shimmery amethyst around her shoulders cowl-wise, with the ends falling behind her back like folded wings, and went to play hostess to Tweeters Arbuthnot.

Starting the cocktails an hour early was no doubt a break in precedent, but Bubbles had risen to the challenge with salmon-roe canapés and a plate of the cheese they'd cut into last night. Joris Groot had evidently taken it for granted he was a member of the party and started the fire. Groot was the only cottager present; Black John must be out volunteering and Wont and Miss Quainley off revising their literary game plan. Radunov was apparently getting on better than he'd expected with Rasputin and Queen Victoria.

Wherever they were, Emma hoped they'd stay there. Tweeters was already in the room; Theonia had offered him a chair. He was settling himself into it, hiking up his pant legs and arranging the tail of his old gray-green corduroy jacket with the same fussy twitchings and flutterings she'd observed on hens going to roost. Emma had the impression that too many people arriving at once might scare him into flight. That would be a shame; she did want to meet this unlikely bird of passage.

Tweeters wanted to meet Emma, too. That was clear from the

way he burst out of the chair like a flushed pheasant, wings outstretched and beak agape. Not to compare him to a bird was impossible. His nose was long and thin and set close to his mouth, which was also long and thin. His chin receded into a longer, thinner neck hitched to a gangling body that spread out at the waist and sloped quickly down to legs as long and spindly as a whooping crane's.

His eyebrows were the birdman's best feature: a luxuriant mix of stiff black and white hairs, jutting boldly out and up over eyes as sharp and beady as a heron's. His forehead sloped all the way to the crown of his head, until it met another great crest of hair thrusting straight back. Definitely a heron, Emma thought; she'd never been this close to one before.

She was going to be given every opportunity to examine this particular specimen as closely as she liked, Tweeters made that evident without delay. Emma hadn't been so expertly backed into a sofa corner since her debutante days. Once he'd got her on the nest, Tweeters folded up those incredible legs and went to roost as close beside her as decorum allowed. With both long, bony-fingered hands resting on his knees, he sat beaming at her through his eyebrows as though he were in fact a heron and she a particularly plump and succulent lady frog.

"Mrs. Kelling, this is indeed a pleasure," he chirped. "I've been longing to meet you ever since Theonia told me about your volunteer work with the Pleasaunce Fire Department. Jumping into nets was quite an enthusiasm of mine at one time. I trained on a trampoline. Do you?"

"Why, no, that never occurred to me," said Emma. "The firemen showed me the rudiments, then I simply began on the first floor and worked up. I'm quite an amateur, really. How did you make out today with the puffins?"

"Ah, my friends the puffins. Fascinating creatures! You know, of course, that they're actually relatives of the great auk? Collateral descendants, I suppose I ought to have said. The Alcidae are a fairly large family, the razor-billed auk being no doubt the closest descendant in the direct line at this time. Then there are murres. You've met the murres?"

Really, Emma thought, this encounter was shaping up just like one of Appie Kelling's family tea parties. She regretted aloud that she had not the pleasure of the murres' acquaintance; nor yet, when pressed further, of the guillemots'. Tweeters seemed particularly distressed that she didn't know the guillemots.

"They nest in rock crannies or burrows in striking contrast to the auks and murres, which don't really nest at all but simply lay their eggs on open cliff ledges facing the sea."

"That would seem a somewhat irresponsible thing to do," Emma replied rather severely. "Don't the eggs keep rolling off?"

Tweeters raised a clawlike finger and waggled it playfully under her nose. "You underestimate the wily alcids. They lay pear-shaped eggs. The advantage of the pear shape, you see, is that when the egg rolls, as indeed it must on occasion, it merely revolves in a circle and winds up pretty much where it had been in the first place. If I had a pear and an apple, I could demonstrate the difference."

"That's quite all right," said Emma. "I can visualize."

"I'm sure you can, you clever lady!" Tweeters nudged himself a trifle closer. "The great auk's calamity was that it couldn't fly. Or wouldn't. It had wing feathers but apparently never got around to developing them properly."

For a moment he seemed quite put out with the great auk but soon recovered his spirits. "All the Alcidae today fly quite capably. In fact, they even fly under water, using their wings to speed them along when they're after a fish, as they so often are."

Tweeters beamed like a proud father relating his toddler's latest escapade. "The puffins are much more domestically minded than the auks and murres. They dig themselves deep burrows and both parents take turns incubating the egg, though I have to admit the female's turn is always much longer than the male's."

"That doesn't surprise me a bit," said Emma.

"However," Tweeters went on in defense of his sex, "the male does a perfectly splendid job as a provider. The chick gets stuffed full as a tick twice every day. Of fish, naturally."

"Naturally," Emma agreed. "How nice for the chick. Does the mother get any, or does she have to catch her own?"

"As a matter of fact, the female puffin takes an equal role in both the fishing and the feeding," Tweeters confessed. He ate some salmon roe in a rather self-conscious manner, then brightened again. "Did you know that puffins' beaks shed their bright colors during the postnuptial molt?"

"That's so apt to be the case once the honeymoon's over, isn't it?" Emma answered with a sad, sweet smile.

"Ah, but puffins are able to brighten up their beaks again as soon as the next mating season rolls around."

Tweeters was well into his double martini now, and his own beak was glowing like a good deed in a naughty world. Emma began to wonder where this conversation might be leading. Tweeters must have decided he was skating too close to the bounds of decorum, though, for he zoomed off on a different tack.

"Puffins don't shuffle along on their tarsi the way other alcids do, you know. They tiptoe around like peg-legged sailors on a toot."

He whirred up from the sofa and began prancing around the hearthrug, imitating the puffin's rolling walk till he'd sent both Emma and Theonia into convulsions. Joris Groot had been making desultory conversation with Theonia as he sketched her in semisilhouette against the firelight. He shrugged, flipped the page, and began caricaturing Tweeters as a puffin with, of course, special attention to the feet. Emma supposed Groot was having a good time in his quiet way, but she did wish he'd take himself elsewhere for a while. She wanted to talk to Tweeters about what she suspected he'd really been doing all day. She did think of asking him to show her the inner workings of the seaplane, but he'd got started on the peculiar nesting habits of Kittlitz's Murrelet and she wasn't sure it would be either polite or prudent to make any such suggestion.

From the Alcidae it was only a short hop to the skuas and jaegers, of which Tweeters had many a scandalous tale to relate. By his account, skuas were perfectly dreadful birds, feeding their young on other birds' nestlings and sometimes even serving up their first-hatched chick to their second. Cousin Mabel would get on well with the skuas, Emma was thinking, when Count Radunov showed up in his navy blue blazer and she realized with a jolt that it was already six o'clock.

Joris Groot folded his drawing pad, put the cap on his black pen and said he guessed he'd better go get washed up for dinner. Tweeters, who'd settled himself back on the sofa next to Emma, got up again and observed with obvious reluctance that he ought to head back home to Boston. Radunov, who'd been eyeing the lack of any noticeable gap between Tweeters and Emma in much the same way as Emma's father would have done fifty years ago, made it perfectly clear without actually saying so that he couldn't agree more.

Even poised for flight, Tweeters was still loath to depart. Theonia took the situation firmly in hand. "I'll walk down to the plane with you, Tweeters. I believe I may have left my gloves on the seat this morning."

"I don't recall your wearing gloves," Tweeters was tactless enough to reply.

"But of course I wasn't wearing my gloves. If I'd had them on, how could I have left them behind?" Theonia pointed out with some acerbity.

Tweeters was gentleman enough to acknowledge the soundness of her reasoning. "Ah, true. Very true. Come along, then, a-hunting we shall go. Emma, would you care to join in pursuit of the wayward gloves?"

At Tweeter's offhand use of the name Emma, Count Radunov nearly lost his aplomb. Emma herself thought it a trifle hard on the count; though Tweeters, as a close friend of the Beacon Hill Kellings, was certainly not committing a breach of etiquette in addressing another Kelling by her first name now that they'd been introduced. At least she could turn down Tweeters's invitation, in fact she'd have been rude to accept.

"I'm sorry," she told her new acquaintance, "but I can't leave my house guests. Perhaps you'll be flying up this way another time?"

"Tomorrow, for instance?"

"Why, yes, I suppose so, if it works into your schedule." She hadn't bargained for quite so enthusiastic a response. "I may be tied up with some domestic problems we're having"—that was putting it mildly enough—"but I'm sure Theonia would enjoy showing you around the island. You may find Pocapuk a disappointment, though. We have no puffins."

"Puffins aren't everything," he told her in a fine burst of renunciation. "There's hang gliding, for instance. You'd be a natural for hang gliding, Emma."

"How kind of you to say so. We must discuss it another time."

"There's also skydiving and hot-air ballooning," Tweeters boomed, as Theonia dragged him practically by brute force out the door.

"Actually, I shouldn't mind a bit discussing hot-air balloons,"

Emma remarked to Radunov once the birdman had finally flown. "I've always had a hankering to go up in one."

Count Radunov was taking a dim view. "Mrs. Kelling, you would not enjoy riding in a hot-air balloon. They offer a particularly depressing combination of total boredom, physical discomfort, frightening bursts of noise and flame, and constant peril of life and limb. Believe me, I know."

"Oh well." Emma was feeling a certain degree of buoyancy, balloon or no balloon. "There's always hang gliding. What can I get you to drink? We seem to be without our usual bartender; I expect Vincent is still searching the island. Did Mr. Sendick catch up with him, do you know?"

Count Radunov did not know. He also didn't know why Vincent should be searching the island, or said he didn't. It occurred to Emma that he hadn't been present on the beach while she was making her report to Wont's crew. She told him now. Radunov was appalled, or said he was.

"And how is the child feeling now?"

"She was doing quite well an hour or so ago when Bubbles brought in the hors d'oeuvres," Emma replied. "Speaking of which, will you have some?"

He glanced at the coffee table and shrugged. Emma saw why.

"Oh dear, Tweeters has finished off most of the cheese and all the caviar. It was only the red kind," she half-apologized. "I'll see what else Bubbles can bring us. Things are really in something of a shambles tonight. Perhaps I ought to—oh, Bernice, there you are. Have you any good news about Sandy?"

"She says she's okay," the girl replied. "She wants to get up and watch 'Dr. Who,' but her father says she can't. And Bubbles says do you need any more ice or anything?"

"Tell him yes and ask if there are any more appetizers. Count Radunov hasn't had any, and the others will be along any minute, I expect. Where's Sandy's father? Is he still outdoors?"

"Nope. I mean no, Mrs. Kelling. He's talking on the phone and he sounds mad as heck. Want me to tell him you want him after he hangs up?"

"Just tell him I'd like to hear whatever news he has, but that if he has more important matters on hand we can manage the drinks and dinner without him. Can you remember all that?"

"I guess so. And more ice, right?"

Bernice took the ravaged serving plates from the coffee table and ran off. She was still wearing her green Smurf shirt and probably wouldn't have time to change. What difference did it make? Between doing two girls' work and playing nurse to Sandy, the poor child had been run ragged all day; one couldn't expect miracles. Emma took the drink Radunov had refreshed for her and went back to her nest on the sofa. Radunov cast a quizzical look at the empty space beside her. She smiled up at him.

"Put on another log, will you, then come and sit here where you can enjoy the fire. I suppose you're wondering why we've been lying about the telephone?"

"Not lying, surely? *Equivocating* would be a kinder word." He placed the log in exactly the right spot, then took advantage of Emma's invitation. "As to why, might it perhaps have been in the interest of preventing the guests from running up outrageous long-distance telephone bills?"

"How perspicacious of you. Vincent says there's been trouble in the past about excessive phone bills, and this is his way of making sure it doesn't happen again. I think we may as well stick with our equivocation for as long as we can manage, if you'll be kind enough to overlook Bernice's little slip of the tongue."

"I am capable of developing instant deafness in whichever ear better suits your convenience. So Groot is changing his shirt, Sendick is combing the wilderness, and Mrs. Brooks is saying good-bye to the whooping crane."

Emma couldn't help laughing. "I'd have said the great blue heron."

"Heron by all means, if you prefer. Ornithology is one field in which I claim no expertise. Then that leaves only our doughty man of letters and his—how would you describe Miss Quainley? She's a bit on the thin side to be a lovebird."

"Shame on you!" Emma tried not to smile, but the effort was too great. "I have no idea what to call Miss Quainley. Secretary bird, perhaps. She was functioning as Dr. Wont's amanuensis this afternoon; or appeared to be. I believe they've decided to call off the treasure hunt and base their story on how the expedition was hoodooed by the ghosts of the Spanish sailors, by the way. Dr.

Wont's clamoring to leave the island. I told him I didn't think the police would let him go, but perhaps he and Miss Quainley have decided to paddle ashore on that so-called raft Mr. Groot and Mr. Sendick have been working on. I can't think why else they're not here."

TWENTY

Did you get Tweeters off all right?"

That was an inane question, but Emma could hardly come straight out and ask Theonia whether she'd handed over the orange juice and the films from the Dick Tracy camera.

Theonia gave her a smile and a nod. "Oh yes, Tweeters is well taken care of. Didn't you hear him buzzing the house as he took off? He wanted to fly low enough to waggle his wings bye-bye, but I managed to persuade him you wouldn't be looking out the window. He'll be back tomorrow, I shouldn't wonder. You know how ornithologists are; once they find an intriguing new species, they can't wait to study it from every angle. Brooks is the same way about the pied grebes."

"Have you thought of suing them for alienation of affections? And can we get you a fresh drink?"

"Perhaps just a spot of sherry."

"Dry or sweet?" asked Count Radunov, somewhat reluctantly getting up off the sofa.

"Dry, by all means. I'm quite—" Theonia stopped. Vincent was standing in the doorway looking like the wrath of God.

"What is it, Vincent?" Emma asked him, struggling to keep her voice low and controlled.

"Murder!" he blurted. "The bugger was hit from behind, just like my Sandy, an' either shoved off the cliff or thrown off by the scruff o' the neck an' the seat o' the pants, they can't tell which. There's some funny rips in 'is clothes. He was unconscious when he hit an' smothered from landin' on 'is face in the mud. Tide must o' been out, which puts it somewheres before three o'clock this mornin'. Maybe a little later but not much. God A'mighty! Of all things to happen here."

"You've made sure there're no strangers around, haven't you?"

"Hell, yes. We've looked under every rock on Pocapuk. No sign o' nobody nor nothin' nowheres. I don't know what to do."

"Have you been in touch with the county sheriff's office?"

"Franklin has. They'll be here when they git here's the best he could tell me. They got some goddamn high mucky-muck from the gov'ment in the county an' another riot goin' full-blast at the toothpick factory. Too much happenin' an' not enough men to handle it, as usual. Everybody's crazy these days."

"Vincent," said Emma, "sit down before you fall down. Count Radunov, pour him some brandy."

"He'd prefer scotch, I believe," said Theonia. "Here, I'll do it. Try this, Vincent."

He took the glass and returned her a wry smile. "What are you, another one o' them mind readers?"

"Certainly. One thing that's worrying you now is whether to report to Mrs. Sabine tonight or wait till you have a solution to offer her. I'd say wait. This isn't going to take much longer. Another day, perhaps. Go ahead, drink it."

Vincent swallowed a big gulp of the whiskey she'd poured. "Brr! That ought to straighten me out. What makes you so sure?"

"Trust me, Vincent. Mrs. Kelling can tell you I'm seldom wrong. Here, have some of this cheese. I'll bet you haven't bothered to eat all day."

"What was I s'posed to do? Sit stuffin' my face while one o' my kids was riskin' his neck draggin' a corpse out o' the water an' another one damn near a corpse herself? If I ever get my hands on the bugger that—" He drained off the whiskey and hurled the empty glass straight at the back of the fireplace. It crashed in splinters behind the logs. Vincent stared into the flames, appalled by what he'd done.

"My God," he half-whispered. "Them tumblers was thirty years old an' this is the first one that ever got broke. I dunno what's got into me."

"You were having a perfectly normal reaction to the stress you've been under," Emma told him, "and that glassware was never anything special in the first place. Don't give it another thought, Vincent. What did your brother have to say about Sandy's condition? Bernice told us she's champing at the bit to get out of bed and watch television."

"Ayuh, but she ain't goin' to, not tonight. Franklin said to give 'er a decent supper. If she keeps it down, he thinks likely she'll be all right. Franklin says it must o' been that glue she gaums up 'er hair with that saved 'er from worse than what she got. An' here I been yellin' at 'er to quit usin' the stuff."

Vincent grabbed hold of the chair arms and yanked himself to his feet. "I better go see what's happenin' out back."

"Poor man," Theonia remarked when he was safely out of the room, "what a hideous spot for him to be in. Well, Emma, what do you suppose has happened to the rest of your house party?"

"Count Radunov and I were just wondering that ourselves. Maybe they're all packing to go home."

Emma found the notion rather comforting, but she might have known it wasn't happening. She was just getting nicely settled to finish her sherry in peace and quiet when Black John Sendick bounced in, full of beans and covered with scratches from blackberry vines. He looked reasonably trim in a buttoned-up blue denim jacket, but Emma suspected a dirty sweatshirt underneath.

"Have you seen Dr. Wont and Miss Quainley?" she asked him.

"No, but I've heard them." He grinned. "They're probably on their way."

Emma suppressed a sigh. "And Mr. Groot should be back any minute. He went to change a while ago."

She thought Black John looked a trifle surprised at that, but he didn't say anything. He mixed himself a rum and Coca-Cola—shades of Emma's youth—and settled as close as he could get to the appetizers. The young novelist was an enthusiastic trencherman at all times, but a day of raft building and searching the blackberry jungles appeared to have given him the appetite of an anaconda. He was worse than Tweeters, Emma thought; she hoped she wouldn't have to send back for a third round of cheese and crackers before Bubbles announced dinner. She glanced at her watch. Twelve minutes to go. It seemed a long time.

Two and a half minutes later, Miss Quainley and Dr. Wont blew in. Emma didn't need a seeress to tell her the two had been having a royal set-to. Ignoring his companion's sulky glowers, Wont marched straight to the bar and poured himself a tumblerful of gin. He plunked in one ice cube, waved the vermouth bottle over the glass in a token gesture, and went to sit beside Theonia, who immediately got up and went to fix a drink for Miss Quainley. The younger woman looked as if she could use one and didn't hesitate to say why.

"I've just had the most ghastly experience! I stopped in to see if Alding was awake and somebody hit me on the head."

"She's having pipe dreams," snorted Wont. "She bumped into the wall."

"I am not! I was nowhere near the wall and I've got a lump the size of an egg. Feel it, Mrs. Kelling."

Emma didn't particularly want to, but she thought she'd better. Lisbet Quainley had pulled her long hair through some sort of gold-colored metal spool affair that perched on the crown of her head, creating a horsetail effect that went a bit too well with her long, thin face. Emma couldn't feel any great swelling as she explored the skull with the tips of her fingers, but she did get a trace of blood on one fingertip. She parted the hair where it felt damp and uncovered a small cut on the scalp.

"It looks to me as if the blow may have fallen on that metal affair you're wearing on your head and driven the edge into your scalp. The cut's nothing to worry about, but you might as well come upstairs and let me dab some antiseptic on it."

"Please don't bother, Mrs. Kelling," the younger woman demurred. "I don't want to make a fuss."

"Huh! Considering the fuss you've already made, I consider that statement wholly untenable," Wont snarled over his gin.

"I hope you know when you're being ignored, Ev."

Emma wasn't about to let the pair of them get away with any childish wrangling in her presence. "And where were you while Miss Quainley was being assaulted, Dr. Wont?" she asked him.

"I was still in my cottage. Miss Quainley had gone on ahead, having expressed the intention of checking, as she put it, on Mrs. Fath. I'd told her I'd catch up with her, which I subsequently did, only to find her on the path in a state of semihysteria."

"You didn't look around for any sign of the person who hit her?"

"I was then and still am disinclined to believe anybody hit her."

Wont finished his gin and went back for more. Emma could have kicked him.

"We'd better go upstairs," she said. Lisbet Quainley noticed the set of her jaw and went.

Like a perfect hostess, Adelaide Sabine had caused a few standard first-aid supplies to be left in the guest bathroom's medicine chest. Emma recalled seeing hydrogen peroxide, Merthiolate, and sterile gauze pads. "Come this way," she told her reluctant patient, and opened the door to her bedroom.

As she did so, she heard a loud thud from outside and felt a strong draft of cold air. Where was it coming from? She distinctly remembered closing her windows before she'd left her room. The sea breeze had become too brisk for comfort. Now the window at the far end of the room, the one Emma herself had never yet opened, was pushed up as far as it could go. She ran over to it, noticed the screen had also been raised, and poked out her head.

The sun porch roof was directly below, a fact Emma hadn't quite realized until this minute. The drop wouldn't have been much for an able-bodied person. From the roof to the ground would have been nothing at all; the wrought-iron trellis could have served as a ladder. She hoped that beautiful clematis wasn't ruined, as if something so inconsequential could matter at a time like this.

"What's wrong?" Lisbet Quainley was fussing again. "My God, not another!"

"I'm afraid so."

Emma started opening drawers. They weren't badly messed up, but they'd definitely been searched. She went back and locked the window, for whatever good that might do, then took her patient by the arm, led her into the bathroom, and sat her on the stool.

"Take that thing out of your hair, I need to get at the cut."

"But aren't you going to see if the burglar took anything?"

"There was nothing to take. I'm wearing my pearls and my wallet's in my skirt pocket. Hold still, can't you? This is messier than I'd realized. Cuts on the scalp always bleed a lot." She swabbed out the cut with peroxide while Miss Quainley squirmed. "There you are, it's only a flesh wound. Keep pressing this pad over the cut till the bleeding stops. Let's go, I need to find Vincent right away."

"What do you bet you'd already have found him if we'd got here a second or two sooner?"

"Miss Quainley! Surely you don't believe Vincent's the one who did this?"

"Why not? Do you know where he was?"

"He'd been in the drawing room with us until just a few minutes ago."

"A few minutes is all it would take," Lisbet Quainley argued. "That's how professional burglars work, get in and out as fast as they can."

"If Vincent had wanted to break into my room," Emma insisted, "he'd have had every opportunity earlier in the day."

"Would he really?"

Not while he was caring for his injured daughter. Not while he was helping his brothers cope with Jimmy Sorpende's lifeless body. Not while he was leading his little band of searchers through the blackberry vines. This would have been as good a time as any, Emma supposed, when he knew she and Theonia were occupied with their guests. And where had Vincent been when Lisbet Quainley was being hit over the head in Alding Fath's cottage? It wasn't impossible that he could have gone straight there after he'd shown that startling outburst of anger and frustration, then rushed back here and gone up the back stairs to the bedroom. Emma assumed there must be a back service stairway, although she hadn't used it or even gone looking for it. The Sabines had been of the old school. They might have been the world's most considerate employers in other respects, but they'd never have permitted their servants to use the front stairs. And the cottages weren't far from the house. How could they be, on an island as small as Pocapuk?

She led Miss Quainley back down to the drawing room, left her dabbing at her skull with the gauze pad, and walked quickly out to the kitchen. Bernice was in the dining room as she passed through, setting the table backward. She said, "Knives on the right, please, forks on the left," and kept going. Neil was at the kitchen table eating chowder. Bubbles was dishing up more chowder into a majolica tureen shaped like a fish. Another house gift, Emma surmised automatically. Nobody else was in sight.

"Where's your father?"

"In with Sandy." Neil put down his spoon and stared up at her. "What's the matter, Mrs. Kelling?"

"Someone was searching my room just now. When he heard me coming, he jumped out the window and escaped over the porch roof."

"Wow!" Neil hopped up and ran into the ell. "Dad! Hey, Dad! Mrs. Kelling got burgled."

Emma heard a chair crashing over and Vincent saying something extremely profane. He'd be along in a second. She said to Bubbles, "Where's Ted?"

The cook kept on bailing chowder. She said again, "Where's Ted?"

By now, Vincent was there to hear. "What happened to you, Mrs. Kelling? What do you want Ted for?"

"I want to know where he's been for the past fifteen minutes. Miss Quainley came in a few minutes ago with a cut on her scalp that she claims she got when she stopped in to see Mrs. Fath and was hit from behind, like Sandy. I took her upstairs to fix her up. When I opened my bedroom door, I heard a loud thump. The window over the porch roof was wide open and the screen was up, so I assumed what I heard was somebody jumping out. My bureau drawers had been searched. I expect we'll find signs on the trellis that somebody used it for a ladder. The intruder might conceivably have been you, but I prefer not to think so. It probably wasn't Neil because when I got to the kitchen he'd been eating chowder and his bowl was almost empty. So that leaves Ted. Where is he?"

"Jesus H. Christ, how the hell do I know? I can't be babysittin'—" Vincent caught himself. "I'm sorry, Mrs. Kelling. Ted was s'posed to finish cleanin' off the tools we was usin' this morning, then come in an' have his supper. I'll go see if he's still in the pony shed."

Which wouldn't prove a thing. Of course Ted would have run back to the pony shed and pretended he'd been there all the time. How could Vincent prove he hadn't? How could she, for that matter? Nevertheless, she told the caretaker, "Find him, then, and hang on to him. As soon as we finish dinner, I want to talk with that young man. And furthermore, Vincent, I don't think Mrs. Fath should be left in that cottage alone any longer. You'd better bring her up to the house right away. Neil can help you put her on the electric cart, can't he? She's not a big woman. There's an extra bed in Mrs. Sabine's room; we can put her there."

"Where Sandy got hit on the head?" Vincent snorted. "We'll put 'er in Ted's room. He can bunk in with Bubbles or sleep on that cot in the storeroom. I don't care which."

As Vincent went out, Emma turned to Bubbles with a half-smile of apology. "I'm sorry to have barged in while you were doing your last-minute touches, but I'm sure you understand why I had to."

"Yeth, Mithith Kelling. Vinthent came thtraight out here after he talked to you. He got two bowlth of chowder and took them into Thandy'th room tho they could eat together. Vinthent'th a good man. You can quit worrying about him."

"Thank you, Bubbles. Believe me, I don't want to. Then you might as well get on with serving dinner. I'll tell the others to come to the table, shall I?"

"Pleathe."

Tonight's meal would be a dismal farce, but what else could she do? Emma straightened her back and walked into the drawing room. Joris Groot was there; he must have just come in. Most uncharacteristically, he was holding the floor, talking loud and fast in that incongruously high voice.

"Damnest thing that's ever happened to me. Just stopped in to see if Alding wanted anything and when I went to leave, the door was locked. From the outside! I didn't know what the hell to do. Alding was asleep; I didn't want to go banging and yelling and waking her up. I thought at first the door was just stuck, so I put my shoulder to it and gave it a kick, but nothing doing. So finally I opened a window and lowered myself down by the hands, which is how I got so dirty. Sorry, Mrs. Kelling, but I knew I was running late because I'd got to fiddling around with my sketch, so I didn't want to go back and change a second time. Anyway, I went back up on the porch and would you believe, the key was in the lock."

"It hadn't been there when you went in?" Radunov asked him.

"No, the door was already ajar; I just walked in. If one of you clowns was trying to be funny—"

"There's nothing funny about it," Lisbet Quainley told him

sharply. She took the gauze pad away from her head and held it out so Groot could see the blood. "This happened to me in Alding's cottage about fifteen minutes ago. Whoever hit me must still have been there when I ran out."

"Where, for instance?" Everard Wont still wasn't buying.

"How do I know? I didn't hang around long enough to search the place. In the bathroom, I suppose, or behind that curtain where Alding hangs her clothes."

"So when I came in, the guy slipped out behind me and locked the door after him in case I might try to follow," said Groot. "That makes sense."

"To you, perhaps." The gin wasn't sweetening Wont's mood any.

Why couldn't whoever it was have slugged the one who most needed hitting? Emma gritted her teeth and said, "I'm told dinner is ready to be served. Will you all please come to the table?"

TWENTY-ONE

"You can't imagine what a relief it is to talk to somebody who hasn't been hit over the head today!"

Emma was on the telephone in the pantry, Theonia in the drawing room using the one that came out of the Chinese box. The two Mrs. Kellings had been catching Sarah and Max up on the events of the day. Considering the sort of day they'd had, that had taken a fair amount of time. Now they were ready to let the Bittersohns get in a word or two.

"Have you got back the report on the orange juice?" Theonia was asking Max.

"Yes. It's laced with what the chemist refers to as a tranquilizing agent. He's going to see if he can pin down which one, but I don't suppose that matters much. The point is that there's just enough of the drug to keep a person who's already been given a dose buzzing along nicely. How did you happen to hit on the orange juice?"

"Through your friend, Count Radunov. I thought it was awfully philanthropic of a man like him to be running a servant's errand. I could see why the others keep popping in on Mrs. Fath; she's one of their group and it's natural for them to be concerned about her. From what he told Emma, though, Radunov was a stranger to them all. So when he came tripping along full of sweetness and light on his errand of mercy, I wondered. When we got to the cottage and found the place practically awash in orange juice already, I wondered a little more."

"Theonia and I were going to take the juice ourselves, but Bubbles the cook practically threw a fit when I went to get it," Emma added. "Did I mention last night that he's a trained nurse? I have a hunch Bubbles suspects somebody's been tampering with Mrs. Fath's food; I can't think why else he's being so ferociously protective of her."

"Could it be that he's keeping her tranquilized himself so that he'll have a patient to take care of?" Sarah suggested. "Didn't you tell us last night, Emma, that Bubbles comes to Pocapuk because he has depressions?"

"What Bubbles said was that he gets depressed working at the hospice because all his patients are terminal cases," Emma corrected. "That doesn't mean he goes nutty, just that he has a compassionate nature. I hope. Anyway, I'm not about to challenge Bubbles on the subject because he cooks like a dream. Unless—good heavens, you don't think he's all of a sudden one day going to sling a handful of arsenic into the lobster bisque and wipe out the lot of us?"

"Aunt Emma, of course I don't. It's just that Bubbles is the most obvious person to be doctoring Mrs. Fath's food because he's the one who's so insistent on not letting anyone else handle it. And of course being both a cook and a nurse, he'd know exactly what to do. If he's keeping her tranquilized, he may be doing it in a spirit of benevolence. Perhaps he thinks she's on the verge of a breakdown and needs a good long rest. Or else he's fallen in love with her at first sight and wants to nurse her back to health so that she'll be overwhelmed with gratitude and consent to become Mrs. Bubbles."

"Makes sense to me," said Max. "I'm planning to overwhelm my own nurse with gratitude if they ever let me out of this damned cast long enough to get at her. So Radunov's on to something, is he?"

"Either on to something or up to something," said Emma. "He told me he writes on all sorts of different subjects; maybe he's doing a little private research on tranquilizers. But why pick on Mrs. Fath? If he wanted to anesthetize somebody, why couldn't he have done us all a favor and chosen Everard Wont?"

"Cheer up, Emma. You may not have Dr. Wont around much longer," Theonia reminded her.

"Oh yes, Max, that's another thing. As soon as I told Wont and his crew that people were getting bludgeoned left and right and everybody was under suspicion, he threw one of his temperaments and demanded to be taken off the island at once. Naturally I told him he couldn't, which in fact was the simple truth, since we don't have a boat available."

"Not to worry," said Theonia. "Tweeters will be delighted to fly us out at the drop of a handkerchief if things get too sticky. Would you believe, Sarah, that Emma's actually succeeded in taking Tweeters's mind off the puffins?"

"Certainly I believe it," Sarah replied. "Man cannot live by puffins alone. But you haven't asked about the necklace. Tell them, Max."

"Gladly. You made quite a haul there, Emma. What you fished out of your Gladstone bag was once the property of the Duchess of Cantilever, stolen from her by a young footman with whom her relationship was somewhat equivocal and sold by the ex-footman to a rich New Yorker who presented it to one of the Floradora Girls who in turn married the by then widowed Duke of Cantilever, thus bringing the necklace back into the family amid much rejoicing. In the fullness of time, the duke passed away and the duchess came back to New York, where she eventually sold the necklace back to the son of the rich New Yorker who'd given it to her in the first place."

"That was the one who bought it from the footman?" Emma did like to keep her facts straight.

"The ex-footman," Max corrected. "He'd been fired as soon as his perfidy was revealed. He never got caught, however. Instead, he changed his name, assumed U.S. citizenship, and eventually became a prominent member of the Harding administration. He got rich on the Teapot Dome scandal, bought back the necklace from the formerly rich New Yorker after the crash in 1929—that was the son of the original rich New Yorker, as you may recall, Emma—and gave it to a certain member of the Ziegfeld Follies, who should probably remain nameless since she later married a nephew of the late Duke of Cantilever and became a pillar of international society. Her granddaughter's now engaged to a member of the present administration who happens also to be a scion of that same prominent New York family who went broke in the crash of 1929 but have since managed to recoup their fortunes."

"Such as how?" asked Theonia.

"In a number of ingenious ways," Max replied, "with a little help from their friends. The dowager Follies lady was actually attending a formal reception for the happy couple last week here in Boston when she was robbed of the necklace and considerably damaged in the process. The Cantilevers and the prominent New York family, all of whom naturally feel they have certain vested interests in the necklace, are each offering rewards for its recovery. Summing it up, Emma, you stand to make something in the vicinity of fifty thousand dollars after taxes on the deal. And Radunov's going to be spitting tacks when he learns what he passed up by acting like a little gentleman."

"Ladderman Bechley's widow, on the other hand, will be quite delighted," said Emma. "Naturally I shall turn the money over to the Firemen's Relief Fund. If it hadn't been for our both being at the benefit, I shouldn't have talked to Adelaide Sabine and wound up here on Pocapuk. At least that'll be some good coming out of this ghastly experience."

"There is one catch," Max was constrained to point out. "You don't get the money until you've also provided evidence leading to the arrest and conviction of the person who stole the necklace and damaged Lady Cantilever."

"But that was most likely Jimmy Sorpende," Theonia protested. "They can't convict him if he's dead. Won't it still count if we can prove Jimmy was the guilty party?"

"I expect so, if you can also come up with the evidence against whomever he was working with."

"Surely we can manage that, though I'm not sure Ted Sharpless is going to be much help. Emma had another go at him tonight after dinner on the strength of our finding out that Jimmy was definitely assaulted before being thrown off the cliff into the mudflats. He didn't budge an inch from his original story. He may have to, of course, once the police start working on him. I hope to goodness they get here soon. But what about my films? Has Tweeters developed them yet?"

Sarah replied. "Yes, he's just brought them up to us from

Brooks's darkroom. You've done an excellent job, Theonia. I'm spreading out the prints so Max can see. Do you know any of the people so far, darling?"

"Radunov, of course," said Max. "He never changes."

"What about Count Radunov, Max?" Emma hoped she didn't sound too personally perturbed. "He's being awfully gallant; one would prefer to know one's not being fawned over by a murderer."

To her relief, Max chuckled. "I don't know, Emma, but I'd say the chances of Radunov's having chucked Jimmy Sorpende off the cliff are fairly remote. Radunov's pretty versatile, but he's never uncouth."

"That's not precisely the answer I'd have preferred, Max, but I suppose it will have to do. Getting back to the photographs, do you recognize anybody else?"

"I recognize Wont."

While Max was still in the hospital, Jeremy Kelling had gone over to entertain him by reading some of the more outrageous lies from Wont's book for which Jem had been personally responsible. The photograph of the author on the back flap had been far more flattering than the one among Theonia's collection, but the sneer was there in both.

After having received the necklace from Tweeters, Max had got Sarah to invite Jem over for a drink, not that Jem wouldn't have come anyway. When questioned as to his impression of Everard Wont as a possible co-conspirator, Jem Kelling had given it as his considered opinion that Wont had neither the brains nor the guts to swipe a lollipop from a sleeping infant.

He had added that Wont was far too busy tripping over his own ego to engage in any activity that needed to be done without public fanfare. In the unlikely event that Wont ever did pull off a successful jewel theft, he'd queer his own pitch by writing a book about it and trying to take the price of the getaway car off his income tax as a business expense.

Wont might, of course, be planning to do just that, one never knew. Thinking of the treasure hunt so conveniently disrupted by hostile pirate ghosts, Emma had to agree that one certainly didn't.

Sarah was the only one who had something new to contribute, and it wasn't much. She recognized Lisbet Quainley, though not by name.

"She was working in one of the Newbury Street art galleries a while back. I can't recall which, but I could take the photo with me and ask around. What do you think, Theonia?"

"It wouldn't do any harm, if you can spare the time. You might try to find out whether Miss Quainley is in fact an artist of any recognizable degree or whether she's enrolled somewhere as an art student, though she strikes me as being a bit old for that. Thirty to thirty-five is my guess. I suppose being so thin might make her look older," Theonia added a bit smugly.

Sarah was mildly amused. "I'll let you know what I find out. While we're at it, what about that other one, the illustrator? Groot, I think you said his name was, Emma. Is he the rather attractive young fellow in the sweatshirt?"

"No, Groot's the fortyish one with the big feet who looks as if he'd been assembled by a committee. Joris is his first name. He told me he's primarily a specialist in drawing children's shoes. Is that possible?"

Sarah had done some illustrating herself. "Oh yes," she replied, "that's entirely possible. Lots of commercial artists specialize in one type of work, particularly where there's a lot of call for it. The shoe industry used to be really big in Boston; I don't know what sort of shape it's in now. Have you any idea whom Groot's been working for?"

"As a matter of fact, yes. He told me he'd just finished doing a whole catalog of children's shoes. Itsy-Bitsy Footsy-Wootsies, he called them. I gather he wasn't trying to be funny, so I assume it must be a brand name. These things do happen. I don't know whether it's a Boston company or not."

"I'll give the Kirstein Library a ring in the morning, they'll be able to tell us. Anyone else you want checked out? What about Sendick? Have you any specifics on him?"

"Just that his grandfather used to read the Black John stories in the *Globe,* and his mother's maiden name was Black. Mr. Sendick talks freely enough, but now that I think of it, he doesn't actually say much. Not about his background, anyway."

"Does he come from around here?"

"I assume he must. He wears a sweatshirt with a picture of Tycho Brahe on it."

"Maybe Sendick's a dropout from MIT," said Max.

"But then he'd be writing science fiction instead of thrillers," Sarah argued. "See if you can pin him down a little, Emma."

"I'll try, dear, though I'm afraid I'm no great shakes as a detective. I did think of one thing I wish you'd do, though. Could you phone Marcia Pence and find out very discreetly whether Adelaide brought a personal maid with her last year? If so, who was she? I meant to ask Vincent but somehow I didn't like to."

"Certainly I will, but why discreetly?"

"Because the Pences, and more importantly Adelaide, still don't know there's anything going on out here. Vincent and I thought it best not to tell them until the situation's been taken care of. Adelaide's so very tottery, poor darling, that Marcia and Peter are already under a dreadful strain. I don't want to give them additional grief until I have to. It's not as though they were in a position to do anything."

Max made some kind of noise; Emma couldn't tell what it was supposed to mean. Just that his cast was bothering him, perhaps. She offered sympathetic murmurs. He replied nobly that the cast wasn't so bad as being dragged to death by maddened wildebeests.

"I'm glad you can look on the bright side, my dear," said Emma. "I suppose I ought to go now, before somebody decides to come for a drink of water or whatever."

"You're out in that pantry all by yourself?"

"Yes, of course I am. This is the only way we could each get to a phone."

"Then be damned careful when you leave. You too, Theonia. This head bopping could turn into an epidemic."

"Don't worry, Max. I haven't turned on the light; they won't be able to find me. Good night, then. Call tomorrow if you find anything."

"It's been tomorrow for quite some time now," Sarah pointed out. "We'll send our pet carrier pigeon, with a note tied to his leg. Tweeters is right here, itching to be let out of the coop."

"I wish you hadn't said 'itching,'" Max fretted. "If they can put a man on the moon, why can't they invent a body cast you can scratch through?"

They ran up another minute or so on Adelaide Sabine's phone bill wishing each other fond farewells, then, somewhat reluctantly, Emma hung up. She closed the pantry door behind her, switched on her flashlight just long enough to orient herself, and started to feel her way out of the kitchen. She'd known this was a big room, but why did it feel so much bigger in the dark? Emma managed to steer herself past the table and the big iron stove without tripping over a chair or a log of wood. She'd got as far as the huge black-japanned flour bin when she stumbled and lost her slipper. That was when she got hit on the head.

TWENTY-TWO

This has gone quite far enough!"

The voice was that of a woman who had chaired a great many meetings. Emma thought it sounded familiar; she realized after a while that the voice was her own. Lights were blazing in her face, Bubbles was waving the ammonia bottle under her nose. Theonia was doing something with a bag of ice cubes. Putting them on her forehead, Emma decided; she was having some trouble sorting things out. So was Theonia, apparently, since it was the back of Emma's head that had sustained the blow.

She was quite clear on that point now. The blow had not been a hard one, more what might be called a disconcerting blow. The real damage had been done by banging her face on the edge of the metal flour bin as she fell. There was a dent in her forehead; she could feel it when she ran her fingers up under the icebag. It hurt, but there didn't seem to be any blood. Contusions but no lacerations. What sort of contusions? A black eye would be most inappropriate for a woman of her years and position. Emma said so. Theonia patted her cheek.

"Just lie still for a moment, my dear. You've had a nasty knock. What happened, do you remember?"

"Certainly I remember. My slipper came off. When I bent over to pick it up, somebody hit me on the head."

"No, dear. You lost your balance and struck your forehead on the flour bin."

"That was afterward."

"You know best, my dear."

Theonia was humoring her. Emma was not about to be humored. She pushed away the ammonia bottle and the ice cubes. She sat up and put a hand to the back of her head. There was one spot that made her wince as she touched it. It was swollen; not hugely swollen like the bump from that blow that missed fracturing Sandy's skull, not gorily swollen like the injury Lisbet Quainley sustained, but definitely swollen.

"Then where," she demanded angrily, "did I get this?"

First Theonia, then Bubbles obliged by feeling her lump. It was not, they agreed, much of a lump. Nothing to worry about, Bubbles reassured her.

Emma did not want reassurances. What she wanted, she realized with some astonishment, was revenge. How ignoble of her! She took hold of the edge of the flour bin to help herself up, but Bubbles put some kind of nursely grip on her arm and drew her effortlessly to her feet without jolting her sore head.

"Now, Mithith Kelling, I'm going to help you upthtairth and give you a thedative. Mithith Brookth, you'd better thleep in the thame room with her tonight. We don't want any more inthidentth, do we?"

"We certainly don't," Theonia agreed. "I shouldn't dream of leaving Mrs. Kelling by herself. Do you feel up to climbing the stairs, Emma, or shall we camp out in the living room?"

"I feel perfectly capable of climbing the stairs," Emma replied with such dignity as she could muster under the circumstances, "and I don't need a thedative."

Oh dear, that hadn't come out quite the way she'd intended. She hoped Bubbles would assume she must have bitten her tongue when she fell. "I'll just take a couple of aspirin," she amplified, being extra careful of her sibilants. "You see, I'm quite steady on my feet. Thank you, Bubbles. Now do get back to bed yourself. Unless you think we should all be out chasing after whoever keeps sneaking up behind people and bashing their heads."

"I think that would be an incredibly stupid thing to do," said Theonia, "and I'm sure Bubbles agrees. Ready, Emma? Perhaps I'd better take your arm."

Emma thought she should explain to the cook what the pro-tem mistress of the house had been doing in the kitchen, then she thought she shouldn't. That was surely not the way things had always been done. Emma started to give Bubbles a gracious nod but thought better of it. Her head was in no shape for nodding. She took the arm Theonia offered and walked slowly and carefully through the house and up the stairs.

She ought to have roused Vincent, she supposed, and made him count noses in the ell. She ought to have sent him or somebody out to make sure none of the cottagers had been attacked. She'd been on the point at dinnertime of suggesting they all double up for safety, but how could she know who was safe with whom? Anyway, the men should be capable of taking care of themselves. Only the women were getting picked on so far, unless one counted the late Jimmy Sorpende. Alding Fath was here in the ell, where Bubbles could look in on her. Lisbet Quainley had already received her blow. Anyway, she had Everard Wont to take care of her. Though it was more likely Miss Quainley was taking care of him, Emma thought cynically.

"Which room do you want to sleep in?" Theonia asked her. "Mine has two beds."

"But only one of them's made up," Emma objected. "Let's use mine. I'll take the chaise, it's quite comfortable and my head may not hurt so much if I don't lie flat. Besides, my room's one of the few places where nobody's been slugged yet."

"I don't know whether that's a plus or a minus, but it shall be as you say, my dear. Just let me pick up my toothbrush and my Queen Bee Replenishing Cream. After tonight I'm going to need all the help I can get. Oh, Emma!"

The room, which had been freshly turned out for Theonia before Sandy was struck down, had now been thoroughly and recklessly searched. Bedclothes were dragged to the floor, mattresses hanging half off their springs. Dresser drawers had been pulled out and dumped wherever they'd happened to hit. Even that moth-eaten old bathrobe of the late Mr. Sabine's had been ripped out of the closet and thrown down in a heap, together with Theonia's traveling dress and sailor hat.

Emma could not recall ever having been more furious in her whole life. She slammed the door of the ravaged bedroom, wheeled around so fast that her blue bathrobe flew out like a chorus girl's skirt, and marched down the stairs.

Theonia hurried after her. "Emma, where are you going?"

"To do what I should have done as soon as this nonsense started. It's quite clear we're dealing with a criminal who's utterly ruthless, damnably persistent, totally lacking in either manners or imagination, and disgustingly inefficient. I can think of no more dangerous combination of traits. Theonia, this is no time to pussyfoot!"

"Then do turn on some lights so we shan't break our necks. You can be as intrepid as you like, Emma, but I'd feel much braver if I didn't keep tripping over the hem of your bathrobe."

Theonia thought she knew what Emma was aiming for, and she was right. She simply hadn't realized how much noise that big ship's bell by the kitchen door could make when rung with might and main by a thoroughly irate former garden-club president.

The bell even roused Alding Fath. Within a minute and a half, Emma had the entire population of Pocapuk Island gathered around the door: some inside, some out, all of them in states of undress ranging from prudish to downright indecorous, all of them demanding to know with ejaculations mostly profane what was going on.

A woman who'd been able to give the keynote speech without benefit of microphone at the open-air benefit of the Pleasaunce Firemen's Relief Fund had no trouble whatever making herself heard above a dozen overexcited islanders. "During the past half hour," Emma informed them, "I have been struck on the head and Mrs. Brooks's bedroom has been recklessly ransacked. This is the fourth time in twenty-four hours that one of us here on Pocapuk has been subjected to violent assault and the third time a room has been searched. The first assault led to the death of the victim; the second time, a skull fracture was only averted by a lucky circumstance. Next time, if there were to be a next time, one of you could wind up dead."

This started a babble that Emma promptly quelled. "This is why I've got you out of bed. The island has been thoroughly searched;

there's no mysterious stranger lurking in the bushes. Whoever's been committing these outrages has to be one of us here now. I don't expect the perpetrator to confess. Whoever you are, you're obviously a thoroughgoing scoundrel and totally lacking in the rudiments of common courtesy. I just want to make it clearly understood that you might as well quit thumping people around and tearing the place apart, because you're not going to find what you're looking for."

"You mean the treasure?" That was Black John Sendick, with his Tycho Brahe sweatshirt on inside out and backward.

"No, I'm referring to an exceedingly vulgar but no doubt fabulously expensive diamond necklace that I inadvertently brought here myself. During the trip on the ferry, somebody had temporarily relieved me of my Gladstone bag and hidden the necklace in the lining with the apparent intention of stealing it back again on the island. The man who was found drowned yesterday morning—"

"His name was Jimmy Sorpende," Theonia put in. "He was a rather inept criminal with a prison record."

"Why the hell didn't you say so before?" bellowed Vincent. He was wearing an ancient bathrobe patterned in one of the Indian designs popular in the late twenties and early thirties. It must have been a family heirloom, Emma thought inconsequentially.

"I have said so," Theonia was telling him sweetly. "Sorry to break in, Emma. Do go on."

"Thank you, Theonia. I don't know what function the late Mr. Sorpende was supposed to perform. Since he was an experienced burglar, he was most likely the one who managed to steal the Gladstone bag out of my bedroom night before last while I was asleep. He supposed, of course, that the necklace was still in the bag. In fact I'd happened to discover it during the evening and put it in the safe, stuffing a piece of costume jewelry under the lining in place of the diamonds. I don't know why I did that, it just seemed a good idea at the time."

"My God!" said somebody in the crowd.

Emma waited for a more enlightened response. It didn't come, however, so she continued. "The fact that Mr. Sorpende was later struck on the head and thrown over the cliff suggests that his accomplice had discovered the substitution and assumed Mr.

Sorpende was trying to appropriate the necklace for himself. The accomplice thereupon lost his temper—I use 'his' in this context as an indefinite pronoun, you understand—and murdered Mr. Sorpende, throwing the worthless bag and costume jewelry over the cliff after him in a further fit of pique. Don't you think so, Theonia?"

"Either that or the accomplice killed Jimmy Sorpende first in order to gain sole possession of the necklace and threw the bag after him simply to get rid of it. We'll probably never know which, but I don't suppose it matters. I might point out that Mrs. Kelling is quite right about the impersonal pronoun. It wouldn't take any prodigious amount of strength to fell somebody with a hard blow to the head, then roll him to the edge of the cliff and shove him off. An able-bodied woman could do it. I daresay I could myself if I put my mind to it."

"You might sit down on the ground and push with your feet," Sendick suggested. "Most people have a lot more power in their leg muscles than they do in their arms."

"Very true," said Theonia. "I must say that hadn't occurred to me, but do go on, Emma."

"Thank you, Theonia. I should perhaps mention that Dr. Franklin says Mr. Sorpende was still alive when he landed. So he wouldn't have drowned as his assailant perhaps expected. However, it was Mr. Sorpende's misfortune to land facedown and be smothered by the mud. Had he landed faceup, he might have survived the fall."

"Then it's manslaughter, not murder," said Black John.

"Why yes, I suppose it would be, now that you mention it," Emma conceded. "You do know a great deal about these things, don't you, Mr. Sendick? Neil, since you're the one who found him, is there anything you'd care to add?"

Neil's teeth were chattering. He was clad only in pajama bottoms and his feet were bare, but he manfully stepped forward and spoke his piece. "J-just that Uncle Frank said they found some pine needles glued to the guy's hair with pitch, like as if he might have been hit with a pine branch or rolled over the ground where the pine needles were. Didn't he, Pop?"

"Ayuh. For God's sake, couldn't you have had sense enough to put something on? Come over here."

Vincent wrapped his son in a fold of his Indian-blanket bathrobe and hugged him close to his side. "Sandy, you scoot back to bed. You shouldn't be up in your condition."

"Oh, Pop!" his daughter protested. "I feel swell, honest. Bernice and I don't want to miss anything. Are you okay, Mrs. Kelling? Gosh, I hope that guy didn't ruin your pretty wig when he hit you."

Sandy did indeed have an embarrassing penchant for the truth. Emma dealt with the faux pas as best she could. "I'm not at all sure my attacker was a male, Sandy. Fortunately for me, the blow was a relatively light one. This bruise on my forehead came from striking the edge of the flour bin as I fell. And I was not wearing my pretty wig, that's only for dress-up. I do have hair of my own, as you can see, though I expect it's a dreadful mess by now."

Emma caught Count Radunov's appraising eye and blushed; she was annoyed with herself for doing so. "And your father's quite right," she went on briskly. "You ought to be in bed. Bernice, so should you. I suppose you all expect me to apologize for dragging you out at this hour. Since it's obvious that whichever of you stole that necklace originally is on a rampage to get it back, however, I thought it more sensible to tell you now than risk finding somebody else either injured or dead in the morning."

"How right you were," Count Radunov assured her. "We are deeply grateful for your solicitude on our behalf and only regret the deplorable incident that prompted it."

He was winding up for further effusion, but Lisbet Quainley cut him off.

"Where's the necklace now, Mrs. Kelling?"

"On its way back to its original owner," Emma told her. "Don't ask me who that is because I don't know. All I know is that it was stolen from the wearer at a charity ball. I sent it to Boston by Mr. Arbuthnot, the man who brought Mrs. Brooks here in his seaplane this morning. By now, it's been turned over to the proper authorities."

Emma knew she was stretching a point there, but she didn't care. Max Bittersohn was certainly more proper than Jimmy Sorpende and his head-bashing confederate. Max would in fact return the jewels to their rightful owners as soon as he'd extracted a reasonable fee for Theonia's services and full payment of the reward to the Firemen's Relief Fund.

Tweeters wouldn't care about financial reimbursement. According to Theonia, he already had more money than he knew what to do with, despite turning it over by the fistful to the Audubon Society and being the sole support of several puffin rookeries. Speaking of Tweeters—Emma cocked an eyebrow at Theonia and then at Mrs. Fath, who was clutching her lurid Japanese kimono around her and looking confused, as well she might.

Theonia nodded and took up the tale. "We should also tell you that we gave Mr. Arbuthnot a sample of orange juice obtained from Mrs. Fath's room. We've received a report of the analysis and discovered someone has been dosing Mrs. Fath with tranquilizers, presumably to keep her from using her psychic powers to reveal his or her other malefactions. Whichever of you is doing this must stop immediately. You're in violation of the federal narcotics law. Furthermore, it's a devastating thing to do to anybody, let alone a genuine sensitive."

"Tranquilizers?" Mrs. Fath had at last been jolted out of her lethargy. "I can't take tranquilizers! They ruin the vibrations. For Pete's sake, why couldn't you just have slugged me over the head, too? You might as well kill me as put me out of business."

"We shall do all we can to help you recover your vibrations," Emma assured her. "In the meantime, Bubbles will be extra careful to make sure you ingest nothing at all, not so much as a sip of water, not even your toothpaste, which he has not personally approved. No food or drink will be left sitting around where anybody could get at it. Do you understand that, Mrs. Fath? You are to put nothing at all in your mouth that hasn't come straight from Bubbles. Furthermore, he's going to taste it first and stay right with you while you eat it."

Lisbet Quainley emitted another of her hysterical giggles. "So if Alding goes spacey again, we'll all know who to blame. Tough luck, Bubbles."

Bubbles clearly couldn't have agreed more, but what could he say? "Yeth, Mithith Kelling. I'll do my betht."

"I know you will." That was not Emma but Alding Fath, sounding a good deal less woozy than she had since the night she arrived. "You've been an angel of mercy to me, Bubbles. I remember that, all right."

"Don't thay that, Mithith Fath! I—I failed you."

"The hell you did," roared Vincent. "Quit being so hard on yourself, Bubbles. How could you know a goddamn raging lunatic was trying to kill us all on account of a goddamn necklace nobody saw fit to tell me about?"

He glared at Emma. She glared right back. "How was I to know you weren't the accomplice? I know it now, of course, because I realize you'd never have struck your own daughter. Though you did let your son risk his neck yesterday morning retrieving that worthless jewelry of mine. I couldn't help wondering then whether you were hoping to recover the diamond necklace at any cost."

"I wasn't risking my neck," Neil protested. "Pop didn't send me, but he didn't stop me. He knew I'd be okay."

"Can't raise a boy to be a sissy," the father growled. "I didn't know what Neil was divin' for, but I'll admit I was curious to know what was there. It didn't stand to reason that feller would go through all the bother o' comin' here to Pocapuk and playin' his amnesia stunt just to run off with a bunch o' junk. You could o' told me."

"Yes, I could, and I'm sorry now that I didn't," Emma admitted. "But just answer me one question, Vincent. If the shoe had been on the other foot, would you have told me?"

"Well, no," he admitted after a struggle, "I don't s'pose I would. Okay, Mrs. Kelling, I guess you got me on that one. All I can say is, when I find which one o' you birds slugged my daughter—"

He didn't bother to finish. He didn't have to. Ted Sharpless winced as though he'd been hit over the head himself. Black John Sendick started to say something, then didn't. Lisbet Quainley giggled again and clutched Everard Wont, who pulled away angrily. Sandy and Bernice were gaping like spectators at a horror show; Neil leaned against his father as if Vincent were the hero who could make the monster go away. It was Joris Groot who broke the silence.

"This," he said, "is one hell of a situation."

"I quite agree," said Emma. "I suppose the best course right now is for everyone to go back to bed and get what sleep we can. Now that our resident criminal understands it's useless to go on smashing and bashing, I should think the rest of us are safe enough. Don't you, Theonia?"

"I sincerely hope so. Good night, everybody."

"With one exception." Lisbet Quainley was still either not trying or not able to suppress those senseless giggles.

The party dispersed to seek what repose each might, with luck, attain. The two Mrs. Kellings went back upstairs. As she was adjusting herself on the chaise longue, it occurred to Emma that amid all that babble and chatter, all those hair-raising revelations, Everard Wont had said not one single word.

TWENTY-THREE

Emma hadn't expected to sleep a wink, but aspirin and exhaustion did their work. She didn't open an eye again until Bernice and Sandy showed up with morning tea. Bernice was carrying the tray; Sandy had evidently just come along to be sociable.

"It's half-past eight, Mrs. Kelling. Pop said we'd better come and make sure you two were still alive. Hi, Mrs. Brooks. Ooh, what a wicked nightie!"

"Well, I see you're bright and chirpy this morning." That was Theonia, Emma was still conducting experiments with her eyelids. "Thank you, Bernice, just set the tray here on the table. Is your head quite recovered, Sandy?"

"My bump hurts when I touch it, but Pop said it was okay to get up before I drove him nuts. You guys won't be late to breakfast; everybody's running late this morning. Bubbles gave Mrs. Fath a couple of soft-boiled eggs for breakfast. He candled them first to make sure nobody'd stuck a hypodermic needle through the shells and squirted in any unknown Asiatic poison or anything. Was that okay, Mrs. Kelling?"

"Quite satisfactory." Emma had all her moving parts in working order by now, as far as she could tell. "How is Mrs. Fath feeling?"

"Okay, I guess. She ate in the kitchen with us so Bubbles could keep an eye on her. Pop sent Neil to her cottage for some clothes, and he brought back all the wrong stuff, naturally. Mrs. Fath's going to give him a course in mind reading as soon as she gets her head back together. Take your time getting dressed, Bubbles didn't even put the muffins in the oven till just a little while ago, and none of the cottagers have shown up yet except Black John. He's wearing a green sweatshirt today; it's got a picture of a moose in a hammock on it. I bet his girlfriend gave it to him. Does Black John have a girlfriend, Mrs. Kelling?"

"Dozens, I should think." Emma was feeling a little brisker now that she'd managed to get half a cup of tea into her. "Refill my cup for me like a good girl, then you and Bernice skip along and help Bubbles with breakfast since you're so full of pep. Mrs. Brooks and I will be down as soon as we've pulled ourselves together."

That might take some doing, Emma thought a few minutes later as she faced the awful truth in the bathroom mirror. As a rule, she was not one to balk at a challenge, but this morning the old Kelling fizz had definitely gone flat. She had to give herself a stern lecture and swipe a glob of Theonia's Queen Bee Replenishing Cream before she could even face the effort of lifting her second-best wig off the block. A good, long wallow in a hot bath with plenty of geranium salts was what she needed, but conscience forbade such indulgence.

Emma compromised on a quick shower and a snatch from *Ruddigore*. "For duty, duty must be done; the rule applies to every one, and painful though the duty be, to shirk the task were fiddle-de-dee. To shirk the taaask, to shirk the task were fiddle-de-fiddle-de diddle-de-dee!"

Not bad. She'd managed that long high note without a croak or a waver. Granted, the piece was written for Richard and Sir Despard, so the note wasn't all that high, but why quibble over details? Somewhat reassured, she dried off on one of Adelaide's sumptuous though faded bath sheets; put on some frisky lingerie Little Em, bless the child, had given her on her last birthday as a cock of the snook to Father Time; and started to work on her face.

There, she told herself, some minutes later, that ought to do it if anything could. Now to snaffle the rose print blouse before Theonia beat her to it and she had to be polite. No, Theonia was taking the blue with the red pinstripe and jazzing it up with the red scarf off her sailor hat. Trust Theonia.

The pink blouse and a few minutes' extra work with a sable brush and a cake of blusher did all Emma could reasonably expect in the circumstances. "Lovely," said Theonia. "You look like a rose without a thorn."

"Apt application's artful aid." Emma rinsed out the brush and set it on the edge of the sink to dry. "I'll bet I'm a better painter than Lisbet Quainley. Shall we go down? I suppose it's useless to hope Sarah will call before noontime."

"Oh, she might. Sarah's unbelievably efficient, you know. I must say the combination of sea air and late-night alarms does stimulate one's appetite. Let's hope the muffins are done."

The muffins were done, the chafing dishes were filled, and the clans were beginning to gather. Joris Groot was at the table with Sendick, stuffing his face as if this were to be his last meal on earth. Alding Fath was sitting where she'd sat their first night on the island.

"Don't worry, Mrs. Kelling," she reassured Emma. "I'm not eating, just visiting."

"I know. Sandy told me about the soft-boiled eggs, which was a very sensible thing for Bubbles to do. It's good to see you up and about, Mrs. Fath. I don't believe you've met my cousin's wife, Mrs. Brooks Kelling. People are calling her Mrs. Brooks to avoid confusion."

"That's good. Been too much confusion around here already, sounds like to me. How do you do, Mrs. Brooks? Say, have I met you before?"

Theonia held out her hand. Alding Fath took it and held it long enough to make Emma aware that something more than a courteous handshake was going on. Then Theonia said, "You're going to be just fine," and went to get herself some creamed haddock.

The haddock was excellent; Emma had some, too. She was at the muffins-and-marmalade stage when Lisbet Quainley showed up bundled into a great mass of sweatering loosely knit in hit-or-miss greenery-yallery splashes interspersed with dirty puce and angry dark red. Aside from its ugliness, the garment was an odd choice, Emma thought; the day was already warm enough for thin cottons.

Everard Wont most likely wouldn't show up for breakfast, Miss

Quainley told the others. She didn't come straight out and say he'd gone back to the cottage after that painful session in the dark of night and drunk himself into a coma, but the inference was not hard to draw. The young woman herself was desperately uneasy, Emma thought.

Alding Fath thought so, too. "What's eating you, Lisbet? Looks to me as if you're wearing that sweater for protection."

"Don't be silly, Alding! I just put it on because—I don't know. Because it was the first thing I grabbed. I didn't want to be late for breakfast. Anyway, why shouldn't I be feeling a few shivers now and then? Maybe you don't know it, but I got hit on the head, too. My scalp was cut open, for God's sake! I was bleeding all over the place."

If one had to endure the pain, one might as well enjoy the publicity, Emma supposed. "How is your head this morning, Miss Quainley?" she asked. "Much better, I hope. Do try the creamed haddock; it's quite delicious and just the thing for a delicate stomach."

"If you say so."

Lisbet Quainley rolled up her unlovely sleeves to keep them out of the chafing dishes while she helped herself to a minuscule portion of fish and a slice of dry toast. Whatever Wont had been drinking, Emma deduced, he hadn't been drinking alone. And where was Count Radunov? Surely that elegant gentleman of fortune hadn't indulged in an unseemly early-morning booze-up.

Emma was pouring her second and final cup of coffee by the time Radunov appeared, dapper as usual but wan around the eyes. He filled a plate at the buffet without appearing to notice or care what he took and sat down to eat it with none of his usual efforts toward affable table talk. Theonia and Alding Fath were talking their highly specialized brand of shop in low tones at their end of the table, but nobody else was saying much of anything. The likelihood that they might be having breakfast with a thief and a murderer or manslaughterer, as the case might be, would naturally tend to put a strain on the rules of etiquette, Emma had to concede.

Vincent came in as she was about ready to abandon any pretense of being hostess and leave the table to whoever chose to preside. "Mrs. Kelling," he said, "I've heard from the county sheriff's office. They say they ought to have somebody out here around noontime."

"Oh, good. I'm sure you'll be as relieved as I."

"Ayuh. Now what do you want done about the big bedroom? Bernice can't handle that mess alone. I don't want Sandy bendin' an' stretchin' and startin' her head up again."

"I should think not," Emma agreed. "Why don't you let us borrow Neil long enough to lift the mattresses back on the beds? Mrs. Brooks and I can handle the rest. It will give us something to occupy ourselves while we're waiting."

"I'll send 'im up whenever you're ready."

Emma laid down her napkin. "Now is as good a time as any. Theonia, come whenever you feel the urge."

Mrs. Fath stood up, too. "I'd better go back to my cottage and get squared away, if Bubbles will let me. It's been nice talking to you, Mrs. Brooks."

"I look forward to continuing our chat, Mrs. Fath. Until later, then."

"What do you think of her?" Emma asked as they went upstairs.

"I think she's a dear." Theonia's tone left no room for doubt. "You can forget the spies gathering information, Emma. That woman wouldn't know how to go about it. She may not be quite so infallible as she thinks she is, but she's honest as far as she goes. Any ambiguities she may have uttered the other night weren't meant to trick you. She was only trying to describe precisely the impressions she was getting, which is not always easy or even possible. People get misled because they color what the reader says with what's in their own minds."

"Now that I think of it, Theonia, that's exactly what happened. All Mrs. Fath actually said was black and white and stones coming out of the sea. Then Mr. Groot picked up with his notion about Shag Rock and the white gulls." Et cetera. "Wont and the rest jumped to the conclusion that she was describing the place where Pocapuk's treasure was buried because that was what they were hoping to hear. Yesterday morning, when Neil came in wearing that old black raincoat and carrying the *Iolanthe* jewelry he'd fished up wrapped in a white towel, it became clear what she'd really meant. Rather amusing, when one thinks about it."

"I suppose so." Theonia didn't sound much interested. "Well, let's get to work. What a mess!"

"It's all my fault for not having told about the safe sooner," said Emma. "I deserve to get stuck with the cleaning up. But you don't. Wouldn't you rather go back and watch Count Radunov eat his breakfast?"

"Don't be morbid, my dear. Ah, here's Neil. Just what we need, a strong back."

The boy grinned and fell to work. Within ten minutes they had the mattresses on their springs, the beds made up, and the drawers back in the dressers.

"Now for the fun part," Emma groaned as she surveyed the jumble of garments and bric-a-brac strewn all over the floor. "You may as well run along to your father, Neil. Mrs. Brooks and I can manage the rest by ourselves. Oh, but first I meant to ask you—were you here last year with Mrs. Sabine?"

He shook his head. "Off-season with Pop a few times but never while she was here. See, Dad's Uncle Winfield always used to come and help Dad, he and his friend Jake Pierce, who lives with him since Aunt May died. Uncle Winfield had a leg shot off in the war when he was a young guy. It never bothered him till a few months ago, but then he started having trouble with his stump and had to go to the veterans' hospital. They finally had to cut off the stump clear up to his hip almost; he's still in a wheelchair. So Dad figured what with my mother being away and everything, Jake would have to stay home and take care of Uncle Winfield this summer instead of coming to Pocapuk. That's how Ted and I got to come instead."

"I see," said Emma. "What I really wondered was whether Mrs. Sabine had brought a maid with her, someone to look after her room and all that, the way Sandy's been doing for me."

"Gee, Mrs. Kelling, I don't know. Mum was on a dig up in Washington County last summer, so Sandy and I went up there with her and camped out most of the time."

"Then you didn't see your father all summer?"

"Oh yeah, we saw him. Uncle Winfield and Jake were here, so Pop didn't mind taking a day off now and then when Mrs. Sabine didn't have anything special going on. He just never talked about the island much; he was too glad to get back to us. This year, with Mum not able to get home on weekends, Sandy and me here with him, and Ches and Wal coming out every day like they do, Pop isn't planning to take any time off. He says I'm too young to be left in charge and Ted's kind of a goof-off and Mrs. Sabine's not here and Pop hasn't quite made up his mind about you. I guess I shouldn't have said that."

Emma laughed. "Why shouldn't you? Your father's wise not to trust any stranger too far, especially considering what's been happening here the past few days. Mrs. Sabine's fortunate to have such a conscientious overseer. Now you'd better scoot along; I expect your father has something else lined up for you to do."

"You better believe it. Pop's got a natural gift for keeping noses glued to the grindstone. See you later, then."

Emma and Theonia went on with the task of straightening up what the would-be burglar had dumped. Adelaide Sabine had obviously been in the habit of leaving a good many personal effects, such as lingerie, nightwear, and casual clothing, on Pocapuk from year to year in order to avoid having to tote stacks of luggage back and forth. That was sensible; Emma would have done the same. Nevertheless, she wished she didn't have to handle these intimate garments. It was too much like an invasion of the old lady's privacy; Adelaide was of a generation to whom such things still mattered.

Oh well, Emma supposed what Adelaide didn't know wouldn't upset her. Had Sarah had better luck than she on the question of the maid? It was getting on for noon; if Sarah didn't call pretty soon, Emma might just give her a ring. What if someone did pick up the extension in the pantry? The sooner all secrets were out, the better for everyone. With one exception, as Lisbet Quainley had so appositely and annoyingly pointed out.

First things first; Emma was too well-organized to leave this job half done. She was hanging Mr. Sabine's ratty bathrobe back in the closet when Bernice tapped nervously at the door and stuck her head inside.

"Mrs. Kelling, there's a telephone call for you. It's your niece."

"Oh, good. Thank you Bernice. Do you want to get in on this, Theonia?"

"You go ahead. I'll be down as soon as I finish here."

Emma didn't stay to coax. Vincent was already in the drawing room with the telephone out of the Chinese box. An Admirable Crichton if ever there was one. Emma gave him a nod and took the receiver he handed her.

"Yes, Sarah. What's up?"

"Quite a lot. To begin with, Mrs. Sabine did have a maid with her last year, a girl about nineteen years old named Cecily Green, the daughter of somebody who worked for the Pences. She was an art student, you may be interested to know. Mrs. Sabine did teach the girl how to open the safe; she was in bed for several days with one of her attacks and didn't want to leave her jewelry lying around loose."

"I wonder why Adelaide didn't ask Vincent," said Emma. "I suppose she didn't feel it was quite the thing to have him performing personal errands in her bedroom while she was actually lying there in her nightgown. So she let this young stranger do it instead. Oh dear!"

"'Oh dear' is hardly the word," said Sarah. "I've done a follow-up on Cecily Green. She was a nice-enough girl from a respectable family but none too swift in the intellect. After she came back to Boston, she started seeing a fellow named Ted Sharpless who came from somewhere up near where you are now. They met in a singles bar, from what I was able to gather. She fell for him in a big way, but her father found out somehow that Sharpless was a convict on parole and made her quit seeing him. That was around the end of April. Shortly after they broke up, Cecily was killed in a hit-and-run accident, or a reasonable facsimile of one. That could have been the real reason why Sharpless skipped back to Maine."

"Sarah!"

"Yes, it makes you wonder, doesn't it? We don't know, of course, whether she told him about the safe just to make conversation or whether he picked her up on purpose to pump her about the Sabine place. As to who killed her, that could have been Sharpless but I doubt it. He was too obvious a suspect. I'd guess he was safely off in some bar with his pal Jimmy, working up an alibi, while the third member of the team went after Cecily Green. If somebody twists the screws a bit, it's a fairly safe bet Sharpless will talk."

"Vincent tells me the county sheriff's people will be here by noontime, so perhaps I'd better go and do some preliminary twisting right now."

"Wait a minute, Aunt Emma, I haven't finished. You also asked me to work on Joris Groot and Black John Sendick. It may interest you to know Footsy-Wootsy was bought out by a conglomerate three years ago. The company had been losing money; the conglomerate quickly ran it into the ground and took a big tax loss; which, of course, had been their objective from the beginning. The Footsy-Wootsy trademark hasn't been used since."

"Then what was Mr. Groot lying for? You don't suppose he's had a nervous breakdown or something and that's the last job he remembers having done? After a lifetime of drawing children's sneakers, suddenly finding out there were no sneakers left to draw might conceivably have a shattering effect on one, don't you think? But what's he been living on in the meantime?"

"Good question, Aunt Emma. I asked our friend Bill Jones about him. Bill's a commercial artist himself." Among other things, but Sarah didn't go into that. "He says Groot did in fact used to be a shoe artist but hasn't had much to do in that line since Footsy-Wootsy folded. Groot's a bachelor, by the way. He still has a studio downtown and doesn't appear to be strapped for cash, but Bill doesn't know what sort of work he's doing. Bill will find out; he's good at that."

"Thank you, Sarah. That does indeed give one food for thought."

"As to Sendick, he's a son of some fairly well-to-do people who live in Beneficence."

"Beneficence? That's not far from Pleasaunce. I wonder if they might happen to be clients of Parker Pence?"

"Good question. Anyway, Black John's been something of a handful, it seems. He went to Boston College and majored in lacrosse, wrestling, track, and soccer, which left him little or no time for academics. After he flunked out, he hitchhiked to Alaska and worked on a salmon-fishing boat for a while, then gravitated to San Francisco, where he became a black belt in karate practically overnight. He's a crack athlete, holds a couple of intercollegiate track records, came in fifth in the BAA Marathon two years ago, and won a Golden Gloves boxing tournament in the welterweight classification while he was still in high school. As for his writing career, he did a series of articles for the *Pacific Salmon-Gutters' Gazette* that were fairly well received, but that seems to have been his chief literary triumph to date. He's generally considered a likable fellow but short in the fuse and a rather wicked practical joker. Does that help any?"

"I can't see how."

Emma sent her love to Max and young Davy. Then, deliberately and carefully, she put away the telephone and locked the Chinese box. So Sendick was a runner, a scrapper, and a wicked practical joker. And Groot was a liar, but why? And why had Everard Wont gone silent all of a sudden? And what would happen if Emma were to go to Wont's cottage and rouse him out of his alleged drunken stupor and tell him the county police were on their way to Pocapuk?

TWENTY-FOUR

Now there was nothing to do but wait. Emma had got the cottagers herded together in the sun porch like pigs in a pen. This was too beautiful a day to be indoors, but she didn't want them roaming around loose when the people from the county sheriff's office arrived. She wanted this horrible business to be over and done with, and she wanted it now.

And then what? Would the cottagers all want to leave Pocapuk? Would she find herself alone here with the servants for the rest of the summer? Surely Adelaide Sabine wouldn't care to keep this entire establishment running just for her; perhaps Adelaide would put it up for sale to avoid the inheritance taxes, leaving Emma there to handle the prospective buyers. That would be the sensible thing to do.

Adelaide would never do it, though. Marcia wouldn't let her. Selling Pocapuk would mean acknowledging that Adelaide's life was over. As an only daughter, Marcia had been particularly close to her mother; she wasn't about to let go of Adelaide until she absolutely had to. That was why Marcia hadn't put her foot down about this slightly insane affair of letting a bunch of totally unknown who-are-theys park here for the summer.

The cottagers were taking their confinement calmly enough at the moment. Black John Sendick was reading a paperback thriller, Joris

Groot was sketching his own feet, or rather his own enormous white-and-baby-blue-striped running shoes. Alding Fath was knitting some indeterminate garment out of shaggy brown yarn, sneezing every so often when the fluff got up her nose. Lisbet Quainley and Everard Wont were sitting together on the glider hammock at the far end of the porch. She had her yellow pad on her knees, he was presumably dictating, although Emma couldn't see that anything much was being taken down.

Count Radunov, on the other hand, was scribbling away like a house afire, glancing up at Theonia every so often as though for inspiration. Perhaps he'd cast her as Queen Victoria, though Emma couldn't think why. The czarina, more likely, though Alexandra hadn't been Theonia's type either. She was wearing the same blue skirt and blouse she'd borrowed yesterday, which was considerate of her. Emma was not yet ready to face the question of who coped with the laundry. Perhaps she wouldn't have to; she might soon be leaving Pocapuk with the rest of them.

Right now the prospect was alluring, and yet this was a lovely place. One could be so happy on Pocapuk, Emma thought wistfully, if one could pick one's own guests. Which of this lot would she have chosen? None, of course, she wouldn't have known they existed. Maybe it was better to get away from one's familiar circle, to open oneself to new associations, new experiences, new ideas. Adelaide's way might have been the right way despite the inherent risks. Maybe Emma had never risked enough, had always been too careful to make sure the net was under her before she jumped.

Well, there was always hang gliding. Radunov seemed to have caught her thought, though of course he hadn't; he looked up and smiled at her. Emma smiled back, then she noticed how badly crushed the clematis outside the porch window was and went back to feeling depressed.

It was precisely one minute to twelve when Brother Lowell pulled up to the dock with two passengers aboard. Both wore trim khaki-and-brown uniforms, Emma observed with ineffable relief. Vincent, Neil, Sandy, and Bernice were all hurrying down to meet them. Ted Sharpless was hanging back. He'd run away, Emma thought, if there were any place to go. Bubbles was not in sight; presumably he was still in the kitchen putting together the picnic lunch they were going to have after a while, provided the sheriff's men didn't haul the lot of them away.

"Charlotte, having seen his body borne before her on a shutter, like a well-conducted person, went on cutting bread and butter," Emma murmured, mostly to herself. Was she the only person left alive who still quoted Thackeray? No, Radunov was smiling at her again.

Again she smiled back, albeit nervously. She'd begun to feel like a kettle coming up to the boil. *Please God,* she prayed silently, *make it happen now*. She couldn't endure much more of this.

Shame on her. That was theatrical nonsense. She would endure as much as she had to, when had she not? When Vincent brought the two deputies out to the porch, Emma greeted them as collectedly as though they were expected guests at one of her lawn parties.

Deputy MacDuff had many stripes on his uniform sleeve; he did the talking. Deputy MacIvor had fewer stripes; he, for the most part, kept his mouth shut.

"I expect you want to be told precisely what's been happening here," Emma began.

"They got a pretty good idea already," said Vincent.

"Ayuh," said Deputy MacDuff. "Let's just get sorted out here. You're Mrs. Kelling and you're an old friend of Mrs. Sabine's. That right?"

"Essentially, yes. Mrs. Beddoes Kelling of Pleasaunce, Massachusetts. My first name is Emma and I'm a widow. To be precise, I've been a close friend of Mrs. Sabine's daughter and her husband, Marcia and Peter Pence, for many years. I never knew Adelaide Sabine very well until she came to live with her daughter about four years ago. Since then we've become quite close, however. That's why I volunteered to take over here at Pocapuk for her when Mrs. Sabine's doctor decided at the last minute that she really wasn't up to coming here herself. She had her staff engaged and all six of her cottages filled, you see. She didn't want to leave her guests in the lurch even though she'd never met any of them. And still hasn't, needless to say."

"Darned decent of her," MacDuff grunted.

What he meant was "Darned crazy of her." Emma shook her head.

"I know it sounds unusual, but it wasn't really. She'd been in the habit of entertaining artists and writers whom she didn't necessarily know socially. She knew she could rely on Vincent to carry on as usual. And lastly, I think she couldn't quite bring herself to give up Pocapuk. Wouldn't you suppose so, Vincent?"

"It's not for me to say," he replied gruffly. "All I know is, I been comin' here to work every summer since I was fifteen years old. Her an' me always got along pretty good, she'd know how I—"

"Anyway," Emma stepped in quickly so that the rest wouldn't notice how close the man was to breaking down, "my first hint of trouble—and a pretty broad one, I must say—came on the ferryboat, when I was drugged and robbed of an old Gladstone bag containing a lot of stage jewelry."

"You sure you were drugged?"

Deputy MacDuff wasn't buying her story. Emma couldn't blame him, but neither was she about to let him think her a liar.

"Quite sure. I grant you it sounds like cheap melodrama, but the same thing happened to me a few years ago in my own house when a valuable painting was stolen. I recognized the symptoms. As it turned out, this robbery was only temporary. Count Radunov here recovered my bag shortly afterward. I'll let him tell you about that."

"Wait a minute," said Vincent. "We might as well get the rest of 'em in here, too, so's you'll have us all where you can get at us."

MacDuff said that was a good idea and presumably MacIvor agreed, so Vincent went and rounded up his staff: the three young ones clearly thrilled to be in on the action, Bubbles fussing at being dragged away from his kitchen, Ted Sharpless scared stiff and doing a poor job of pretending he wasn't. They squeezed themselves in as best they could: Bubbles in the one extra chair, Neil and the girls on the floor, Ted perched on the doorstep leading from the porch into the dining room as if poised for a quick getaway.

Radunov picked up the ball, MacDuff kept it rolling from him to the next. This was no country bumpkin; the deputy handled the questioning smoothly, with as little help from Emma as she could hold herself down to. She'd chaired enough meetings to know when to speak and when to yield the floor. Deputy MacIvor noted down the salient information with an occasional assist from Vincent when a word came along that he didn't quite catch.

Merely taking down the various testimonies ate up more time than Emma had anticipated. Once Deputy MacDuff was satisfied that they'd covered the ground, Vincent declared a sandwich break, which the men from the sheriff's office appreciated as much as the rest. And now, thought Emma, to serious business. She took a last sip of tea, patted her lips with her napkin, handed the cup to Sandy, and reopened the meeting.

"I must tell you, Deputy MacDuff, that my cousin and I have some family connections who are private detectives. We've been in touch with them by telephone and managed to collect some information for you. To begin with, the man Neil fished out of the water was named Jimmy Sorpende. Perhaps you'd already learned that?"

No, they hadn't and MacDuff didn't seem any too pleased that the Kelling ladies had got the jump on them. "What else do you know about him?" he demanded.

"He had a prison record. We don't have the details, but I expect you can get them easily enough. Unless some of the people here could fill you in."

Vincent caught the inference fast enough. "How 'bout you, Ted?"

The young man only glowered and sneaked a furtive glance in Emma's direction.

"I'm sorry, Ted," she told him, "but two people are dead and three more have been physically assaulted, of whom I'm one, and I'm not about to let it happen again. You'd better tell what you know."

Ted stayed mute. Vincent didn't.

"Two dead? Who's the other one, for God's sake?"

"A young art student from Boston named Cecily Green."

"Cecily Green? You mean that kid who was here last summer with Mrs. Sabine?"

"That's right. You no doubt remember that Mrs. Sabine was far from well even then and had to stay in bed for a while. During that time, she taught Miss Green how to open the safe so that she could put Mrs. Sabine's jewelry away for her."

"Why the hell didn't Mrs. Sabine ask me?"

"Because she thought the task more suitable for a lady's maid than a man in your position, I assume. You must remember, Vincent, that Mrs. Sabine has very old-fashioned ideas about how to run her household. Anyway, sometime in May, Miss Green was killed by a hit-and-run driver who still hasn't been caught. A month or so before that she'd become friendly with a young man named Ted Sharpless, whom she'd met in a singles bar. Her father had taken exception to the acquaintance and made her break off the affair. You were living in Boston yourself at the time, weren't you, Ted?"

"So what if I was?" he snarled. "Couldn't there be two guys with the same name?"

"I suppose there could, but it appears this particular Ted Sharpless came from the same part of Maine where Miss Green had spent last summer. I realize young fellows like you don't like to take advice, Ted, but I strongly recommend that you quit trying to make your position worse than it already is. Cecily Green told you about that safe in Mrs. Sabine's upstairs closet, didn't she? And you passed on the information to Jimmy Sorpende."

"Okay, she told me. What the hell, it didn't mean anything to me. I only told Jimmy for a joke."

Emma raised her eyebrows. "Theonia, would you care to comment?"

"Indeed I should. I'd like Mr. Sharpless to explain why, if he thought Miss Green's story was merely a joke, he took pains to memorize the combination and write it down for Jimmy Sorpende to bring here with him."

Vincent boiled over. "And I'd like to ask you, Mrs. Brooks, how you knew Sorpende had the combination with him."

"I didn't," Theonia replied with one of her Mona Lisa smiles. "I only made the suggestion to see what sort of reaction I'd get. Then you did find the combination."

"I found a cardboard match folder from a Boston bar with some numbers written on the inside when I went through his pockets trying to find out who he was. I gave it to Lowell when he took the body ashore."

"And Lowell turned it over to us, as was right and proper." Deputy MacDuff showed Emma a small plastic envelope that contained a water-soaked remnant with a few figures still readable on it. "Is this the combination, Mrs. Kelling?"

"Yes. I know because it also happens to be Marcia Pence's telephone number. If you want to try it yourself, I can take you upstairs and show you the safe."

"Later, maybe. Go ahead, Sharpless. So you killed your girlfriend to shut her mouth about tipping you off to the safe."

"I didn't kill her! Cecily was hit on Huntington Avenue outside the art museum at half-past nine on a Wednesday night. I was tending bar at the Gone Goose 'way the hell and gone over in Dorchester. I didn't get off duty till one o'clock the next morning. Ask the Boston cops; they'll tell you. I've got an alibi you couldn't break with a fucking chain saw."

"Watch your language, Sharpless," snapped MacDuff. "Where was your friend Sorpende that night?"

"Working at a dog track halfway to Rhode Island. Want me to draw you a map?"

"Never mind, just tell me the name of whoever you and Sorpende were working with."

"I wasn't working with anybody! Jimmy was just a guy I happened to meet in a bar, that's all. Maybe he was working with somebody; I wouldn't know about that. We weren't real buddies or anything."

"Then why did you let him have the combination to Mrs. Sabine's safe?"

"I told you why."

"I know what you told me. Now tell me the truth."

Ted was crumbling around the edges by now. "Jim said he'd make it tough for me if I didn't," he growled.

"Make it tough for you how?"

"Aw, I got busted on a D and D and did three months. Jim was going to spread it around that I had a record if I didn't come across."

"That so?" said Deputy MacDuff. "According to the bulletin we received a while back, you've done two years of a three-year term for aggravated assault with dangerous weapons: namely a pair of hobnailed boots, a knuckle-duster, and a tire iron. You've been in violation of your parole since shortly after you were taken in for questioning with regard to the apparent hit-and-run accident that killed Cecily Green of Boston. Speaking of which, how did the Green girl's father get to know you were a convict? The report says that's why he'd broken off the connection between you and his daughter. Did Sorpende rat on you after all?"

"I guess so."

Ted was lying, of course, thought Emma. Mr. Green could have found out easily enough by seeing Ted's name in the newspaper or asking around the neighborhood barrooms. Jimmy must have had some other hold over Ted; probably there'd been an earlier violation of his parole. Regardless of decorum, she whispered to Theonia, and Theonia nodded.

"Excuse me, Deputy MacDuff," Emma said. "I have a question. Ted, you said you first met Jimmy Sorpende at a bar. How did that happen? Did somebody introduce you, or what?"

"What difference does it make?"

"Quite a lot, I should think. Please answer my question."

"Answer her question, Sharpless," said Deputy MacDuff.

Ted shrugged. "Okay, no big deal. The bar was crowded, see. I was up there ready to order and this guy behind me stuck a five in my hand and asked me to get him a beer. So I did and looked around and he's over at a table waving to me. So I went over and gave him his beer and he wouldn't take the change. So I sat down with him and we got to talking, that's all."

"That's what I thought," said Emma. "What it amounts to is that Jimmy Sorpende picked you up. Could that have been because he already knew you were in fact not a released prisoner but a parolee who could be sent back to jail for consorting with a known felon, namely himself? I don't suppose you realized then what Jimmy was up to, but I expect you found out fast enough when you'd told him your little tale about Cecily and then balked at giving him the combination to the safe."

"I didn't want to get Cecily in trouble."

"But when it came to the pinch you decided better her than you. You're a charming fellow, Ted. Did Jimmy Sorpende tell you why he wanted the combination?"

"He told me he knew a guy who'd pay for it, and we could split the money."

"What would this person have wanted it for?"

"A place to stash something was all I could think of."

"And how right you were. What was he planning to stash?"

"How should I know? It was none of my business."

"And did you get your share of the money?"

"Nah. I never laid eyes on him again till he showed up here in that beat-up wet suit."

"Then how did you know he was at the dog track the night Cecily Green was killed?"

"I heard. See, I'd told the police Jimmy was a friend of hers, so they checked him out. I had to tell them something, didn't I? They were leaning on me. I figured if I told them she'd found another guy they'd leave me alone. Besides, I—I guess I felt as if I owed Cecily something. She wasn't a bad kid. Just stupid."

"In other words, you knew perfectly well Cecily's death was no accident, and you thought Jimmy must have been responsible. That was why you set the police on him, wasn't it? You hoped to get enough on him so that he wouldn't tell on you. Did Cecily actually ever get to meet Jimmy?"

"How do I know? And what difference did it make? They wouldn't believe Jimmy anyway, and she wasn't around to say."

MacDuff shook his head. "You're a winner, Sharpless. How come you got that bartending job? Since when did bars start hiring convicts?"

"It was only for one night. A guy got sick and they needed somebody in a hurry. The head bartender got hold of my name and called me up, so I said sure."

"Was the Gone Goose one of your regular hangouts?"

"No, I never went in there before."

"Then how did the bartender get hold of your name and phone number?"

"I don't know, he never said."

"You don't expect me to believe that, Sharpless."

"I'm telling you, I don't know."

Ted Sharpless was desperately keeping his eyes on his own sneakers, black ones with white stripes along the sides and a small hole over the left big toe. Emma Kelling drew a deep breath.

"That's all right, Deputy MacDuff. If Ted really doesn't know, I believe I can help you."

Really, this being clouted over the head was getting monotonous. Through the pain, Emma could hear the crash of a breaking window and a great deal of shouting. By the time she realized what was causing her temporary blindness and straightened the wig he'd pushed down over her eyes, Joris Groot was through the broken window and off down the path to Shag Rock Point, with almost the entire population of Pocapuk Island pelting after him.

came back empty-handed in a minute or two. "Mithith Kelling, there'th a telephone call for you."

"Telephone call?" Everard Wont was vocal again. "What's all this about telephones? I thought you said there wasn't one."

"Far as you're concerned, there isn't," snapped Vincent. "Speakin' of which, Professor, since you're so hell-bent on gettin' off Pocapuk, you better go get your stuff together right now. My brother won't mind settin' you ashore, but he's got to get goin' pretty quick. The deputies have to file their report."

Emma could have kissed him. "Theonia," she said, "that must be Sarah. Would you talk to her? Tell her I'm tied up right now with a departing guest."

"Of course," Theonia replied. "Don't bother getting the other phone out, Vincent, I'll take it in the kitchen."

She walked out with the cook. Emma leaped to the attack. "Neil, would you please drive the luggage cart around to Dr. Wont's cottage and help him with his bags? We mustn't keep your uncle waiting. Dr. Wont, it's too bad your project hasn't worked out, but I have to say I had small hopes of it from the start. Now, does anybody else want to leave with Dr. Wont? If you do, please say so right this minute. As far as I'm concerned, the rest of you are quite welcome to finish out the summer here with me on the one condition that you never so much as breathe another word about Pocapuk's treasure in my presence."

Wont had most likely not intended to quit Mrs. Sabine's free fleshpots now that the danger was past, but what could he do? Seething, he jerked his chin at Lisbet Quainley. Sighing, she got up and followed him out of the house.

"I had a feeling she'd go," said Alding Fath. "I wonder if that means I'm getting my powers back."

"I expect we all had the same feeling," said Emma, "so I'm afraid this one's not a fair test, Mrs. Fath. Or may I call you Alding?"

"Sure, go right ahead. Glad to have you."

"And you must call me Emma. Now that we've been through so much together, I think we're entitled to use first names. Don't you agree, Alexei?"

Count Radunov was, as she'd expected, both gratified and amused. "My dear Emma, I could not agree more. Speaking of

TWENTY-FIVE

I guess I still have a lot to learn about building a raft."

Ruefully did Black John speak and well might he say so. The makeshift raft on which Joris Groot had made his insane attempt to get away from Pocapuk had started to fall apart even before Vincent, Lowell, and the two deputies had collected themselves and gone for the boat. They'd still been too far away to do any good when the last two logs went their separate ways and Groot tried to swim for it. All they'd been able to retrieve was one white-and-blue running shoe, size eleven and one half.

"Cussed fool," Vincent was fuming, "if he'd had brains enough to grab on to a floatin' log we'd o' saved 'im easy enough."

"For what?" said Emma. "Groot would have been convicted of grand larceny, criminal assault, manslaughter, and no doubt the deliberate murder of Cecily Green. He'd have spent the rest of his life behind bars drawing pictures of other prisoners' feet. I suggest you stop blaming yourself for something you couldn't prevent and fix us all a drink, yourself included, if you can forget for once how things have always been done around here."

"I'll get thome thnackth." Bubbles left the porch to which they'd all automatically gravitated again despite the broken window, but psychic powers, I observe that yours must be developed to a high degree. How else could you have hit on the lumpish Groot as the villain in our melodrama?"

"Don't laugh at me, Alexei. I'm no detective, but I do know a little about people. Things kept piling up. To begin with, I always tend to distrust blank-faced people on general principles. Then Vincent told me Jimmy Sorpende's clothing showed signs that he might have been picked up bodily and heaved over the cliff, which suggested an assailant who was big and strong. I have to admit Black John here was the first who came to my mind."

"I bet I was the second," Vincent grunted.

"Well, there was that possibility," Emma admitted, "but we've already talked about that. Another thing that made me wonder was watching him and Black John building that raft. Groot was yelling at Dr. Wont and waving a big hammer around in quite a bloodcurdling way. Not that one could blame him because Dr. Wont is surely the most infuriating bird ever hatched, but it did show that Groot wasn't always the placid fellow he seemed to be. What really struck me, I think, was our poker game. He was trying to cheat and got furious when it didn't work."

"Because you cheated back." Alexei Radunov was having a lovely time. "I thought I was the one you suspected of marking the deck."

"You were naturally my first choice," Emma replied sweetly.

"Thank you, dear lady, but you overestimate my guile. You used the old fingernail trick, did you not?"

"Only because he used it first."

"What's the fingernail trick?" asked Black John.

"One makes tiny nicks in the edges of the cards or else little dents in the backs. Somebody was making nicks, I could feel them as I shuffled. So I merely added a few extra nicks here and there as the cards came around and waited to see which of you got thrown off his game. We used to pull that sort of trick on each other during our weekly poker games when my husband was alive. Everybody's winnings went to the Firemen's Relief Fund anyway, so cheating was just part of the fun."

Radunov burst out laughing. "Emma, you continue to amaze me! So it was a case of *falsus in uno, falsus in omnibus*."

"Exactly," Emma replied. "Groot also lied to me about Footsy-Wootsy."

"The cad! Had I but known, I'd have challenged him at once."

"Alexei, I am in no mood for frivolity. Footsy-Wootsy was the name of a shoe company he claimed to have done work for recently. My niece checked them out and found they'd gone out of business three years ago. And then Groot told that absurd yarn about getting locked inside Alding's cottage when in fact he must already have been there and hit Lisbet Quainley on the head, then rushed up here and searched my bedroom, getting himself filthy when he jumped out my window and climbed down the trellis."

The real clincher had been the hole in Ted Sharpless's sneaker that matched the New Year's Eve drawing in Joris Groot's sketchbook, but Emma decided not to mention that. A lady didn't have to tell all her little secrets. Anyway, Deputy MacDuff had taken both the sketchbook and the model into custody by now. And here came Theonia with a tray of hors d'oeuvres.

"Ah, there you are, Theonia. Bernice, would you take this tray and pass it around? What did Sarah have to say?"

"Just that she'd unearthed a few more facts. Lisbet Quainley lives on a small inherited income and occasional jobs of an artsy-craftsy nature. She does paint, but nobody seems to feel she has much in the way of talent. Her outstanding characteristic appears to be a penchant for getting mixed up with totally impossible men."

Emma exchanged smiles with Alding Fath. "Tell us something we don't know, my dear."

"The big thing is that Sarah's and Max's friend Bill Jones has managed to find out what Joris Groot had been doing since he lost the Footsy-Wootsy account. He'd picked up some free-lance work drawing jewelry for newspaper ads. He was good at finicky detail, as you know. He'd also been working as a part-time waiter for caterers handling lavish affairs like the one at which the Cantilever necklace was stolen. There'd already been a couple of similar robberies; the caterers were getting worried."

"As well they might," said Radunov. "That sort of thing could put them out of business in a hurry. But they hadn't begun to suspect Groot?"

"Bill didn't say so. Groot was such a quiet, dull-looking fellow that they probably wouldn't have noticed him particularly."

"Unless they found out he had connections among the jewelers," Radunov suggested. "That's probably how he got on to a fence willing to handle what he stole."

"Or else to somebody who egged him on to steal," Black John added. "How did Jimmy Sorpende fit into the picture?"

"I don't know how they got together," said Theonia. "I have a feeling Groot made the mistake of thinking he could use Jimmy for odd jobs whenever he wanted him and shut him out of the big ones. It looks to me as though Groot may have been acting on his own when he decided to bring the necklace to Pocapuk. This would have seemed an ideal place to lie low for the summer at no expense to himself. He may have meant to stash the necklace in Mrs. Sabine's safe until after the party dispersed for the winter and collect it when he thought it was safe to approach his fence. As to how he wangled an invitation to join Dr. Wont's group, I suppose Lisbet Quainley fixed it up."

"That's right," said Alding Fath. "Lisbet hangs out in some back-street restaurant that caters to writers and artists, she told me on the ferry. I guess you do, too, Black John."

"Sure, Tintoretto's Taverna. I go mostly for the spaghetti; a guy can't drink and stay in shape. Anyway, Tintoretto's is the sort of place where everybody gets to know everybody. I'm not really one of the regulars, but Groot used to be there practically every night and so did Liz. They'd have these high-flown discussions about art, Liz doing all the talking and Groot giving a grunt or a nod about once every five minutes. Then Liz started bringing Ev around. I don't know how she latched on to him, but she does seem to have some kind of magnetic attraction for losers. A couple of months ago Ev lined up this Pocapuk deal and started looking for recruits."

"Who shouldn't have been hard to find," said Emma rather caustically.

"You'd have thought so," Black John replied, "but it meant tying yourself up for a whole summer on a project that sounded pretty hopeless in a place nobody knew anything about with a jerk nobody could stand. But then Joris said he'd come because he'd been wanting to try his hand at illustrating a book and this seemed a good chance. Liz wanted to be with Ev, God knows why. I wanted to get out of town for the summer, and it was either Pocapuk or listening to my folks nagging me about why didn't I quit making believe I could write and find myself a job that paid something. Alding, what about you?" .

"Ev sent for me. He'd heard about me through a woman who'd got me to locate some jewelry she'd lost and figured I was just the one to locate Pocapuk's—sorry, Emma. At first I didn't want to come because I didn't like the vibrations from Ev's letter, but this other feeling came through that I ought to do it regardless. So I wrote back that I'd come if he'd send me a round-trip ticket, and he did, so here I am. What's to become of me I don't know, but I'm not going to worry about that till I have to. Go on about Joris and this Jimmy boy, Theonia."

Theonia rearranged her red scarf. "Of course now that they're both dead we can only conjecture. After discussing the matter with our cousin the detective, though, I should say Jimmy Sorpende either knew or suspected Joris Groot had the necklace in his possession and had no intention of cutting Jimmy in on the takings. Jimmy therefore followed Groot to Maine and onto the ferry. He couldn't have known it was the discovery that he was traveling with a bona-fide clairvoyant that sent Groot into a panic. We don't know ourselves, but odds are, it was. Anyway, Jimmy would certainly have seen Groot drugging Emma's coffee and stealing her Gladstone bag. That would have been his cue to step back into the picture, and by then Groot would have been only too glad to leave Jimmy literally holding the bag. I expect he gave Jimmy orders to keep it hidden until the next-to-the-last stop, then leave it in the men's room and go ashore."

"The idea being that one of us would find the bag and either return it to its owner or carry it ashore here," Radunov put in. "It would have occurred to neither of them, one assumes, that the finder might simply turn the bag over to the ferryboat captain. And in fact the plan worked."

"Only Jimmy didn't go ashore," said Theonia. "What he must have done was sneak down into the hold and steal a diving suit and a snorkel out of somebody's car. He'd then have stashed the bag as Groot told him to, hid somewhere until the ferry was almost to Pocapuk, slipped overboard, and swam under water to the island. Jimmy was probably hiding under the dock when you all came ashore and waited there till he was reasonably sure you were out of the way. When you happened to catch sight of him, Emma, I expect he was doing a quick reconnoiter to see where he might plausibly drag himself ashore suffering from amnesia and wait his chance to steal the bag back. He probably knew Ted Sharpless was already on Pocapuk and wouldn't dare refuse to help him."

Vincent snorted. "Catch me ever doin' another favor for a jailbird!"

"Now, Vincent," said Alding Fath, "they're not all like Ted Sharpless."

"Yeah, Dad," said Sandy. "All you have to do is let Mrs. Fath check 'em out for you first."

"Mind your tongue, young woman." But Vincent's lips were twitching. "What beats me is how Groot knew Sorpende was on the island. I never said."

"I expect the meeting came as a shock to them both," Theonia told him. "What must have happened is that they both came prowling after the necklace at more or less the same time. I think Jimmy got to it first, being the more experienced burglar. Groot either trailed him and let him take the risk of stealing the bag out of Emma's bedroom or else happened on him after he'd got it. I don't know how Jimmy planned to get off the island."

"Figured we had a boat he could steal," said Vincent.

"I suppose so. Anyway, Groot apparently slugged Jimmy with a pine branch and chucked him over the cliff, then searched the bag, found only Emma's jewelry, and tossed the whole business after Jimmy in a fit of temper. He may possibly have gone down and searched Jimmy's body after that; we can't know because of course the footprints would have been washed away when the tide came in."

"Could o' shoved Jimmy's face in the mud to make sure he smothered," Vincent suggested. "I wouldn't put it past Groot after the way he went for Sandy. He must o' been half crazy to go searchin' the house in broad daylight."

"It's a mercy he didn't kill more of us," said Emma. "There's nothing more dangerous than a thoroughly disorganized scoundrel. Well, Theonia, is that the end of your report?"

"Just that I'm supposed to tell you Tweeters Arbuthnot was awfully sorry he couldn't come today. His pet toucan is molting and he felt he had to be there in its hour of need. He's engaged a toucan-sitter for tomorrow, however, and will be here to pick me up. But first he wants to take you for a little hop to see the puffins."

"I'm not sure I'll be quite in the mood for puffins."

"He also mentioned hang gliding."

"Oh?" Emma began to perk up. "I wonder what one ought to wear?"

"Emma, you wouldn't!" cried Alexei Radunov.

Theonia laughed. "I assure you she would, but could you put off deciding for a few minutes, Emma? Bubbles wants us in the kitchen. You too, please, Vincent."

This was a change; Vincent looked as puzzled as Emma felt. However, they both followed Theonia without demur. As they were going through the dining room, Vincent asked her, "What's he want us for?"

"I'm sure he doesn't want us at all," Theonia surprised him by replying. "It's just that there's one more bit of unfinished business I'd like to clear up before I leave."

TWENTY-SIX

Bubbles definitely hadn't been expecting them; he was at the sink washing vegetables when they walked in. "Oh, hi. What'th up, Vinthent?"

The boss cocked his head at Theonia. "Ask her."

"We came to see what you have in your flour bin," said Theonia.

"No!" Forgetting to shut off the water, Bubbles rushed across the kitchen and spread-eagled himself in front of the bin. "You can't! It'th mine!"

"What the hell's eatin' you?" Quite effortlessly, Vincent took his pudgy friend under the armpits and set him aside. "Get me a long-handled spoon or somethin'."

Meek as a whipped dog, Bubbles slunk over to the pegboard and took down a huge skimming ladle with a handle fully a yard long. Vincent stuck the ladle down as far as it would go and began to stir. Half a second later, he was staring down at a length of chain looped around the handle and two ancient coins resting in the scoop. He blew off the flour and they shone bright gold.

"Mighty Jehu, Bubbles! Who have you been robbing?"

"Pocapuk," moaned the cook. "I found the treasure."

"I'll be damned!" Vincent was stirring up a miniature whirlwind by now. "What's all these pebbles in here for?"

Theonia picked one out of the ladle and rubbed it on her sleeve. "I believe they're rough-cut emeralds," she told him mildly. "Vincent, do be careful. You're getting flour all over the kitchen. Emma, get a dishpan or something to put these in. How much more is there, Bubbles?"

The cook only shrugged his shoulders.

"Why the hell couldn't you have packed it in plastic bags or somethin'?" Vincent had flour up his nose by now and spoke through a run of sneezes. "Why didn't you let on you'd found it? Christ, Bubbles, you weren't plannin' to steal the stuff? Not you."

"Yeth, I wath!" Furious, desperate, almost in tears, Bubbles sounded like a defiant six-year-old. "I need it for the hothpithe. Our funding'th run out. We'll have to clothe the doorth if we don't get money thomehow. I can't thand that, Vinthe."

"Okay, simmer down." Vincent reached out a huge, floury hand to pat his friend's heaving shoulder. "I can see how you feel. But damn it, Bubbles, use your head. How did you think you were goin' to market pirate gold?"

Bubbles sniffed a mighty sniff. "I wath planning to pray for guidanthe."

"You'd o' guided yourself straight into jail, that's what you'd o' done. Don't you know there's rules and regulations about buried treasure? This ain't your land, it's Mrs. Sabine's. If anybody's got a right to this stuff, she does. Where'd you find it, anyways?"

"Right down in the cove, over by Alding'th cottage. I wath digging for clamth our firtht day out, and there it wath. I jutht thcooped up the treasure with my clamming rake and hid it under the quahogth. I wath planning to go back for more, but the cottagerth came and I haven't had the chanthe."

Vincent stood there shaking his head for a long minute, then he heaved a sigh that came all the way from his boots. "Can you beat that? Right in front of our noses all this time. It must o' got hove up in the winter storms or somethin'. Earthquake, maybe. Bubbles, I'm jiggered if I know what to do."

"The first thing," said Theonia practically, "is for us to keep our mouths shut."

"And the second is to get Parker Pence out here," Emma added. "He handles all Adelaide's business; he'll know what to do. I'll phone him at his office tomorrow. This may be a break for you,

Vincent. Knowing Parker, I can guarantee he won't let this island go out of the family so long as he thinks there might be one single emerald left under those mudflats. If the Pocapuk legend is true, there ought to be a great deal more treasure where this came from."

She reached into the dishpan and picked up one of the dull green pebbles. "I must say there's something awfully convincing about an emerald as big as one's thumb. You'll surely get some kind of finder's fee in any case, Bubbles."

"But that won't be enough to keep the hothpithe going!"

"How do you know it won't? However, I expect there'll be all sorts of red tape to untangle before anybody gets anything. In the meantime"—Emma tossed back the emerald and turned to the stricken cook, her eyes asparkle and her face aglow—"we'll run a benefit."

This was no elderly woman oppressed with the weight of her long-gone youth, her lost beloved, her dying friend, by a decaying house, and an unsolved list of catastrophes. This was Emma, booted and spurred and ready to ride.

"So let's start getting organized. Theonia, you're much cleverer with your hands than I; you'd better take the Gladstone bag back with you and get the fairies' jewelry in order. Then you can begin studying your role."

"What role? I'm no actress."

"Of course you are. We need a Fairy Queen for *Iolanthe* and you're the very one. I think I'll ask Alexei to be the Lord Chancellor," Emma added meditatively. "He already knows the songs. And can't you just see him with dear little gauze wings sprouting out of his shoulder blades? I'll invite him to stay at my house for the duration."

Theonia smiled. "That'll give the ladies in the garden club something to buzz about."

"Yes, won't they have fun? The proceeds from the performance can go to the hospice fund, but that won't be till next April. Right now is when we've got to get cracking. A lawn fete here on Pocapuk before Peter starts dredging and word gets out about the treasure, don't you think? We'll bring people out in boats and have a gala tea with music and perhaps a make-believe treasure hunt with lots of funny prizes. I'll alert my orchestra and work out the details. Vincent, you'll see to the advertising and the boats. Bubbles will manage the food; Neil can help me plan the treasure hunt. Sandy and Bernice must have quaint costumes. With mobcaps, I think, unless we can get hold of that awful hair goo of theirs and bury it somewhere."

"Don't rap the goo," said Vincent. "It saved my kid's life, don't forget."

"True enough. Very well, then, Sandy may have her goo, but she'll keep it under her cap. Which reminds me, Bubbles and I still have another bit of business to clear up."

"Thuch ath what?" the cook asked nervously.

"Such as your keeping Alding Fath doped with tranquilizers because she'd come too close to the truth about your secret cache when she was telling fortunes at the dinner table that first night. Naturally when she mentioned black and white and jewels she didn't mean Shag Rock, as Joris Groot tried to make us believe, she was talking about the emeralds in the flour bin. Furthermore, it was you who hit me on the head when I happened to stumble in the wrong place, wasn't it? What did you use, a rolling pin?"

"Heaventh no! Jutht a big wooden thpoon. I didn't want to hurt you, Mithith Kelling, but I wath dethperate about the hothpithe."

"All right, Bubbles, I understand. Now you leave the hospice to me and concentrate on nursing Alding Fath's vibrations back into working order. Peter will need her to help find the rest of Pocapuk's treasure, I daresay, and I shall enjoy having her around."

There'd be time for quiet cups of tea and pleasant chats now and then. There'd be Black John Sendick dashing about in his absurd sweatshirt and perhaps even writing something scary enough to be salable now that he'd had a taste of real-life horrors. There'd be Alexei Radunov to play courtier when he wasn't too involved with Rasputin and Queen Victoria. There'd be Sandy, Bernice, and Neil to do her every bidding, there'd be Vincent to make sure they did it right. There'd be Tweeters Arbuthnot dropping by on his way to see the puffins. There'd be no time for hang gliding if she was to rescue Bubbles's hospice from penury and failure, but not even Emma Kelling could do everything. Granted, they'd got off to a shaky start, but all in all this was shaping up to be quite an agreeable summer.